FOR SALE
by OWNER

OTHER BOOKS AND AUDIO BOOKS
BY MARLENE BATEMAN

Crooked House

A Death in the Family

Motive for Murder

Light on Fire Island

FOR SALE
by OWNER

a novel

MARLENE BATEMAN

Covenant Communications, Inc.

Cover image © *Romantic Couple Winter Outdoor Ice Skating*, YinYang; courtesy of istockphoto.com.

Cover design copyright © 2016 by Covenant Communications, Inc.

Published by Covenant Communications, Inc.
American Fork, Utah

Printed in the United States of America
First Printing: October 2016

22 21 20 19 18 17 16   10 9 8 7 6 5 4 3 2 1

ISBN 978-1-62108-898-1

To *my* Kenzie

ACKNOWLEDGMENTS

MANY THANKS TO JOHN WELLS, Monica Miles, Jennie Stevens, Leah Hansen, Anna Smith, Holly Horton, Geri Main, and Tammi Nesi, who read the manuscript and gave many helpful suggestions. I also want to thank Holly Horton for her editorial expertise. A special thanks goes to my terrific editor, Stacey Turner. In addition, I owe a debt of gratitude to the great cooks that tested the cookie recipes: Virginia Kendall, Stacey Turner, Monica Miles, and Mariah Goodrich.

CHAPTER ONE

THE ROAD SHONE LIKE SILVER as the twin beams of the Camry's head-lights tracked over the wet interstate. As McKenzie Forsberg exited the freeway, butterflies rose in her stomach then crashed and burned. Had she made the right decision? Back at home in Chicago, it had seemed utterly right and sensible, but now all sorts of doubts were creeping in.

A sign loomed ahead, announcing they were entering the city of Lake Forest, Illinois—population 18,756. Kenzie glanced over at her daughter, Sara. "Still excited about moving here?"

"I thought we were just visiting." Sara's reply was muffled because she had her nose pressed against the window in order to stare at the brightly colored Christmas lights illuminating the houses they passed.

"Well, yes. We won't move until after Christmas. You're not worried, are you?" Moving could be unsettling. Kenzie had moved when she'd been around Sara's age, and it had been fine. But then, her family had only moved five miles to the outskirts of town to a home that bordered the woods—a home where her parents still lived.

"Not really. Grandma and Grandpa are here."

"And you already have a bunch of friends." Sociable and outgoing, Sara had made a number of friends during their visits to Lake Forest.

Turning from the window, Sara pushed the long honey-blonde hair, which was so like her mother's, away from her face. "Did you have a lot of friends when you lived here? I mean besides that one boy?"

"Quite a few. Of course, Lake Forest was a lot smaller back then. That made it easier to make friends." As for the boy, they'd been best friends for two magical years.

"I haven't seen Kaylee and Ali since last summer." There was a complaining note in Sara's voice. "You're always too busy to come and visit Grandma and Grandpa."

They had been over this too many times for Kenzie to address it now. Besides, they were here now—partially due to the stern lecture her older brother had given her. Tom had pointed out that she hadn't come for two years and that she *had* to come this year since neither of their two brothers could make the trip.

Although Kenzie had hoped to arrive before nightfall, she was now glad they hadn't since it allowed them to enjoy the Christmas lights as they drove through the quiet residential neighborhood. When Kenzie turned on Oak Leaf Drive and pulled up in front of her brother's house, a huge smile broke out on her face, and she clasped the steering wheel in delight. She was home—really and truly. She had lived in this spreading old house for the first ten years of her life. She turned off the engine and just sat in satisfaction, eyeing the Christmas tree with twinkling lights, which was framed in the front window.

"Here it is—the old homestead. I hated to move, but at least we stayed in the same town so I got to keep all my friends." Kenzie gazed fondly at the reddish-brick house that had always been special to her, with its wrap-around front porch and snow-covered roof.

"They sure have a lot of lights," Sara exclaimed in wide-eyed admiration. Clear lights swooped in crescents from the porch railing, while multicolored lights outlined eaves and windows.

"Now remember, don't tell Uncle Tom that we're going to buy his house. I want it to be a special surprise."

"I won't tell," Sara promised.

"He's going to be so excited." Kenzie smiled. "I'm going to write up a certificate, put it in a big box, wrap it up all pretty with a big bow on top, and give it to him on Christmas."

"You mean you're not going to tell him *now*?" Sara made it sound like she'd have to keep the secret for an eternity instead of only seventeen days.

"I probably won't be able to wait that long," Kenzie admitted, eyes glowing as she sighed in complete and utter happiness. The house was perfect. All doubts about moving back disappeared. This was right— she could feel it in her bones. She'd spent so much time thinking, praying, and making plans—and now it was all coming together! A bubbly feeling like ginger ale tickled her chest. How awesome to come back and live in her childhood home! She needed this—oh, how she needed this. Two years of wrenching turmoil had left her drained, making this moment extra sweet. She was coming home! Just seeing the house poured balm on Kenzie's soul.

Tired of sitting, Sara opened her door. "Come on, Mom!"

Kenzie pushed a button, popping open the Camry's trunk. As they went to the trunk, she said, "I hope you won't be too disappointed when Grandma and Grandpa move."

Sara frowned. "I wish they weren't leaving right when we're coming here."

"They've talked about moving to Arizona for years," Kenzie reminded her, pulling out a sack of presents and shutting the trunk.

"Why can't Grandma and Grandpa stay here?" Sara sounded forlorn.

"Grandma said the house is too big for them."

"Maybe when they know we're moving here, they'll decide to stay!"

Some of Kenzie's excitement evaporated at the thought. But no. She wouldn't think about her father now. Not when she was so full of excitement and happiness. "I wouldn't count on it, sweetheart," Kenzie cautioned. Her parents had always planned on moving to a warmer climate when they got older—even if they hadn't mentioned moving for some time.

A few inches of snow covered the lawn, but the sidewalk was clear. On the front porch, Kenzie let Sara ring the bell to announce their arrival, then she opened the door, and they stepped onto a woven rug.

Mandy hurried in, her smile bright as she wiped her hands on a kitchen towel. Kenzie's sister-in-law had an abundance of thick dark hair, which curved just above her shoulders. She wore her typical happy expression, and, as always, she was warm and welcoming. "Oh, I'm so glad you're here!"

When they hugged, Kenzie could feel the slight bulge of the baby Mandy was expecting in five months.

"It's so good to see you!" Mandy exclaimed, her friendly face alight as she hugged Sara.

"Where are your kids?" Kenzie asked, surprised she hadn't been surrounded yet.

"At your parents'. Your mom picked them up this afternoon on her way home from the store. She made Brian's sheep costume and wanted him to try it on one more time in case she needed to make any last-minute alterations."

They hung their coats in the closet, and Sara wandered off. Kenzie went with Mandy to the kitchen, where she'd been making a fruit salad, most likely for the dinner Kenzie's parents were hosting that night. Her sister-in-law folded whipped cream into the fruit and stirred while Kenzie licked the cream off the beaters. "I don't know why you even added fruit. This is great all by itself."

As Mandy put away the mixer, the back door opened, and Tom walked in. Kenzie's brother was a big bear of a man with a square, friendly face and hair he'd cut short when his hairline began receding. Tom smiled in delight and enveloped her in a hug that made it hard to breathe. Kenzie was about to beg for mercy, but Tom loosened his hold in the nick of time. The man didn't know his own strength.

"How were the roads?" he asked, going to give his wife a hug and a kiss.

"Great. It only snowed a little, and it melted as soon as it hit the road."

"Good." Tom slid his arm around Mandy's waist and asked her, "Did you tell Kenzie about the change of plans?"

"Not yet. She just got here a few minutes ago."

"What's going on?" Kenzie asked.

Tom said, "I know you talked Mom into having a family dinner tonight so I'd be there to break the ice with Dad, but you'll need to do a little chipping without me. The bishop called. Butch is sick, and I need to fill in for him at tithing settlement tonight."

Mandy did her best to support Tom, who stayed busy as a counselor in the bishopric even though it put a crimp in family plans. "Of course it would happen on the night of Brian's school play!"

"I'll be there," Tom reassured her. "The bishop only needs me for an hour."

An hour! Kenzie scoffed inwardly. Translated, that meant almost two since it took twenty minutes to drive to the ward house in Gurnee. Then, add a little more time since Tom enjoyed talking and could chat for days. Kenzie hid her disappointment, telling herself not to worry.

After all, Mandy and the kids would be there to dispel any tension. Mandy knew all about what had occurred between Kenzie and her father and, being one of her most loyal friends, had stuck by her through the dark days of her divorce. Kenzie had considered asking Mandy if she and Sara could stay at their house during their visit, but she'd discarded the idea, knowing her mother would be hurt—and she'd been hurt enough by this schism between father and daughter. Kenzie would not inflict any more hurt—though staying with Mandy would have made things easier.

After picking up Sara and swinging her around in his version of a greeting, Tom kissed his wife good-bye. "I'll be back as soon as I can, but if I get held up, I might have to meet you at the school." He gave Kenzie another hug before rushing off.

Mandy stretched plastic wrap over the salad and said, "All set. Let's go."

Since her children would be riding with her to the Christmas play, Mandy would drive her minivan. She locked the front door behind Kenzie and Sara, who both waited on the front porch until the garage door creaked open. Mandy backed out, waving as they went down the steps.

Suddenly, Kenzie's breath caught in her throat, and she stopped as her heart gave a great thump. On the front lawn, a blue-and-white realty sign stood among the holiday decorations. When she and Sara arrived, it had been blocked from view by a large inflatable igloo with penguins skating inside. But now the sign—with a big red SOLD plastered across it—was plainly and painfully visible.

CHAPTER TWO

KENZIE'S MOUTH OPENED, BUT NO words came out. Her eyes were wide and staring. Sara came close, concerned as the taillights of Mandy's van glimmered red in the darkness.

"Are you okay, Mom?" She turned in the direction Kenzie was staring and saw the sign. "Does that mean Uncle Tom and Aunt Mandy sold the house?" Sara asked worriedly.

The profound shock manifested itself as nausea. Crossing her arms over her stomach, Kenzie hoped she wasn't going to be sick. "Um, I'm not sure," she said, refusing to accept the evidence of her eyes. Still, how many meanings did *sold* have? Sold was sold. But it couldn't be. Her head was spinning so fast it was a miracle it didn't fly off.

Mechanically, she got into the car, checked for traffic, and pulled onto the road. Tom *couldn't* have sold the home without telling her. He wouldn't do that to her. But then, Tom didn't know she wanted to buy it.

She hit the steering wheel in frustration, causing Sara to jump. *Why* hadn't Tom told her he'd sold the house? Or Mandy? They talked frequently and hadn't said a thing, which meant the sold sticker had to have been put up recently. She tried to remember the last time Mandy or Tom had mentioned the house. Lately, all they'd talked about had been her upcoming visit. Yet Kenzie knew selling the house was very important to Mandy—she and Tom had their eye on buying the Steadman home a few blocks away. It was a large four-bedroom home, which would give them the extra room they needed for their growing family.

"What's the matter, Mom? Is it that sold sign?"

Kenzie's throat tightened, and she tightly gripped the steering wheel as another wave of nausea hit. "Yes."

"Does that mean we aren't going to buy their house?"

Something in Kenzie rebelled. It was too much. It was *all* too much! She was tired of accepting whatever life dished out. A difficult divorce when she and Larry were supposed to live happily ever after. A pervert at work, and a boss who wouldn't stand up for her. A father who made outrageous accusations. Kenzie had carefully formulated her plans, and then she'd *prayed* about them. She'd felt a confirming flood of warmth in her chest that she'd made the right decision, for Pete's sake. This *couldn't* be happening. She wouldn't let it. No, sir. She wasn't about to take this without a fight. "No, it does *not* mean we aren't buying the house." Kenzie spoke with real determination. "I'll talk with Tom and get it worked out."

"But how can you if someone else bought it?"

The corners of Kenzie's mouth turned down. "Aye, and there's the rub."

"Is that another quote?" Sara groaned. "You're always saying weird things that some guy said. I don't know what you mean."

In high school, Kenzie had fallen in love with Shakespeare, a love that had endured despite her major in business administration. "That *guy* is Shakespeare—and the quote is from *Hamlet*. It means there's a problem." A *biiiiig* problem. But there had to be something she could do. One of the reasons Kenzie had risen to upper management at Midwest Computers was because of her ability to solve problems. She'd come up with something.

In a few minutes, Kenzie pulled into her parents' driveway, which was lined with candy cane lights. Miniature lights sparkled on bushes and trees in the yard. A large pine wreath hung on the door, and icicle lights dripped from the roof. She and Sara grabbed their luggage and wheeled their cases toward the sprawling tan brick house.

They were no sooner inside than Kenzie's mother rushed toward them. Elaine bent to hug Sara, kissed her on the cheek, then wrapped her arms around Kenzie.

When they pulled back, Kenzie stared at her mother in surprise. "When did you get your hair cut?"

Elaine touched her short steel-gray hair that was cut in a feathery do. "A couple of months ago. I decided I wanted wash-and-wear hair."

"I like it!" It fit her mother's petite features and brought out the blue of her eyes.

"Me too," Sara piped up.

Mandy came over and lifted a few strands of her mother-in-law's hair. "I told her it made her look ten years younger."

Slowly, Kenzie's muscles softened and relaxed. It *was* good to be back. The house was spacious, with a large family room showcasing a tall Christmas tree in the corner and an adjoining dining room that opened onto the kitchen. Kenzie flung her coat over the side of the couch just as her father walked in. Tall and lean, Allen Dahlquist liked to wear sweaters such as the tan one he had on now. He wore his gray hair a little long, so he always looked overdue for a haircut. He gave Kenzie an awkward, lopsided hug, leaving a few inches between them. They stood there self-consciously until Sara ran over and threw her arms around her grandfather.

A big smile creased his face. "How's my girl?"

"Good." Then, hearing chatter from her cousins, Sara ran off to join them.

"How was the drive?" Allen asked. "Were the roads clear?"

What was it with men and roads? "It was fine. The snow was light and wasn't sticking."

He listened intently as if she were revealing top-secret information. "Good, good."

The conversation came to another standstill.

Her mother rescued them. "We're so glad you could come!" There was such relief in her voice that Kenzie knew she was thinking about her two sons. As if reading Kenzie's mind, Elaine went on. "They wanted to come, but it's Nate and Jocelyn's year to spend Christmas with her folks, and Randall and Denise can't travel, not with Denise being eight months pregnant. We were going to be mighty lonely."

"Gee, thanks," Mandy said wryly.

"Oh! You know what I mean."

"Sorry, I had to tease you," Mandy said. "Unless this place is packed with bodies, you feel let down."

"Well, let's not stand here." Elaine became brisk. "We've got a play to go to tonight. Kenzie, why don't you take your bags to your room and wash up. Mandy, the children are playing video games in the office. Tell them to turn it off. Dinner's just about ready."

After she'd rolled in the luggage, Kenzie went to the office, where her father was rounding up the children. Fourteen-year-old Adam jumped up to hug her. He was as tall as Kenzie and as lean as his grandfather. Hillary, with her long straight hair, was eleven and had her mother's friendly smile. Seven-year-old Brian wore a fuzzy white costume and black gloves.

Full of importance, he announced, "I'm going to be a sheep in the play tonight."

"If we make it in time," his grandfather said gloomily as they went down the hall.

Elaine overheard and glanced at the clock. "We've plenty of time, dear. Now, Brian, take off that costume. The last thing we need is for you to spill gravy on it. "

Once everyone was seated at the long dining room table, Allen said the blessing, and they began passing around the oven-baked chicken, mashed potatoes, and gravy. Kenzie had hoped for a few private moments with Mandy but had to settle for talking to her from across the table as she passed the biscuits.

"I saw a *sold* sticker on the sign in your yard. When did that happen?"

"A couple of days ago." Mandy cut open her biscuit and buttered it. "We haven't had many people look at it, so this offer came out of the blue."

Kenzie's stomach clenched. It sure had. Steadying herself, Kenzie smoothed out the napkin beside her plate as though it was the most important thing in the world. As she lifted her glass to take a drink, her hands shook to think that deciding to move back might be the most foolish thing she had done in her life.

Her sister-in-law rambled on. "I'd been so anxious because Tom and I wanted to buy the Steadman home before someone else scooped it up, but we couldn't until we sold our home. But now we don't have to worry. We already made them an offer, and they accepted."

Allen had been listening. "Why are you buying another home anyway? Isn't the one you have good enough for you?"

Mandy had been in the family long enough to take her father-in-law's outspokenness in stride. She glanced at Kenzie, who commiserated with her eyes, then explained, "We needed a bigger house and more bedrooms, especially with the baby coming."

Allen stopped gnawing on a drumstick and frowned. "I had five brothers and two sisters, and we had three bedrooms in the whole house. One for my folks, one for the girls, and one in the basement for the boys. We got along fine."

"A lot of things have changed since you were young, Grandpa," Adam said. "Now we have fire, the wheel, agriculture—"

Kenzie had been on the verge of telling Mandy she wanted to buy the house, but her father's comment stopped her. Really, it would be better to wait until they were alone. The last thing Kenzie needed right now was one of her father's callous comments.

Dinner went better than expected, and Kenzie was grateful for Mandy's presence. Even though the children kept the conversation going, there was an underlying tension. Several times when Kenzie glanced at her father, his eyes were on her, and each time their eyes darted away.

Right at the end of dinner, Tom breezed in.

Kenzie looked at her watch. "An hour, huh?"

"Brother Martindale talked and talked." Tom held out his hands to show how helpless he had been. "He was starved for conversation, while I was plain old starving." Tom kissed his wife, took a chair beside her, and started dishing up. "How much time do I have?"

Mandy answered, "We ought to leave in ten minutes."

"Ah, well, a two-piece chicken dinner instead of four."

"You just eat; I'll butter a biscuit for you," his mother told him.

"Thanks. I'll shovel fast." Tom attacked his plate.

When Elaine asked how Tom's work was going, he took a drink of water to wash down a huge bite before answering. "Kind of slow lately." He threw a sly look at Kenzie. "I'm nothing like my sister. Mom and Dad have always been so proud of you, a big-shot executive director, while I'm only a lowly realtor and a colossal disappointment."

"I wouldn't say a *colossal* disappointment," his mom said with a twinkle in her eye.

"Thanks, Mom," Tom said wryly. "I feel so much better now."

Her father asked Kenzie, "So, how is work going with you? Busy as always?"

It took an effort not to frown. Her father *would* have to get in a little dig about her being busy and not visiting often enough. The truth was she had some big news, but now was not the time to announce it, so she kept her answer generic. "There have been a few changes, but it's always busy." She'd tell them all about it soon enough.

CHAPTER THREE

KENZIE AND SARA RODE WITH her parents in their Honda Accord. There was little parking near the elementary school, and her father finally pulled onto a side street to find a spot.

"We'll have to walk a ways," he said.

After a block, Sara complained, "My hands are freezing."

Glancing over at her, Allen asked, "Don't you have any gloves?" He then gave Kenzie a reproachful look.

Kenzie gritted her teeth. His intimation was clear. It was a poor mother who let their child go gloveless on a cold December night. Chalk up another black mark against her. What could have happened to Sara's gloves? Usually she kept them in her coat pockets.

Inside the school, they found Tom, Hillary, and Adam standing just inside the lunchroom, which was filled with rows of chairs facing the stage. They took their seats, saving one for Mandy, who was backstage helping Brian into his costume. The play started with the audience clapping loudly after each number. It was great fun to watch the children perform and listen to their sweet young voices sing the familiar carols.

Despite being on hands and knees, Brian managed to give a wave from a black-gloved "hoof" as his group sang, "While Shepherds Watched Their Flocks by Night." As they sang, the shepherds gently herded the "sheep" as they meandered about the stage. One sheep enjoyed his role a little too much, darting here and there with one or more shepherds chasing him in hot pursuit, much to the audience's delight.

During the program, the audience was occasionally asked to join in singing, and even if they were slightly off-key, their enthusiasm fit right in with the littler carolers on stage.

After the program, Brian found them. He asked eagerly, "Did you see me? Did you see me?"

"We sure did," his grandmother assured him. "You did an amazing job."

"I think we have Oscar material here," Tom said proudly, throwing a meaty arm around his son's shoulders. After further congratulations on Brian's stellar performance, they made for the tables where cookies and punch had been set out. They were waiting in line when Tom recognized the man in front of him. His son was also wearing a sheep costume and appeared to be a year or two older than Brian.

"Jared! How are you?" Tom shook the man's hand. "I think you know most everyone, but I don't believe you've met my sister, McKenzie Forsberg. Kenzie, this is Jared Rawlins, and his son, Corey, the amazing sheep." His brows drew together. "Wait a minute, what's singular for sheep?"

"One sheep—two sheep," Kenzie said. "You did a great job, Corey," she told the little boy, who had bright eyes and tousled, soft-brown hair like his father.

"Thank you."

"Nice to meet you, McKenzie," Jared said, his black eyes on her. His smile was warm and friendly.

He was nice looking, and Kenzie figured he was near her age, perhaps a few years older. "Actually, I usually go by Kenzie."

"Sorry," Tom said to Jared. "I got mixed up—I hardly ever see her, you see."

Kenzie dug an elbow into her brother's side, and he grunted and staggered as if mortally wounded. She shook her head at him as they picked up their cookies and paper cups of punch, then moved off to the side to stand in a small circle.

Jared nodded toward Sara, and he asked, "And this is your daughter?"

"Yes, this is Sara."

"Nice to meet you, Sara," Jared said. "How long are you going to be visiting?"

"Until after Christmas," Sara replied. "Then we have to go back because I'm going to stay with my daddy for New Year's Day."

Elaine said, "We're so happy Kenzie and Sara were able to come out for a nice long visit."

A woman with short highlighted hair walked by, holding hands with a little girl. The woman paused. "Hello, Jared!"

He turned and smiled. "Hi, Pam."

She flashed him a big smile and came closer. "Great play, wasn't it? Corey was so cute."

"Thanks." Jared put a hand on his son's shoulder and spoke to the little girl, who wore a shimmering white gown and had a gold halo above her head. "You made a great angel, Kaity."

"Thank you," she replied solemnly, pink cheeks showing her pleasure.

Pam and her daughter left, and Jared explained to Kenzie, "Pam is the assistant manager at my café." He tilted his head a little. "Tom told me you work at some type of computer business in Chicago. What do you do?"

She flashed a sideways look at her parents. Once again, this wasn't the right moment to announce her news. An older couple had stopped to talk to them, Tom, and Mandy. "I'm the executive director at Midwest Computers. I assist other managers and work with clients and the public. Kind of a jack of all trades," she said depreciatively.

"I've heard of Midwest; they have stores all over. I'm impressed." His tone was so complimentary that Kenzie came close to blushing. Jared was not only good-looking, there was something about his open, friendly expression that drew her. And she liked the interest she saw in his eyes.

Without thinking, her eyes went to his left hand. No wedding band. Yet not all men wore them. And he had a son. Perhaps he was divorced as well. Kenzie enjoyed their conversation and was pleased as he listened with real interest and laughed at her little jokes. She felt witty and appealing. And his attention was so different from Matt's at work—whose bold gaze had become too familiar. Jared's friendly talk and banter caused no sense of uneasiness.

Then, afraid she might be showing too much interest, Kenzie spoke to Jared's little boy. "So, Corey, who made your sheep costume?"

"It sure wasn't me," Jared answered for his son. "I can make a lot of things but not costumes. Fortunately, the school had some extra sheep costumes to lend out."

Tom overheard and said, "Jared does a lot of woodworking."

"Oh really?" Kenzie said. "What do you make?"

"Toys mostly. Cars, trains, airplanes, things like that."

"Wow, you must be very talented."

"Not really, but it does take patience—and a lot of trial and error. If you'd like to stop by sometime, I'll show you some of the things I've made." Jared's eyes held hers a moment.

Now that was an invitation she was definitely going to accept.

Soon, the children became bored and started punching each other. Holding onto Brian as he tried to punch his older brother, Mandy told Tom, with a hint of desperation, "We need to go."

It was with regret that Kenzie told Jared good-bye and went with the others down the polished hallway to get their coats.

"It looks like you had an enjoyable evening," Mandy told Kenzie.

Deliberately misconstruing her sister-in-law's words, Kenzie replied, "The play was a lot of fun."

"You know what I mean. I think Jared was smitten with you."

Tom grinned as he shrugged on his coat. "And I detected quite a bit of interest from you on my 'romance-o-meter.'"

"Don't be silly." Kenzie was glad of the darkness that hid her blush as they went out the heavy metal doors.

"Jared's a nice guy," Mandy continued. "He has his own business too—opened a café in town. He's a widower—his wife died a few years ago. From what I've heard, it was really hard on him."

So, he wasn't married. Not that it mattered. She wasn't looking for a relationship. But still—

The family clustered on the sidewalk, their breath foggy in the cold night air. Mandy gave her a hug. "Thanks for coming. We'll see you tomorrow."

"Wait a minute!" Kenzie interjected. "I thought you guys were coming over to the house."

"It's almost nine. Time for bed," Tom said. "School tomorrow."

Rats. She'd hoped to talk to Tom privately. Oh well, she'd just go and talk to him at his office tomorrow.

Once they were back at her parents' home, she and Sara hung their coats in the utility room, then went to the kitchen, where her parents were getting a drink of water. Kenzie was dragging. The long day was beginning to show on her.

She told her parents, "I'm beat. I think we'll unpack and go to bed."

"Do we have to?" Sara whined. "I'm not tired, and I don't have school."

"But you do have homework you can work on tomorrow," Kenzie reminded her. She'd gotten homework assignments from Sara's teacher because she'd taken her out of school before Christmas break.

"I bet you fall asleep before your head hits the pillow," her grandpa teased, then he held out his arms for a hug.

Elaine told them, "If you need anything, just ask. There are extra blankets in the closet."

"Thanks." Once again, she'd have to wait to tell them her news. Her body was screaming for bed.

She and Sara stayed in the bedroom Kenzie had used after moving so many years ago. The same curtains, splashed with yellow and blue flowers, framed two windows, and her old dresser with rectangular mirrors was against the same wall. The only thing that had changed was the bed. Instead of a twin, it was now a queen. Kenzie put their suitcases on top of the yellow and blue bedspread and began putting clothes away. It didn't take long.

Sara changed into her pajamas while Kenzie brushed her teeth in the attached bathroom.

Sara came in. "It's been a long time since we've been here for Christmas," she said, squirting too much toothpaste on her brush.

Kenzie was about to deny it, then added up the months. They hadn't been back for the holidays since her divorce. Two years. She murmured an agreement.

But Sara wasn't ready to let it go. When they were back in the bedroom, she faced her mother, a slight figure in fuzzy pink pajamas. "Why are you mad at Grandma and Grandpa?"

"I'm not mad at them."

Plopping on the end of the bed, Sara said, "You act like you are."

"Well, I'm not." When Kenzie saw her words had done nothing to change Sara's quizzical expression, she sat and wrapped her arms around her daughter. "Well, I guess I am a little mad at Grandpa."

"Why?" Sara's curious, china-blue eyes drilled into her own.

"Hey, we've talked about this." When Sara first realized something was wrong between her mother and grandfather, Kenzie had talked with her—explaining it on a child's level. But apparently, being in the same house with her grandparents had roused some of Sara's old questions and concerns.

"Grandpa said some things that hurt your feelings."

"That's right."

"Sometimes Grandpa says things that aren't very nice," Sara admitted. "Why won't you tell me what he said?"

"Because it's between him and me." Kenzie smoothed her daughter's hair.

"Did he say sorry?" When Kenzie shook her head, Sara leaned against her. "You've been mad a long time."

True. Kenzie was ashamed at how it still bothered her. "I know. I need to forgive and let it go. And I have been trying." Kenzie held her daughter close, her chin on Sara's strawberry-scented hair. Two years was too long to hold on to hurt feelings, yet she'd been unable to get past the wave of hurt that stabbed her heart each time she thought about what he'd said. Even now, Kenzie wondered how her father could have said such terrible things. He'd been judgmental, chauvinistic, self-righteous, and—and just plain *mean!*

Closing her eyes, Kenzie stopped the internal reverie. She could not—*would not*—allow negative thoughts to run away with her. She would be understanding and forgiving. Before leaving Chicago, Kenzie had decided to talk to her father, even though she didn't relish the idea. It was sure to be upsetting. Still, what was more painful? Years of inward seething or a few agonizing minutes of talking? She'd swallow her pride and go to him, even though *he* was the one who should have been coming to her. And she'd be taking a chance. A heart-to-heart talk might *not* make things right but result in more hurt—especially if her father remained true to character and spewed forth more poisonous comments.

Sighing heavily, Kenzie slipped down and kneeled beside the bed. "It's late, so we're going to skip our scripture reading, but let's have prayer."

Later, as she lay beside her daughter, Kenzie peered through the window. How lovely the pines were with moonlight turning them to silver. Beginning to drift off, Kenzie made plans. First on the list, and underlined twice, was driving to town and talking to Tom about the house. After all, the house was the foundation for all of her plans. If she was to begin a new life—and she was—then she *had* to have that house. One way or another.

CHAPTER FOUR

HANGING THE SHEEP COSTUME ON a chair in the dining room so Corey didn't forget to take it back to school, Jared went to his son's bedroom. Corey was sitting cross-legged on his red car-bed—a special bed his grandfather had made. The sides were cut to look like a race car. Headlights were painted on the front, black wheels on the sides, and the number *87* on the "door."

"You did really good in the play tonight, son." Then Jared teasingly added, "You looked and acted just like a sheep."

This was a mistake, because Corey promptly leapt out of bed, got on his hands and knees, and began ambling around the room bleating, "Baaaaaa! Baaaaaa!"

"Okay, Mr. Sheep, did you brush your teeth?"

"Baaaaa!"

Jared eyed his son thoughtfully. "Is that a yes-baaaa or a no-baaaa?"

Nodding his head energetically, Corey intoned, "Baaaaaa!"

"All right. Now, do you want to go outside with the other sheep, or do you want to sleep in this nice comfy bed?"

His son considered a moment, making Jared wish he'd kept his mouth shut. Then with an amazingly nimble leap, Corey soared onto the bed.

"Wow, I had no idea sheep were so agile," Jared said, pulling the covers up.

"Dad, can we get a sheep when we move into our new house?"

Jared chuckled as he tucked his son in and sat on the edge of the bed. Every day, Corey asked what they could do or get when they moved into their larger home. "I'm not sure the backyard is big enough to handle a sheep. And I'd have to check zoning restrictions."

Corey crinkled up his forehead. "What's that?"

"Laws that tell you what animals you can or can't have where you live."

This clearly made no sense whatsoever to Corey, who frowned deeply.

"You're pretty excited about moving, aren't you?"

Corey nodded. "When *are* we going to move?"

"I'm not sure. There are a lot of things to do first. I've already filled out most of the paperwork to get a loan, but we still need to sell *our* house. Then, we'll have to take care of a lot more stuff—finalize the loan, work with the title company—*then* we can move."

His son was horrified. "That'll take forever!"

"Nah, we'll be in the house before you know it." Still, Jared understood his son's feelings. He'd put off getting a new home, wanting to wait until his business was stable enough to provide a secure living. Starting a new business had been a big risk—so many failed the first year—but he'd survived that hurdle. Jared had taken Corey house hunting a number of times, and his son loved every house he saw. It had been hard to explain to his nine-year-old that this home or that one didn't have certain features Jared wanted. But now, he'd found the perfect house.

"You like it here in Lake Forest, don't you?" Jared wanted to make sure. Corey nodded. "I'm glad. I've always wanted to live here. It's a special place."

"If you like it so much, why didn't you and Mom live here?"

"Because your mom wanted to live in Rockford. Her family was all there. But I have a lot of good memories about this town."

"I wish Grandma and Grandpa lived here. And Uncle Lee and Aunt Karen and—"

"Okay, I get the picture," Jared said, cutting him off. "But we'll be with all of them for Christmas. So, did you have fun tonight?"

"Yeah. But next year I want to be a Wise Man." Corey pulled an arm out from under the comforter and scratched his neck. "Dad, who were those people you were talking to tonight?"

"I thought you knew Tom and Mandy and their kids."

"I mean the old people, and the lady with the long hair. And that girl."

Jared chuckled. "They were Tom's parents, Allen and Elaine Dalquist. And the lady is Tom's sister, Kenzie. The girl is her daughter, Sara. I think she's about a year younger than you."

"Do they live here?"

"Mr. and Mrs. Dalquist do. Don't you remember going to their house last year after we put on a program at the rest home?"

"Oh, yeah."

Jared went on. "Kenzie is their daughter. She and Sara are visiting from Chicago."

"That lady was pretty."

That was a fact. And nice too. It had been a long time since someone had caught Jared's attention the way Kenzie had. He'd enjoyed talking with her. Usually he was shy and a bit tongue-tied around people he didn't know, but he'd had no problem at all talking with Kenzie Forsberg. She made it so easy; it was like Jared had known her all his life. And it had been nice of her to talk to Corey.

Then Corey asked, "Dad, when we move, can we get a dog?"

Was there an animal his son *didn't* want? Jared stood and stretched. "We'll see. Now, time to close those peepers. Good night." He bent, kissed Corey's forehead, then slipped out.

After turning on the TV and checking the latest football and basketball scores, Jared locked the doors. He peeked in once more on Corey. His son's arm was sticking out, so Jared tucked it under the blanket. Gently, Jared ran his hand over the boy's fine hair, then turning, studied the picture on the dresser. The glass frame reflected the moonlight coming through the window, so it was too dark to make out his wife's features. Still, Jared knew it from memory. Hard to believe Robin had been gone four years.

Well-meaning people assured him at the funeral that the pain would eventually go away. Jared hadn't believed them. But time had proven a great healer. Gradually the pain had diminished although it happened so slowly that Jared was not aware of it until he looked back after six months, then a year, then two. Having an active boy to care for helped distract him, but it took a long time to realize—and accept—that he wasn't being disloyal to his wife's memory if he went on with his life.

It wasn't until after moving to Lake Forest that he began to date. But he felt so awkward and uncomfortable that it was easier not to. To his surprise, a number of women approached him. He'd accepted their invitations, mostly because he realized it took a lot of courage to ask and he didn't want to make anyone feel bad—but the only dates that had gone really well were with Pam. Many times he thought how blessed he'd been to have found an employee so bright and personable. Since they worked together, it was easy to plan and go to concerts or movies. Pam was a valuable employee—and a good friend as well.

Jared left his son's door open a foot so he could hear if Corey called to him in the night. In his own bedroom, Jared dropped his keys in a small wooden bowl on the dresser. The bowl was one he'd made himself. Jared loved working with wood and was eager to get back to it now the café was doing well and he no longer had to work all hours of the day and night. His love of woodworking was another reason Jared wanted to get into a bigger home. He had a lathe, band saw, drill press, chop saw, router, and a few other pieces of equipment but no room to use them. His current home didn't have a garage, only a carport, so he'd packed his equipment away in an old storage shed.

And it wouldn't hurt to have more room in the house. When he sat on the edge of his bed to take off his shoes and socks, Jared's knees were only three feet from the dresser. With a swish, Jared threw his rolled-up shirt into the hamper in the corner. He looked forward to having a bedroom that was bigger than a postage stamp.

He recalled his son's comments about Kenzie being pretty. She most definitely was, but there was something more about her. Kenzie had a friendly, lively air and a kind of wholesomeness that showed on her face. You could tell just by talking with her that she was a nice person. And those big brown eyes and long honey-blonde hair didn't hurt either. Kenzie Forsberg was someone he'd like to get to know a little better. What luck she was Tom's sister—that would make it easier to make an excuse to see her once in a while. And he meant to do just that.

CHAPTER FIVE

THE NEXT MORNING KENZIE HAD a hard time finding a spot in the large parking lot west of Main Street. People were out in force doing their Christmas shopping. Crossing the lot, Kenzie pressed the lock button on her key fob, and her car honked. She liked to think it was her car's way of saying, "I'm good now—all locked up—don't worry about me."

When Kenzie pushed open the door to Dahlquist Realtors, the chimes at the top jangled raucously, announcing her arrival. The reception area was small but neat. Chairs lined two sides, a low coffee table was spread with colorful magazines, and a wooden coat tree stood in the corner. Two large windows gave plenty of light, and at the far end a long counter usually housed one of the realtors who worked there. Tom insisted everyone take a turn staffing it, but today it was empty.

Tom's office was to the right and, befitting his status as broker and owner, was large and nicely appointed. Its large window allowed him to keep an eye on the reception area. When Tom looked up from his computer and saw Kenzie, he waved her in. Bookshelves lined one wall, and the window by the filing cabinets had its blinds half closed against the morning sun.

"The last two weeks before Christmas is the worst time in the world for realtors, so I'm not having anyone man the front desk," he explained. As Kenzie slid into a chair near his L-shaped oak desk, he remarked, "You're up bright and early. I thought you'd take advantage of your vacation and sleep in a bit."

"I stopped sleeping in when I started working at Midwest Computers."

"I hear you." Tom shifted in his chair, making it creak under his weight. "It was nice of you to take time off and come out early so you could see Brian in the play. He was so excited when you called and said you were coming early especially to see him."

Kenzie had initially planned a ten-day trip—not two and a half weeks—but when Brian called to ask if she could come, she couldn't disappoint him.

"The play was great. And it's fun to be back in Lake Forest. There's just something about a small town—it's comfortable, you know? Like an old pair of slippers."

"A pair of slippers you don't wear very often," Tom lowered his brow and said sardonically. "I thought maybe you'd become allergic to small towns after living in the big city."

"Not at all. Chicago's great, but it doesn't have the same ambiance as a little town."

"From what I've been able to gather, your staying away was because of some argument with Dad. You never have told me what happened."

Kenzie eyed Tom. "That's because it's private." Even as she spoke, the hurt quivered there in her heart—simmering just below the surface. Would she never overcome it?

"I'm your big brother. I have rights." He grinned boyishly.

It was tempting to tell him all. Tom was the big brother she'd always looked up to and confided in about almost everything. But not this.

He persisted. "That *is* why you haven't been back for Christmas the last few years, isn't it?"

"Partly, but I was also busy with work."

"No one's buying that." Tom shook his head. "Work is a convenient excuse you pull out whenever I suggest you drive out and spend a couple of days. You know what you're doing, don't you?" He went on without waiting for a response. "You're shoving the problem with Dad down into the bottom of your briefcase and hoping it'll stay there, but it's just moldering away, like a forgotten ham sandwich."

Kenzie made a face. "Ugh. That's a terrible metaphor."

"Come on and tell your big brother. I've got a shoulder to cry on."

But crying was the last thing Kenzie intended on doing. She'd been there, done that, and vowed no more. But she knew Tom—now that he'd taken the lid off the subject, he'd never let it go unless she gave him something. Maybe he'd be satisfied with the Cliffs Notes version.

"If you must know, Dad made some hurtful insinuations."

He stared at Kenzie as if she'd turned into a zombie. "That's *it*? You're letting what *Dad* says get to you? Dad, who once told Mom when she dyed her hair blonde that it looked like she was wearing a pile of straw on her head?" Tom chuckled. "You know how tactful Dad is—*talk first, think second* is his motto. Whatever he said, I'm sure he didn't mean it."

Kenzie held so still she might have been a wax-work. When she spoke, her voice was deadly flat. "You don't know what he said."

Their eyes locked—fire shooting from hers. Tom backed off. "You're right. I don't. And it's not like you to be offended easily; after all, you grew up with him the same as I did, so it must have been something pretty bad. Have you talked to him about it?"

Logical first step, but one she hadn't taken. At first, anger had stopped her. It had been the deep, bottomless kind of rage that hardened her insides and made her wary of speaking lest terrible things come out. Later, hurt rose and mixed with the anger. It was beyond belief how he had never learned to bridle his tongue. Didn't he know her at all? Obviously not. After, she'd been left with a wound the size of Texas, which she stuffed down in a corner to lessen the hurt. But Tom was right. Kenzie had let it go on way too long.

"I know I've been acting like a two-year-old, and I *am* going to talk with him, but I came to see you because I wanted to talk about something else."

Tom leaned back in his chair and put his feet up on the desk, crossing them at the ankles. "Talk away."

"Last night, I noticed there was a *sold* sticker on your *For Sale* sign."

Tom's face split into a wide grin. "Yeah. Mandy's pretty excited. She's had her eye on the Steadman home ever since they told us they were going to put it up for sale. We made an offer on it yesterday morning, and they accepted."

The tinkle of chimes came from the outer room. Jared Rawlins, wearing jeans and a blue shirt, walked toward the reception counter.

"I'm in here," Tom called, waving when Jared saw them through the window.

What a time for an interruption! But then again, since it was Jared . . .

Jared's eyes, which were as dark and warm as she remembered from last night, widened with pleasure when he saw her. "Good to see you, Kenzie." It sounded like he really meant it too, although she detected a little boyish shyness.

"You too. That was a great play last night."

"I'd say Corey stole the show," Jared said proudly. "He's a character actor, you know—really got into the part. In fact, after we got home, he stayed in character for a while, would only speak to me in 'baaas.'"

They laughed, then Kenzie said, "Maybe he'll be an actor when he grows up."

"He'll have to expand his repertoire. Not many movies cast a sheep as the lead character. Even in *Babe*, they were only supporting characters." Jared grinned and took a chair close to Kenzie, his eyes on her face. "It's nice you could come and visit your family for Christmas."

"It'll be a nice break. It's been a few years since I've been home for the holidays—as Tom keeps reminding me." She shot a look at her brother.

"Kenzie's a bigwig with Midwest Computers in Chicago," Tom explained. "She's always saying it's hard to break away."

"A lot of our sales come at Christmastime," Kenzie reminded him.

Jared was sympathetic. "I'm a firm believer in the old saying, 'Strike when the iron is hot.'"

"Exactly." She arched an eyebrow at her brother then said, "But it is good to be back. I have a lot of wonderful memories growing up here. I'd forgotten how relaxing a small town can be."

"If you'd come back a little more often, you wouldn't forget," Tom bantered.

Kenzie rolled her eyes then turned to Jared. "So how do you like it in Lake Forest?"

"It's been great." Jared was enthusiastic. "Of course I've always loved this area, so I jumped at the chance to come here."

"Mandy told me you opened a restaurant in town."

"Jared's Café. Best place in town to get a bite to eat. You'll have to stop in. I'm kitty-corner across the street."

"I'll stop by." Kenzie was rewarded by Jared's genuine look of pleasure. It was amazing how drawn she was to this personable man.

"I can personally vouch for the club sandwich on twelve-grain bread," Tom said. "Goes great with the broccoli-cheese soup. Jared bakes his own bread on the premises. When you walk in, the smell lifts you off your feet."

Kenzie turned to Jared. "You bake bread? I'm impressed."

"Don't be," Jared replied shyly. "It's my recipe, but I have a baker who does all the work. I'm just the manager, janitor, and sandwich-maker all rolled into one."

"I'll have to check it out."

"Come by for lunch sometime. Bring Sara. It'll be on the house."

Over the years Kenzie had learned to guard her heart, never letting herself become attached to people or places despite her dream of having both. But she felt a swoop of joy that seemed to have its origin in nothing at all except the presence of this man. And the way he looked at her—like she was someone worth a second look. That was a boost to her ego. And the feeling was mutual. It had been some time since she'd been so attracted to a man.

Taking his feet off his desk, Tom asked, "What can I do for you, Jared?"

"I was wondering how things are going on my house—if you'd had any interest since I dropped the price. I'm a little anxious about selling."

"Understandable," Tom assured him. "I'm glad you let me set up a lockbox so anyone can show it anytime. I've got several people lined up to see it. Do you know Carlos and Tracy Perez? They run the travel agency just down the road. I'm trying to arrange for them to see it next week."

"That's great."

"So you're selling your home too?" Kenzie spoke up, interested. "Small world. Did you know Tom had his home up for sale?"

Jared winked at Tom. "Well, it's not for sale anymore. I bought it."

The smile that had been on Kenzie's face froze, cracked, and fell right off. Her eyes darted to Tom, then back to Jared. Maybe she hadn't heard right. "Um, say that again."

"I'm buying Tom's home—I put an offer on it a few days ago."

Kenzie's chest tightened just as it had last night when she'd seen the *sold* sticker. She stared at Tom. "I didn't know until last night that you'd even had an offer. You'd been telling me for months that no one was interested. In fact, the last thing you told me before I came was that you weren't even showing it."

"I wasn't—until Jared came by," Tom said mildly.

There was a fluttering of anxiety as she turned to Jared and said the first thing that came into her mind. "But, but you can't buy Tom's house." Kenzie was aware she sounded panicky, but she didn't care.

Tom looked bewildered. "And why not?" Kenzie groped for words, but he went on, "Maybe no one has ever explained the process of selling a house to you, but if a person puts their home up for sale, it's because they want someone else to buy it."

"But we're talking about *your* home!"

His brow furrowed. "Yes, and soon it will be Jared's home." Tom spoke slowly as if dealing with someone of limited intelligence.

Kenzie cried out, "But I wanted to buy your house!"

Tom's broad face looked even more puzzled now. "Why would you want to buy my house?"

"I'm moving back to Lake Forest."

Astonished, Tom asked, "Well, that's news. When did you decide to do that? You haven't said a word." Then he frowned. "And just when were you planning on sharing this little bit of news with the family?"

"Well, I was going to tell you on Christmas."

Tom threw up his hands. "That's over two weeks away! And you were just going to sit on this until then? And if you wanted the house, why didn't you *say* something? You *do* realize I've had it listed for six months." He shook his head. "I really can't believe that in all the times we've talked, you've never said a *word* about moving back. Not one single, solitary word." If his words had been visible entities, icicles would have been hanging from them.

Rising, Jared shuffled his feet awkwardly, embarrassed at being caught in the crossfire of a family spat. He edged toward the door then nodded politely. "Um, I'd better get back to the café. Let me know if anything develops, Tom. Nice to see you, Kenzie."

Tom acknowledged his departure with a brief glance then returned his steely gaze to Kenzie. It was his big-brother laser glare which used to intimidate Kenzie, but no longer.

"You *can't* sell the house," Kenzie told him.

"Too late. It's sold."

"It's only an offer. Can't you turn it down?"

Tom leaned forward. "What's gotten into you, Kenzie? No, I can't turn it down. I've already accepted it and signed on the dotted line."

"But it hasn't gone through yet," Kenzie said desperately. "It's not final."

"I signed an agreement that I would sell Jared my house," Tom replied gruffly in a voice that would brook no dissention. Then he asked, "Are you really going to move here?" She nodded. "But why? I thought you were happy where you were."

"There are a lot of reasons." Kenzie rubbed her throbbing right temple. "For starters, I want Sara to have the same kind of childhood I did." Kenzie had never forgotten the magic of her childhood and wanted the same for her daughter. "And Sara has always loved it here."

"Like you used to." Tom made it sound like an accusation.

"You may not believe it, but I still do. And I'm tired of living in the city. You're just a face in a crowd there. Oh, I love the theatre, museums, and all of that, but Chicago's within driving range. I don't want to live there anymore. It's a different kind of life—you don't know who your neighbors are, and there's a bar on every corner. I'm tired of six-lane freeways, shootings in parks, and being afraid of walking on the street after dark. I started feeling like I was in a rat race and the rats were winning."

Tom leaned back in his chair. "I had no idea." His voice had lost its hard edges. "Part of this has to be your fancy job. You're always under so much pressure."

"I used to be under pressure."

"What does that mean?"

"I quit my fancy job."

"Just like that?"

"Yep."

"Wow. I thought you loved it." Tom rubbed his jaw. "Did you think it through? At times you can be a little impulsive and act without considering the consequences."

Sometime, Kenzie would tell him about Matt and the larger reasons that led to her resignation.

He asked, "What are you going to do now?"

Kenzie's face brightened. "I have a new job."

"Already? Where?"

"Reliance Software. I've known the executive vice president for years—we've been at a lot of conferences together. So when I started looking around, I called to see if they had any positions available, and he said they needed a general manager at their new facility in—get this—Munderlein."

"Wow." Tom was suitably impressed.

"I'll say. Being offered a job only ten minutes from Lake Forest was like a blessing straight from heaven." Kenzie smiled. "And despite my 'impulsive nature' as you put it, I thought a lot about the job before deciding. I prayed about it and had a good feeling, so I accepted it. I'll have a lot of the same responsibilities I had at Midwest, so it all works out perfectly. Except now I need a house."

"And you wanted mine." Tom appeared troubled. "I still don't know why you didn't say something sooner."

Because she was an idiot. Out loud, she said, "I wanted to surprise you for Christmas."

Tom scoffed. "You surprised me all right."

CHAPTER SIX

AFTER DINNER, WHILE EVERYONE WAS still at the table, Sara hurried to the kitchen and proudly returned with a plate of Peanut Butter Blossom Cookies[1], which had a chocolate Kiss in the middle.

"These are awesome!" Kenzie praised, taking one.

Sara wanted to share the credit. "Grandma helped me make them." She held out the plate to her grandfather.

"They look so good I'm going to take two," Allen said. "These are one of my favorites, you know. You can't do any better than having chocolate and peanut butter in the same cookie." He took a bite. "Hmm, and they're nice and soft too."

"Just the way you like them." Sara threw her grandmother a knowing glance. Kenzie caught the exchange. Her mother must have mentioned that during their cookie-making session. She'd told Kenzie the same thing when she was little.

"It was nice to have Sara's help today," Elaine said. "I want to have a lot of different cookies for the party after we go caroling. So I'm making extra and freezing some from each batch."

"We're going caroling?" Sara asked, taking a drink of milk.

"Well, it started out as caroling but morphed into a Christmas program. A bunch of people go to different rest homes on Christmas Eve and sing carols. You remember going with us, don't you?"

Sara thought hard. "I think so."

"It's been so long since Sara's been here for Christmas, she's forgotten," Allen grumbled, looking from underneath hooded eyes at Kenzie.

---

1 The recipe for Peanut Butter Blossom Cookies can be found at the end of the book.

The sting of rebuke felt like a slap. Taking a deep breath, Kenzie let it slide.

Elaine wanted to make sure Sara remembered. "A lot of people in town get together every year and form groups that go to different rest homes and put on a program. We always invite a few close friends to come here afterward to visit and have cookies and hot chocolate."

"Grandma, what's a rest home?"

Elaine blinked. "Hmm, I don't think they're called that anymore."

"They're assisted living centers now," Kenzie said.

Sara still looked confused, so Elaine went on, "They're places where older people live who need someone to help take care of them."

They started to clear the table, with Sara carrying dishes while Allen put food away.

Standing by the sink, Kenzie asked her mother, "Is it all right to just rinse the plates before putting them in the dishwasher, or do you want them gone over with a brush?"

"Rinsing is fine." Elaine shook her head as she put the rolls in a plastic bag. "I've always thought there ought to be a support group for women who can't put dishes in a dishwasher without cleaning them first."

Once done, they went into the family room. Kenzie knelt near the fireplace on the tan carpet beside a cardboard box she'd brought out earlier. Before she opened it, she asked, "Is it all right if we put out a few of our own decorations?"

"Of course," Elaine assured her. "It's nice to have familiar things. Traditions are very important at Christmas."

Scurrying over, Sara reached into the box and pulled out a ceramic Christmas house. Tossing the bubble wrap aside, she ran over and showed it to her grandparents on the couch. "This is mine. Look, it has a cat on the front porch." She set it on the coffee table then ran back. Kenzie handed her a large snow globe. Sara shook it and, once more, ran over to her grandparents to show them the tiny village caught in a snowstorm.

"That is really something," Allen said, admiring it. "Why don't you put it by the TV, and we can give it a shake whenever we want to make it snow. What else do you have?"

Setting the globe down with the utmost care, Sara went and pulled out a slightly bedraggled penguin. A striped scarf adorned his neck, and his red hat had a pom-pom on the end. She held it up for her grandparents to admire.

"His name is Poppy the Penguin."

"Poppy has always been one of Sara's favorites." Kenzie studied the scruffy penguin. "I tried washing it, but it didn't turn out too well."

"That's all right. He's in better shape than I am," Allen remarked.

Sara gave Poppy an affectionate squeeze then gave it to her grandmother to hold.

When she came back, Kenzie handed her a music box which looked like a small pond. Sara wound it, and two tiny bears began dancing erratically across the glass surface. Then Kenzie pulled out the last item, a small wooden reindeer.

"I remember that!" Elaine said. "Tyrone gave it to you."

"I'm surprised you remembered after all these years," Kenzie said.

"How could I forget? You two were so close. That was a magical Christmas."

"You say that about every Christmas," Kenzie reminded her.

With a half smile curving her lips, Elaine replied, "That's because each Christmas *is* magical."

Kenzie went to a narrow table that stood against the wall by the kitchen and rearranged the gold and silver glittery candles so there was room for the reindeer in the middle. Her mother was right—that had been a magical time. Tyrone had made the little wooden reindeer himself. It had been the best Christmas of her life.

"Okay, Sara, it's bedtime. Give Grandma and Grandpa a hug."

Sara threw herself at them and, after giving them big kisses, grabbed Poppy the Penguin. After their bedtime routine of scripture reading, teeth brushing, and prayer, Kenzie kissed her daughter good night and returned to the family room.

Her father was reading a novel, and her mother was working on a Sudoku puzzle. Kenzie plopped down in an overstuffed chair. "I talked to Tom today about his house."

"What about it?" Elaine asked, the book open on her lap.

"I told him I wanted to buy it."

They were as astonished as Tom had been.

"Why on earth would you want to buy Tom's house?" her father asked curtly.

There were at least a million reasons—most of them were too deep and nebulous to verbalize. For the last few years, her world had been so chaotic that Kenzie felt a driving need to return to a time when life was uncomplicated and not whirling out of control. Her divorce had been emotionally draining, and leaving Midwest after eleven years had been almost as distressing. It wasn't fair to have to quit because of a creepy coworker. Kenzie needed a place where she could slow down, catch her breath, and regain her equilibrium. She'd come back to Lake Forest to regain a sense of security and to provide her daughter with a stable life. Buying the home she'd grown up in had been the keystone to all of her plans. She just *had* to have the house. It seemed impossible to compress all feelings into words her parents could understand.

Instead, she downplayed what she'd been facing recently. "Life has been a bit difficult the last few years," Kenzie began. "I wanted to buy Tom's house because I wanted—no, I needed—a place where I could start over."

"Start over? What kind of talk is that?" Allen asked. "You've got a good job. Why would you want to throw in the towel?"

She *knew* her father wouldn't understand. "I needed to make some changes in my life. I decided moving back to Lake Forest would give me and Sara the stability and foundation we need right now."

Elaine squealed in delight. "You're coming back?" She struggled to get up, and finally Allen gave her a boost from behind. She hurried over to her daughter and hugged her fiercely. "How wonderful! I'm so excited!"

Her father remained seated. "That's some news." His face and voice were like stone. "Glad you finally let us in on your little secret."

"It wasn't a secret," Kenzie shot back.

"No? Well, you hadn't said a word until now," her father declared balefully. "We're always the last to know anything."

Kenzie was readying a sharp retort when her mother glanced anxiously down the hall toward Sara's room. Kenzie bit back her words, but her father went on, oblivious as always.

"Tom's been trying to sell his house a good long while. Why didn't you say something before now?"

She'd expected this and prepared a rebuttal: House sales were slow. Tom said he hadn't been showing his house. He'd priced his home high even though he knew it would put off buyers. He thought it would take up to a year to sell. Last but not least, Kenzie wanted her offer to be a special Christmas surprise to Tom and Mandy.

Kenzie began to ramble—something she did at times, though not often. When she realized what she was doing, she stopped abruptly. Allen stared, looking like someone had hit him on the head with a shovel. None of her reasons had seemed to penetrate her father's brain.

He came out of his catatonic state, shaking his head in disgust. "Nothing like planning ahead. And now you've blown your chance. You had to gamble you could get it before someone else did. Well, you lost that bet."

Spurs of indignation pricked Kenzie. She took a deep breath then another as she'd been taught. Why did he always have to be so negative and derogatory? She was preparing a scathing response which had nothing to do with the topic at hand but everything with her father's callousness, when her mother spoke up.

"I knew you loved the house, but I had no idea your feelings ran so deep. Of course, we did live there until you were ten—it's natural for you to be attached to it."

"I was so glad you kept the house and rented it out instead of selling it when we moved. And when Tom got married and bought it, I thought it would always be in the family."

"It could have been," Allen said. "If you'd said something."

There he went again—spouting off and making things worse.

Her mother must have sensed her irritation, for she asked hurriedly, "When were you thinking of moving back?"

"As soon as possible."

"Oh my!" Elaine was clearly surprised.

Allen narrowed his eyes. "What about your job?"

Time for another revelation. "I quit."

Her father stared, then raised and lowered his shoulders. "Just like that? You're making $95,000 a year, and you just *quit*?"

Elaine frowned at him. "Will you calm down? Kenzie is an adult— she knows what she's doing." Then she turned to her daughter and asked worriedly, "What *are* you doing?"

"What's best for me. There were some things going on at work, and I had to make a change." Kenzie refused to look at her father. She was *not* going to get into the reasons behind that now. She'd had enough of his negativity for one night. "Besides, I've got another job lined up."

Elaine sat down as if her legs had given out. Apparently, all these revelations were taking a toll. Faintly, she asked, "What kind of job?"

"It'll be a lot like the one I had at Midwest—I'll be a general manager and have a lot of the same responsibilities: recruiting and training staff, writing company policies, making sure day-to-day operations run efficiently and projects are completed on time." She stole a look at her father. Apparently her list had soothed him. He didn't seem quite as disgruntled as before. "I'm hoping something will work out so I can still buy Tom's house. I know he got an offer, but after all, isn't an offer just that—an offer? It's not set in stone."

Her parents exchanged glances, and Kenzie went on. "I need to find a place to live until I can get things straightened out."

Elaine piped up. "You can always stay with us, dear!" Her mother seemed so hopeful—her heart was in her shining blue eyes. "We'd love to have you and Sara."

"I appreciate that. But what if the worst happens and I can't get Tom's house? It might take me a while to find another place. Then, once you move, I'd need to find someplace else to stay. I think it'd be easier for me to find my own place now."

"What do you mean? *Once we move?*" her father barked.

"Mom told me you were going to move to Arizona. She told me the two of you had flown out and looked at homes."

Blinking rapidly, Elaine stuttered, "Well, yes, but th—that was months ago. We *thought* we wanted to move there, but when we flew out and looked around—well, it was so hot, and people had all these *rocks* instead of lawn. And, I told you, dear, that we hadn't found a house. So your father and I took some time, talked it over, and decided we didn't want to move away from Tom, Mandy, and the children."

"Why didn't you tell me?" Kenzie cried.

"Why?" her father asked in a low, biting voice. "So you could change your mind about moving here?" He rose slowly—as if it took all his energy he had to stand. "You wouldn't have taken that new job, would you, if you'd known we'd decided to stay." It was a statement, not a question.

"Honey," her mother said in a distressed voice, "I know I talked to you about this, but you always seemed so distracted."

Vague memories surfaced of her mother calling her at work when she'd had deadlines, her boss on her back, meetings lined up, a conference call waiting—

Her father went on, his voice flat. "You wouldn't have planned to move back if you'd known we were going to be here."

It was rare indeed when Kenzie couldn't think of anything to say. Her silence was all Allen needed. Stiff legged, he went to stare out the window at the dark pine trees.

Elaine's gray head bowed, and Kenzie said earnestly, "Mom, I didn't decide to move back just because you were leaving. I—I didn't remember you telling me you were staying. I've been so swamped at work that it's been hard to keep my head above water."

Elaine's eyes were bright. "I shouldn't have called you at work. And you've been so distracted and busy the past few months that I never mentioned it again. It went clean out of my mind." She forced the corners of her mouth up to reassure Kenzie that all was well.

But all was not well. For a moment, Kenzie considered going over and putting her arms around her father. But he stood so still and silent. His back was a granite mountain—solid and unyielding. Unbidden came the memory of his words shortly after she'd told her parents that Larry wanted a divorce. Even now, the sharp hurt felt like a fingernail torn to the quick.

Kenzie turned and walked out.

CHAPTER SEVEN

STANDING BEHIND THE PLEXIGLASS SHIELD, Jared moved like a dancer between the metal bins of tomatoes, onions, pickles, cheese, and condiments, expertly arranging sandwiches to customers' specifications. He was pleased—they'd had a good lunch crowd today. Although orders had slowed, there were still a fair number of people seated in the cozy cherry-red booths and chairs at white tables. The walls were a honey tan with textured wallpaper in a darker tan below the chair railing. Jared had picked out the floor himself—black and white tile. He enjoyed the gentle murmur of conversations in the background. A few people were busy on iPads or cell phones.

A new batch of bread must have just come out of the oven in the back, for Jared inhaled the delectable aroma. He handed a plastic tray with sandwiches, chips, and empty cups to a couple. They headed for the drink machine. Jared started on the next sandwich then heard a familiar voice. It was Kenzie Forsberg. Asking for him.

His chest swelled in pleasure as Pam pointed him out. He was working on an order for two women when Kenzie walked over. What big brown eyes she had. And that smile—it was as breathtaking as he remembered it being on the night of the Christmas play. Still, that scene in Tom's office had definitely been odd. Feeling suddenly awkward, Jared fought the impulse to hold back and scuff his toes like a little boy. How strange Kenzie hadn't told her own brother she wanted to buy his house until it was too late.

"I'll be right with you," he told Kenzie. Working swiftly, he slapped slices of cheddar on the fresh bread; added lettuce, yellow peppers, and tomato; squirted on condiments; then skewered it all with a long toothpick. Jared placed the second sandwich in a cardboard container with its mate and handed the tray to the women.

"You've got a nice place here," Kenzie said, looking around at the green silk plants resting on low walls which divided tables from one another. "I came in to see if I could talk with you, but it looks like you're busy."

"I can get someone to take over," Jared assured her. Then he asked, "Are you hungry? Would you like a sandwich?"

She sniffed the air appreciatively. "It smells so wonderful. You don't have to ask me twice. As long as I can have a piece of fudge too. You don't play fair, putting fudge and all those desserts in a display case you have to walk past before you even order a sandwich."

"Yeah, I'm ruthless that way."

She went back to the dessert case and pointed to the chocolate-walnut fudge. Jared used a square of white tissue paper to pick out a piece and hand it to her. "Fudge—nature's way of making up for Mondays."

She laughed and took a nibble.

Jared told Pam to put the order on a special ticket; then he went back to the sandwich display case. "So what would you like?"

Kenzie eyed the menu hanging on the wall. "What's good?"

"Everything." He liked the way her eyes crinkled when she smiled.

"Oh, you do make it difficult." After a moment, she rattled off, "Twelve-grain bread, turkey, provolone, and run it through the grill."

"You've done this before."

While her sandwich was heating, Jared slapped together a sandwich for himself. When hers came out with the cheese nicely melted, he added the fixings. Jared then signaled to a boy in the back to come take his place. He tossed his gloves in the garbage and, still wearing his white apron, came out the far side, passing a high counter where a number of people sat on red-cushioned stools. Jared led Kenzie to a booth near the back. It wasn't until they were seated across from each other that Jared realized he still had on his chef's hat. Quickly, he swiped it off and laid it beside him.

"Sorry, my sister thought the hat made me look legit."

"It fooled me." Kenzie took a bite. "Oh, this *is* good!"

"Of course. The hat never lies."

Kenzie pulled apart her small bag of Sun Chips. "So how long have you lived here?"

"About three years. I moved here from Rockport."

"Mandy told me your wife had passed away. I'm sorry."

"Thank you." He picked up a quartered pickle from beside his sandwich and took a bite. "After I lost Robin, I stayed in Rockport a while—you know what they say about not making any major decisions for a year." He gave a slight shrug. "I stuck to that, but even before the year was up, I knew I wanted to get away."

"How did Corey take it?"

"He misses his grandparents, but he adjusted. He loves it here now. So do I—it's a beautiful area."

"It sure is." Kenzie wiped her mouth with a napkin. "So are you renting?"

"Nope. I bought a little house. Something small and inexpensive because I wanted to make sure I could make a go of the café before I bought something larger. Plus, I didn't have a lot to put into a house, not with starting a new business."

"I'm sorry about what happened yesterday with Tom."

"Don't worry about it."

"I should have told him before that I wanted to buy his house, but Tom said the market was really slow, that he hadn't been showing it, and a lot of things that lulled me into a false sense of security. So I wanted to surprise him." Kenzie went on for several minutes then stopped. "I don't know why I'm talking so much. Tom says it's one of my faults."

"I don't know why." To tell the truth, he would have been happy to listen all day. Jared took another bite. How amazing it was to be sitting here and talking with Kenzie like they were old friends when he barely knew her. Usually he found it hard to talk with women, especially beautiful ones he had just met.

He asked, "So you're moving back here to Lake Forest?"

"Yep."

"What about your job?"

"I quit. I'm going to work for Reliance Software."

She must be a real go-getter. And confident. She'd quit her position, and not only did she seem fine with it, she'd already gotten another one. Kenzie must be good at what she did. "When do you start?"

"In January."

"Good luck. I'm sure you'll do well." Jared didn't know why he'd added that last part—except she looked very capable.

"Thanks. Actually I'm kind of nervous. I've been with Midwest so long that going to a new company is a leap of faith. Of course, I didn't tell Tom I was worried—he thinks I was being impulsive to quit my old job. But I had my reasons."

Ah, so Kenzie wasn't quite as sure of herself as she appeared. Yet Jared liked that this attractive, charming woman had a vulnerable side. He was about to ask why she'd quit, but right then, a short young man with small ears walked by carrying a basin and a wet cloth.

"Hi, Jared," he called in a voice a shade too loud.

"Hi ya, Scott!"

Scott looked at Jared with a happy expression then glanced at Kenzie, who smiled at him. He went to the next booth and started wiping the table.

Dumping the chips onto her napkin, Kenzie asked, "What made you decide to buy Tom's house?"

There was no easy answer because there were so many reasons. Some were more important than others, but the bottom line was a deep inner belief that this home was the one for him and Corey. "I looked at a lot of houses, and this is the first one that really felt like home to me."

When Kenzie looked at him encouragingly, he went on. "I like the idea of sitting on the front porch in the evenings, reading the paper, and waving at the neighbors as they walk by." That sounded foolish, but Kenzie nodded and seemed to understand. "And Corey loves the huge backyard. He keeps asking for livestock. His latest request is a sheep."

"Wonder where that came from?" Kenzie grinned and picked up the last half of her sandwich.

He liked watching her eat; she was so pretty.

"What?" Kenzie asked, a hand going to her face. "Do I have something on my face?"

Her comment broke him out of his reverie. "Sorry, I didn't mean to stare." What was the matter with him? His face reddened, and he shifted in his seat, trying to think what to say. The truth? It was worth a shot. "It's just that, uh, you're really pretty."

Now Kenzie blushed. "Compliments and terrific sandwiches—no wonder you do such a great business."

They talked further. Once Jared glanced over and saw Pam studying him intently. Did she need his help? Nah, she would have sent Scott to get him. There were only a few people in line.

Kenzie followed the direction of his gaze. "Do you need to get back?"

"It's all right for now."

She cleared her throat "Um, the reason I asked what made you decide on Tom's house is because there are a lot of homes for sale in Lake Forest."

He sipped his water with an uneasy feeling that he knew what she was getting at. "Yeah, and I've seen most of them."

"Well, like I said, there are an awful lot of homes, and I hoped you might be able to find something else you'd like just as well."

"So you can buy your brother's house."

Kenzie gave a nervous little laugh. "That's the idea."

"Did I mention I've looked at a *lot* of homes?" Jared kept his tone polite, but his throat felt tight.

"You did, but you see, I was hoping to buy Tom's house."

"That makes two of us."

"Couldn't you find another one?" There was pleading now in her voice. Kenzie's smile was big and full of purpose. "Tom's home means so much to me. I don't know if Tom mentioned it, but it used to be my parents' home. I grew up there."

It was incredible. Did she even know what she was asking? "And you want to know if I would consider buying a different home."

"Well, yes. I spent the first ten years of my life there. I have a lot of memories tied up in that house."

"I've already made an offer on it—an offer which was accepted," he said flatly.

"But like I said, there are lots of other houses around."

"I've found the house I want. I don't need to see any more." Jared crushed his napkin into a tight ball and threw it onto the tray.

The brightness faded from Kenzie's face. "I don't think you understand how important this house is to me—and to my daughter. If you would withdraw your offer," Kenzie said sweetly, "I'm sure Tom wouldn't charge you any penalty."

"He sure won't because I'm not going to withdraw it." He folded his arms across his chest.

Kenzie's face pinked up. "I hoped you'd be reasonable. That home is a part of my childhood, my history. I made plans to move here just so I could live there. It's the only house I want in Lake Forest. This, this is very important to me."

Oh great, now her voice had turned trembly. But he had to stand firm. "Like you said, there are a lot of homes up for sale. I'm sure you'll find one that will suit you just as well." Jared waited. What would she come up with next?

Kenzie's eyes fixed on his. Her lips tightened as though she did not like what she saw. "You know, Tom has a lot of experience. He'll figure out a way to help me get the house."

Quirking an eyebrow, Jared said, "Is that so? I didn't get that from him while I was there. Are you saying Tom changed his mind after I left?" When Kenzie hesitated, Jared knew he had her. "I didn't think so." It was clear he'd gotten to her by the way her face reddened. A riled-up Kenzie was something to see—her eyes positively sparked fire.

"Are you calling me a liar?" she asked.

"Should I?"

In a huff, Kenzie rose, crumbs falling from her lap. She stalked off, and Jared had to hurry to make it to the door in time to open it for her. She tossed her head, took a step, then turned back. "That house means so much to me," she begged. "Won't you reconsider?"

Jared hated to disappoint her, but the house meant a lot to him too. "Afraid not."

CHAPTER EIGHT

"Need more tape," Kenzie said, using the last of her roll on a brightly wrapped package. Mandy handed her another roll, and Kenzie slipped it into the dispenser. They'd all gone to church that morning and had dinner together. Kenzie's parents had offered to watch the children so she and Mandy could wrap presents undisturbed at Mandy's house. Tom had gone back to church to help with tithing settlement.

"It's nice of you to help me wrap," Mandy said. She and Kenzie sat on her bed, surrounded by rolls of wrapping paper. Mandy leaned over to reach a video game and a book, then swung her head to get her dark hair out of her eyes. "Tom tries to find time to help now and then, but we usually end up having a wrapping marathon on Christmas Eve." She handed the book to Kenzie. "That's for Hillary."

"I'm glad to help," Kenzie said, meaning it. "Wrapping is one of the fun parts of Christmas." She and Larry used to savor it—and it didn't take long to wrap presents for one child.

"Hey, now that you're moving back, we'll be able to do this every year!"

Kenzie wasn't sure about that as she folded paper around the end of the book. "It's fun to wrap for one or two, but the pleasure diminishes exponentially for each additional person."

Mandy laughed. "I agree. Thank goodness Adam started helping the last couple of years." She cut a piece of red-and-white striped paper and laid a pair of jeans for Tom in the middle. "I am soooo happy you're moving here. So tell me, are you excited about your new job?"

"More nervous than excited—new people, new expectations. I'd gotten really comfortable at Midwest. It was hard to leave."

"Will you still be an executive director?"

"My official title will be 'general manager.'"

"That hasn't quite got the zing of 'executive director,' does it?" Mandy wrote a tag, stuck it on the package, and tossed it into the pile at the foot of the bed. "I mean, they have general managers at Burger King."

Kenzie crumpled a piece of leftover paper and threw it at Mandy, who ducked and giggled. "So what if it's a different title?" she asked. "It means the same thing."

"I hope you won't be as stressed there as you were at Midwest."

"My friend who works there says it's a different atmosphere from Midwest. Plus, I'll be leaving one huge pressure point behind—Matt Renault."

"Is that the guy who—"

"Yep."

Mandy gave a mock shudder. "Glad you're getting away from that pervert. And now that you're here, you can start meeting cute guys. I've already started a list. I know you're coming here for a reason—to find someone and fall in love."

"Last thing on my mind." Kenzie taped green paper over a pair of pajamas for Brian.

"Come on, don't you miss being in a relationship?"

"My 'relationship' with Larry was enough to last a lifetime."

"You've got to put that behind you. I know it was horrible and you went through a lot, but now you're moving on with your life." Mandy reached for the curly ribbon. "You're going to fall in love here—I know it."

"You're a hopeless romantic."

"Is there any other kind?" Mandy unrolled red paper with polar bears and snipped away. "Leave it to me," she implored. "I'll take care of everything. Give me a few weeks, and I'll have your weekends filled for the next three years."

"Forget it. I've got more important things to worry about."

"Like what?"

"Like figuring out how to get Jared interested in some other house. I'd planned on buying this house, remember?"

Mandy looked dismayed. "But he already put an offer on this one."

"Does no one in this family know what an offer is? It's a proposal, a suggestion, a proposition—something that's utterly breakable. I just need to find the loopholes that will get you and Tom off the hook and let me buy it."

When Mandy dropped her scissors and turned astonished eyes upon her, Kenzie went on—a bit defensively now. "I've got to do *something*! I've got a new job and no place to live. And think of Sara. I've already uprooted her, and now we don't even know where we'll be living."

She'd always prided herself on being a responsible parent. Her main objective in moving to Lake Forest was to provide a secure home for her daughter with lots of family support. Also, she needed some stability in her own life. The only reason she hadn't unraveled during her divorce was due in large part to Mandy, Tom, and her mother. She didn't just *want* this house; she *needed* it.

Picking herself up and gluing herself together after Larry left had been hard enough, but then she'd had to deal with that scumbag, Matt Renault. Because of him, she'd had to search for a new job. Everything she'd gone through had been exhausting—emotionally and physically—and she was ready for a break. She just *had* to get this house.

"You're welcome to stay with us," Mandy assured her as she tore cellophane off a new roll of paper. "And I'm sure your folks would love to have you."

Neither one of those were viable solutions. Mandy and Tom's house was full, and Kenzie wasn't comfortable moving in with her parents, not with the way things were. The house wasn't big enough for her, Sara, and her father's mouth.

Finding a great job minutes from Lake Forest had been nothing short of a miracle. And the thought of buying her childhood home was a dream. Simply thinking about moving into the home she'd known as a child brought a deep, warm comfort and a security that had been sorely lacking in her life the past years. They said you couldn't go home again, but by George she was going to try!

Pulling off a piece of tape, Kenzie grimaced to think of how indifferent Jared had been when she told him how much the house meant to her. He'd even had the audacity to say *she* could find another home. How *dare* he? The keystone to her plans to move back depended on buying Tom's home. Somehow, she had to figure out a way to buy this house, or everything would collapse like someone blowing on a house of cards.

There was a thump as Mandy tossed another present on the pile. She surveyed the presents they'd wrapped with satisfaction. "I'm bushed. Let's call it good."

"I'll be glad to wrap more."

"You've been a good Samaritan long enough."

"Is there anything else you need help with?"

Mandy tilted her head. "Have you been talking to Tom?"

"No, why?"

"It was the way you said that. I thought he might have mentioned my little painting project. He doesn't want me overdoing because I'm pregnant."

"What are you painting? Something for Christmas? A table for the kids? A wagon?"

"Bedrooms."

"*Bedrooms*? Why on earth would you paint the bedrooms when you're moving?"

"Honestly, for someone so smart, you sure can be dumb. I want to paint the bedrooms at the Steadman home."

"But you've got so much going on with packing and moving. Plus you're pregnant."

"Gee, thanks for clearing that up—I'd wondered what this bulge in my stomach could be." Mandy rolled her eyes. "But think about it. What's the worst thing about painting? I mean besides taping?" She went on, "Moving the furniture. That's why this is the *ideal* time to paint. The house is empty—the Steadmans have already moved to a retirement complex."

"I'm with Tom—I'm worried you're trying to do too much."

"I checked with my doctor—as long as the house is well ventilated, the paint is water based, and I don't get on ladders or get too tired, I'll be fine."

Now was the time to offer her services. The only problem was Kenzie hated painting. Maybe *hate* was the wrong word. *Loathe*. Yes, that was it. But what else could she do?

Trying to keep the funeral tone out of her voice, Kenzie asked, "Do you want me to help?" Then she repeated in her mind, *Say no. Say no. Say no.*

"That would be *fantastic!* Thanks!"

Kenzie nailed a smile on as she picked up scraps of paper, scissors, and tape.

Mandy piled the wrapped presents in a large black garbage sack. "I'll take these over to your folks and hide them in their garage. Then her sister-in-law offered her an out. "Since you can be a little reckless, I'll give you a chance to back out gracefully. I can tell by that weird look on your face that you're not too excited about painting. You look like a martyr at the stake just before they light the match."

"Of course I'll help. But this face is as good as you're going to get. Don't expect me to be a ray of sunshine."

Mandy threw her arms around Kenzie. "You *are* wonderful. We'll do it next week."

"Yay. I can't wait," Kenzie murmured in a melancholy tone.

"We'll have fun. You'll see."

"Right. Then as a treat afterwards, let's scrub your garbage cans." Then Kenzie had a great thought. "Wait a minute—you can't paint. You haven't closed on the house yet."

"You forget this is a small town. We do things differently here. Tom's known the Steadmans all his life. They trust him implicitly. I've already asked them about painting, and they said we can do whatever we want."

"Carte blanche, eh? Aren't you taking a big chance? What if something happens, and you don't get the house?"

"The only reason we wouldn't get the house is if we couldn't sell this one. Mandy winked at her sister-in-law, adding, "And that's not very likely—not when we have two buyers ready to kill each other to get it."

CHAPTER NINE

"The trick to making Mexican Wedding Cookies[2] is not to handle the dough too much," Elaine explained to Sara and Hillary, who stood beside her at the kitchen counter. Adam and Brian had begged off, preferring to play video games, and were ensconced in the office.

"Mix the dough just enough to blend the ingredients. If you overdo it, the cookies will be tough."

The girls happily rolled the dough in their hands to make balls. They placed each piece on the cookie sheet as carefully as if it were a crown jewel.

"I *like* making cookies," Sara said happily as she rolled another ball.

"Me too," Hillary added, flattening her ball slightly.

What fun it was to be making cookies with her granddaughters! Spontaneously, Elaine gave each of them a hug. "I like making cookies too—with you!"

"Do you think Grandpa would like to help?" Sara asked.

"Hmmm, probably not." Elaine glanced over to the family room, where Allen was sitting contentedly by the fireplace reading the *Ensign*. "But he'll be glad to help us eat them."

Sara giggled, then she looked at the large bowl of cookie dough. "We're sure making a lot."

"I'm going to send some home with Hillary, and I want enough to take to the rest home and to serve at the party afterwards."

Elaine slipped a cookie sheet in the oven as the girls rolled more balls. When they were done with the next sheet, Hillary had had enough and left to join the boys.

---

2 The recipe for Mexican Wedding Cookies can be found at the end of the book.

As she and Sara continued working, Elaine couldn't help saying, "I'm so glad you and your mom came for Christmas."

"Me too. I asked if we could come last year, but Mom said no." Sara's cookie fell apart, and she frowned at it like it was misbehaving on purpose.

Elaine showed her how to squish it back together. "I guess your mom had a lot going on at work."

"I don't think so." Sara sounded doubtful. "I think she was still mad at Grandpa."

Oh, dear. So Sara knew all about it. But that was inevitable, Elaine supposed. At times, the tension between Kenzie and Allen was as noticeable as the nose on her face. And the sad thing was that it didn't have to be that way. How many times had she told Kenzie and Allen to talk and work things out? She might as well have talked to a stump. Elaine had delicately broached the subject again yesterday, but Kenzie had brushed it away, spouting meaningless words about talking when the time was right. Elaine had heard it too many times to put any stock in it now.

Sara went on conversationally, "Mom told me that Grandpa hurt her feelings."

Glancing at Sara out of the corner of her eye, Elaine was hard-pressed to keep her voice casual. "Did she say what Grandpa did?"

"Mom wouldn't tell me." Sara started to fidget. "Grandma, I have to use the bathroom."

"You go right ahead." Sara hopped down, and Elaine went to the sink to get a glass of water. At least Kenzie hadn't burdened her daughter with the telling. Sipping the water, she looked over the backyard and on to the woods beyond. Memory swept back to that midsummer weekend nearly two years ago when everything had unraveled.

Kenzie and Sara had arrived for an unexpected visit. Without Larry. Vaguely, Kenzie explained Larry was busy, but Elaine knew something was up by her daughter's restlessness and slightly disjointed way of speaking.

Later that night, Kenzie told them in a broken voice that she and Larry were getting a divorce. The three of them stayed up late, and the tissue box was nearly empty by the time the three of them finally went to bed.

But it was the memory of the next day which remained imprinted indelibly on her mind. That morning, Kenzie's eyes were red and swollen, prompting Elaine to decide to make Kenzie's favorite for dinner—chicken fettuccine. She'd gone to the grocery store, and when she returned she was surprised to see her husband chopping wood in the hot sun.

Carrying her bags, she walked over to where chips were flying. Looking around, she remarked, "I don't see Kenzie's car."

"She left." Allen paused to raise an arm and wipe the sweat from his brow. Then he carefully positioned another log on the chopping block.

"She didn't go to the store, did she? I told her I was going to get the groceries."

The axe flashed in the sun and came down hard, splitting the wood with a crack. "No, she went home. Said to tell you good-bye."

The grocery sacks were like dead weights, pulling her arms to the ground. Elaine couldn't take it in. "I don't understand. Kenzie said they weren't going back until after church tomorrow." She glanced around as if she might see Kenzie. "Why would she go home?"

Allen paused and leaned on his axe. His face was red, and his shirt was soaked through with perspiration. "She didn't like what I had to say."

The grocery sacks slipped to the ground. They were filled with special things Elaine wanted to cook for her daughter and granddaughter. Boneless chicken for the fettuccine. Cantaloupe, grapes, and watermelon for a fruit salad. Walnuts, coconut, and chocolate chips for Sara's favorite layered cookie bars.

Ugh. Elaine's stomach felt like she'd swallowed one of the melons. She loved Allen, but for heaven's sake! He *had* to learn to control his tongue. Speaking in carefully regulated tones, because that was the only way she could stay in control, Elaine asked, "What did you say to her?"

"We were talking about the divorce. I asked her what went wrong— why Larry left. That's all."

The defensive tone in her husband's voice put Elaine on alert. Sometimes, Allen wasn't aware when he offended people by what he said, but this time he knew. Oh, yes, he knew. He just didn't want to admit it. It must have been very bad if Kenzie, who had grown up with him, had been offended enough to leave.

In a voice like steel, only an octave higher, Elaine ground out, *"What did you say?"*

When he told her, Elaine's lips went white, and even though the sun was beating down, a shiver ran through her.

Leaving the groceries scattered on the ground, Elaine turned and stumbled into the house. She sat at the kitchen table, holding her head in her hands and refusing to look up when the door opened and closed. Sounds told her Allen was putting groceries away, but he didn't speak. There was no need. Elaine knew Allen had said more than he was admitting. Probably much more. But she couldn't talk to him now. It would have to come later, once she'd calmed down enough not to throw the melon at his head.

So Allen had asked Kenzie why Larry had left her. That would be the crux of the matter—the thing Allen couldn't understand. Allen loved Larry like a second son. So when Kenzie had told them they were getting divorced, he had to deal not only with his daughter's pain but the knowledge that he was losing Larry. Ever since Larry had asked for Kenzie's hand in marriage, he could do no wrong in Allen's eyes. And so now, it was nearly inconceivable for him to wrap his mind around the fact that Larry had been—was—a jerk.

But Elaine had seen things her husband hadn't during the nine years of her daughter's marriage. She always pushed the worries aside, though, since Kenzie and Larry seemed happy—for the most part anyway. But at times, Kenzie made little comments that made Elaine afraid all was not well. A further, telling change was when they stopped sitting close and no longer held hands. And sometimes, when Kenzie and Larry spoke to each other, the words were polite but their tone and body language said something else entirely, indicating a widening gulf.

More disturbing were the times Elaine noticed Larry staring a little too long at another woman. It might be for a waitress or a sales clerk that Larry turned his charming smile on. And at their Christmas Eve parties, Larry often seemed a little too animated and attentive to unattached women.

Elaine came back to the present when Sara tugged at her blouse. "Grandma, the timer's going off."

"Oh, dear, it certainly is." She bustled over and slipped on an oven mitt.

As she set the cookies on a cooling rack, Sara asked, "What were you thinking about? Mom and Grandpa?"

Elaine peered into her granddaughter's blue eyes, which were so like her own. How astute Sara was for her age. "I was indeed. Those two need to talk and work things out." She put a ball of dough on the cookie sheet and flattened it slightly. "If someone hurts your feelings, go talk to them about it—don't let it go on, or you'll keep being sad."

Sara dusted her hands with flour and rolled another clump of dough. "I think Mom's sad about a lot of things—not just Grandpa."

"She is?" Elaine's chest tightened.

"Yeah. She tries to hide it, but I can tell." Then Sara added confidentially, "I think she's lonely."

That was bound to happen—after being married for so long. "I thought your mom went out on dates."

"Sometimes." Sara grimaced. "But she usually comes back in a bad mood."

Oh, dear. That didn't sound good.

Sara went on. "I wish Mom could find her friend for Christmas."

"What friend is that, dear?"

"The one Mom knew when she was little—the one she played with in the woods."

"Oh, yes, Tyrone. Such a funny name, but don't tell her I said so, okay?"

Sara grinned as her grandmother handed her the last bit of dough. "I won't. But Mom said she liked him a lot. It would be cool if she could find him."

Elaine put the last batch of cookies in, and they washed their hands at the sink. "Well, honey, Tyrone moved away a long time ago. Back when he was a little boy."

"He could have come back. Mom told me Tyrone liked it here. Do you think he could be here?"

It wasn't very likely. But who was she to squelch a child's hope at Christmastime? "It's possible. It might take a bit of Christmas magic, though, for Tyrone and your mom to find each other."

A huge grin split Sara's face. "I like Christmas magic!"

"Me too. It's pretty powerful stuff."

"Can we read that book—*Christmas Magic*?"

"About the little girl who goes outside and finds there's Christmas magic in the air?"

"Yeah!" Sara cried. "And her pets were singing 'Jingle Bells.'"

"And the mice were baking Christmas pies."

"And the snow people she built came to life and started dancing. Can we read it, Grandma?"

"Sure. You get it while I wash this bowl."

When Sara returned, Elaine took the last batch of cookies out, and the two of them went to the family room. Sitting by the fireplace, they took turns reading. Sara's face was glowing when they turned the final page. "See! I bet Tyrone's come back. Mom just has to find him." For some reason, reading the book had fueled her hope.

Elaine smoothed a stray wisp of hair from her granddaughter's face. "Well, the book certainly says there's a lot of magic in the air at Christmastime, making dreams come true." Although she didn't hold out much hope that Kenzie would meet Tyrone, Elaine *did* hope her daughter would meet someone special.

As if reading her mind, Sara said solemnly, "Mom needs someone so she's not lonely."

Giving her granddaughter a squeeze, Elaine asked, "How could she be lonely when she has you?"

Sara considered. "I'm in school a lot though. I told Mom she ought to have a baby, but she didn't think so."

Oh, dear. What could she say? "Having a baby is a big responsibility. A baby needs a mommy and a daddy."

"That's what Mom said." Sara pursed her lips. "But I still think she needs someone."

"But, honey, don't you like it with just you and your mom?"

Sara nodded vigorously. "But I want Mom to be happy. I don't want her to be alone."

"She's not alone. She has you."

"I think she'd like a grown-up friend."

CHAPTER TEN

THE TIRES CRUNCHED ON THE gravel driveway as Kenzie pulled up to her parents' home the following morning. As she grabbed the grocery sacks out of the Camry's trunk, Sara came out of the house and bounced down the front porch steps, wearing her purple coat and matching hat and gloves.

"Where are you going?" Kenzie asked.

"To the woods."

"Sounds like fun. Want company?"

Her daughter said eagerly, "Yeah!"

"Let me take these inside." Sara followed her in, and after putting the food away, Kenzie pulled on her gloves and grabbed her daughter's hand. The road in front of her parents' house dead-ended a third of a mile away with a parking lot for people who wanted to hike in the woods. While growing up, Kenzie felt privileged to live next to the woods—a gateway to her own special kingdom.

They crossed the backyard to the metal gate and went through. Taking the well-worn path, Kenzie and Sara walked through woods of oak and hickory. The branches of the ash trees were thin and bare in contrast with bulky green pine trees scattered here and there. Cold had turned the ground to iron and made the snow crunchy. Silence reigned supreme, and it was so restful and peaceful there that Kenzie wasn't sure how she had ever survived without being able to walk daily in this fairyland of trees and serenity. There was only an occasional bird or squirrel to witness their passing. The woods had always been Kenzie's favorite playground—the first place she went as a child when she finished with homework or household chores.

This was where she had spent two enchanted summers with Tyrone. Every day they did something new, fun, and exciting. One time, they collected pinecones, thinking they could sell them in town and become millionaires. Another time, they pretended to be Indians and stuck tall dried grass in their hair and shirt collars. They often laid in an open meadow, watching puffy clouds drift by and calling out any shapes they discovered in the constantly changing panorama.

Kenzie stepped over a fallen tree. What was Tyrone doing now? Was he happy? Did he ever think, like she did, about the summers they had spent together?

She and Sara were deeper in the woods now. The bare branches of the trees rubbed against each other, whispering scratchily in a light breeze which was sweet with the scent of pine.

"You're thinking of him, aren't you?" Caught up in the solemn stillness of the woods, Sara spoke in a whisper. It was almost as if they were wandering in a sacred place.

Kenzie was startled. Could Sara read her mind?

"You know—that boy."

"Actually, I *was* thinking about him." Kenzie had told Sara all about those magical summers. Her daughter had been fascinated—but Kenzie wasn't sure if it was because it was hard to imagine her mother had ever been a young girl or because it sounded so magical. Whichever it was, Sara listened spellbound whenever Kenzie talked about going on picnics, fishing in the pond, or catching grasshoppers.

"He liked to catch bugs," Sara recalled.

"I'll say. I wasn't too crazy about it but asked my mom for a net anyway. I'd chase after grasshoppers and other flying bugs while Tyrone went for the creepy crawlies. Like under rocks and rotted logs. Ugh." Kenzie shivered, making Sara laugh.

"What did you do with the bugs you caught?"

"Put them in quart jars. My dad punched holes in the lid so they had air. But every day before we went home, I made Tyrone turn the bugs loose. Far away from me!" Kenzie smiled. "Tyrone wasn't too happy—he wanted to keep them—but I insisted. I'd go off a ways, and he'd lay the jar on its side. When we came back the next day, the bugs would all be gone."

How carefree her childhood had been! How foolish she'd been—longing to grow up. She'd had no understanding of the difficulties that came from adulthood. Kenzie scuffed her toes in the snow. You could get blindsided when you least expected it.

A little over two years ago—still reeling from Larry's revelation and his demand for a divorce—Kenzie had come home to lick her wounds in Lake Forest. Shortly after her arrival, Kenzie had come here to meander the shady trails that had occasional patches of sunlight crossing her path. She'd walked for hours, but it wasn't far enough to leave the pain behind.

Her visit had ended abruptly after that dreadful talk with her father. His words had wounded her beyond measure, and without thought, Kenzie had packed and left. She always regretted not telling her mother good-bye, but hurt and anger had overridden all else.

Sara took her hat off and, stuffing it in her pocket, went off the trail, following deer tracks in the crusted snow. As she approached a clump of oak trees, her presence set off the insolent squawking of starlings.

Kenzie trailed after her. The old axiom that the wife is always the last to know had certainly been true in her case. There had been signs, of course, but they were easy to ignore when you trusted your husband. It was only when Kenzie looked back that she was able to see what she had missed. At the time, she hadn't given it a second thought when Larry exited his e-mail the second she walked into the room. The same went for his complaints about how his boss kept forcing him to work late. First it was once a week, then twice. How strange when Larry refused to let her use his cell phone when her battery had run down. And why the anger when she asked about unusual charges on their credit card bill? But she didn't worry until Larry began picking absurd things to fight about—as if cooking too many potatoes or planning a movie night with friends was a call to arms.

His decision to stop attending church had come as a shock. A crisis of faith, a friend told her, and Kenzie took care not to push or prod. She counseled with the bishop and determined to be a loving, supportive wife. How proud she'd been of herself for not making something out of nothing. Until the day Larry sat her down at the kitchen table and acted astounded when she didn't know he'd found someone else. He'd fallen out of love, he'd said. He needed to start a new life. The conversation was one-sided. All about what Larry needed, what he wanted, and what he was and wasn't going to do.

And because of Larry's new life, Kenzie got a new one as well.

The pain took a long time to ease, but eventually it did. And when, after a year and a half, she heard Larry's new love had left him for someone else, she didn't rejoice as she might have in the early days. Instead, it just seemed sad.

When an icy snowball hit her leg, Kenzie jumped. Behind her, Sara burst out laughing and laughed even more when Kenzie tried to make her own snowball—the icy snow refused to stick together.

Fearlessly, Sara ran to her mother. "It doesn't hold together too good."

"I noticed."

They returned to the path. All around was the muffled quietness of winter-cold air. The pale winter sunshine shone down from a vault of tender blue, burnishing Sara's head as she gazed at the dark pines and the brown dappled expanse of leafless trees.

"I love it here," Sara said contentedly, tilting her head at her mother. "You do too, don't you? Is that why you wanted to move here?"

Looking at her daughter's smooth, pink cheeks, Kenzie smiled. "Part of it. I do love it in the woods. Coming here brings back a lot of awesome memories."

Sara made a halfhearted attempt to skip, but her boots made her clumsy, and she abandoned the attempt. "Maybe you'll meet that boy here. Tyrone." She made a face. "What a dumb name. Sounds like a dork."

Inhaling, Kenzie said sharply, "It's *not* a dumb name! And Tyrone was *not* a dork!" Sara was startled by her mother's vehemence, and Kenzie added more gently, "He was my friend and a *really* nice boy."

"Sorry." Sara was full of remorse.

Kenzie took her daughter's hand. "It's okay. Tyrone really was wonderful. He was smart, kind, thoughtful, and a lot of fun to be with."

"And he was your best friend."

"He was." Kenzie arched an eyebrow. "So remember, you can't judge a dork by his cover—I mean, by his name."

Sara giggled as they rounded a curve.

"Tyrone was very self-conscious about his name—said he hated it and was going to change it when he grew up."

"You really liked him, didn't you? I can tell by the way your voice changes when you talk about him."

Really? She'd had no idea.

Sara went on. "Me and Grandma were talking about him yesterday. I think Tyrone moved back here."

Kenzie scoffed. "To Lake Forest? I don't think so."

"What happened to him?"

"I don't know." Kenzie held her daughter's hand a little tighter. "I wish I did."

They returned to the house. That night after dinner, they played games together for family home evening. Sara had great fun sending her grandparents' tokens back to home as they played Sorry. Allen and Elaine pretended great anguish each time, adding to Sara's delight. When the hour grew late, they packed up the games.

"It's time for bed, Sara," her mother told her.

Sara protested, "I don't want to—I'm not tired."

"Do you want to go Christmas shopping tomorrow?" Her little daughter nodded solemnly. "Then you need to get some sleep."

"Or you could wait a few more days, and you and Grandpa could go together." Elaine winked at Sara. "You see, Grandpa always waits till the last minute to do his shopping."

Allen bent across the table toward Sara. "I only do that to give your grandma time to buy what she wants. Then I don't have to go shopping at all."

"Actually, your grandfather always buys exactly what I want," Elaine confessed to Sara. "He must be a mind reader because he always picks perfect gifts. I don't know how he does it."

Allen smiled smugly but said nothing.

Kenzie grabbed Sara's hands to help her up, but Sara pulled back. "I want to play another game."

Her grandfather nudged her. "If your eyelids droop anymore, you won't be able to see where you're going. You'll bump into the furniture and get bruises on your legs. Then we'll have to carry you everywhere because you won't be able to walk. And if you can't walk, you won't be able to go Christmas shopping."

Sara giggled and, giving up, let her mother escort her to the bedroom.

CHAPTER ELEVEN

AFTER BREAKFAST, ELAINE, KENZIE, AND Sara left in high spirits for their shopping trip. They drove to Jo-Ann's to buy rhinestones for a present Sara was making for her grandparents. She'd outlined her hands on half a dozen pieces of colored foam and, after cutting them out, glued pictures of herself on each thumb and finger. She was also working on a poem, which she planned to glue in the palm of each hand. After adding rhinestones and tying a ribbon at the top, Sara would hang the handprints on the Christmas tree for her grandparents to find Christmas morning.

Next was a stop at the dollar store so Sara could buy presents for her cousins. Then they went to downtown Lake Forest and to the shops on Main Street. By twelve thirty, everyone was dragging. When Sara asked if they could have lunch at Jared's Café, Elaine agreed. Kenzie would have preferred eating the Tic Tacs she had in her purse, but Sara and Elaine were oblivious to her reluctance, and away they went. With a heavy sigh, Kenzie followed.

Pam recognized them and gave them a warm welcome. She looked especially cute today with her short hair tucked behind her ears. As luck would have it, Jared—wearing his white chef's hat—was behind the counter making sandwiches.

"I like to make sandwiches to suit the customer," Jared told Sara when they got to his prep station. "Maybe I should sprinkle some princess powder on yours since you're so pretty. "

Sara beamed. "And what about my mom's sandwich?"

With a mischievous expression, Jared responded, "Oh, she gets extra pickle."

"Gee, thanks," Kenzie said wryly, taking her tray.

They sat in a booth near the window so they could watch Christmas shoppers pass by.

"Heavens, it feels wonderful to sit down!" Elaine said. "My feet are aching—along with the rest of me."

She wasn't alone; Kenzie was also glad to take a break. They chatted easily as they ate. Kenzie was nearly finished when she noticed Sara put the rest of her sandwich on the tray. "Are you going to be able to finish your sandwich, sweetie?"

"I'm full," Sara said in a woebegone voice.

"That's too bad. I was going to buy you a piece of fudge when you were done."

"Maybe I could eat a *little* more," Sara said, reaching for her sandwich.

Kenzie glanced toward the candy counter and saw Pam looking in their direction. Pam went over to Jared, putting a familiar hand on his arm as she talked. She then glanced back at Kenzie.

Scott, the stocky young man who cleaned tables, spoke to a customer then started wiping crumbs off a nearby table. Sara tilted her head in curiosity then asked, "What's the matter with that man?"

Kenzie answered, "I think he has Down syndrome. People with that sometimes need a little help learning things, but that's okay. His name is Scott."

When the young man walked past them, Sara spoke up in a friendly voice, "Hi, Scott."

The young man stopped, looking a little puzzled. "Hi."

Kenzie hurried to introduce herself, Sara, and Elaine. Then Scott said to Kenzie, "I remember seeing you before. You were talking with Jared." He then went back to his work.

When Elaine finished her sandwich, she went to the restroom. While she was gone, Sara looked up at her mother with big blue eyes. "I heard you talking with Grandma and Grandpa last week. Grandpa thought you decided to move here because they were moving away. Did you?"

"Of course not."

"Grandpa sounded hurt."

"I know, but he didn't need to be. Lately, Grandpa gets hurt by almost anything I say." Kenzie had to be honest. "And sometimes I do the same thing—feel bad when he doesn't mean to hurt me. It's a bad habit we've gotten into."

Sara nodded like she understood. "I know you're still mad at him."

This wasn't something she liked admitting, but . . . Kenzie took a deep breath. "Yeah, I guess I still am. I shouldn't be, but he hurt my feelings—a lot."

"Can't you forgive him?"

"That's exactly what I need to do." Kenzie put an arm around her daughter and squeezed. "But I decided to move here because I believed it was the best thing for us, not because I thought Grandma and Grandpa were moving. I think it's great they're going to stay."

"Me too!" Sara smiled hugely.

What would be even greater was if she could buy Tom's house. She hadn't given up. Inwardly she sighed. It didn't seem likely, so why was she still hoping? Maybe it was the season—there was just something about Christmas that made you believe in sugarplums and impossible dreams. She'd come home thinking everything would turn out the way she wanted, but she should have known better. Life always had plenty of monkey wrenches to throw into the works.

Picking up their napkins and cups and putting them on the tray, Kenzie thought about what Mandy had said—that she had come back to Lake Forest to fall in love. Ha! Kenzie had a lot of reasons for returning, but falling in love was not on the list. And yet . . . perhaps she was ready for a relationship.

And what of Sara's belief that Tyrone was in Lake Forest? Wishful thinking or premonition? Certainly she and Tyrone had developed a deep and special bond. An idea struck her—could her childhood friendship have been a subconscious motivator behind her decision to return?

As her mother approached, Kenzie glanced at Jared. Of course he would pick the same exact moment to look at her. Their eyes caught and held. He actually was quite good-looking—striking, even, in that white chef's hat. Jared gave her a slight smile then went back to work.

"Well, girls," Elaine said, picking up her sacks. "Ready to go?"

Sara slid off the seat and led the way to the candy display. Kenzie had such a hard time deciding between fudge flavors that Elaine finally asked Pam to give them two of each.

As they pulled their coats off the coatrack, Kenzie told her mother, "I have one more stop to make. Do you mind taking Sara home?"

"Of course not, but we can come with you."

"I wanted to see Tom at his office."

"Oh, I see. How are you going to get home?"

Inspiration struck. "Why don't you two go to Sweet Pea's Ice Cream, and when I'm finished, I'll walk over and meet you there."

Sara's eyes lit up. "Yeah! Let's do that!"

"I thought you were full," her grandmother teased.

"I'm full of *sandwich*. Grandpa told me you can never be too full to eat ice cream. It just melts and fills in around the food in your stomach."

Once outside, they separated, with Kenzie cutting across the street to Tom's office. Fortunately he was in. He came around and gave her a hug.

"You look nice today," Kenzie said, admiring his cream sweater and striped tie. Although her brother was a big man, he was not overweight and wore his clothes well.

"Thanks. What brings you to town?" Tom settled into the padded chair behind his desk.

"A little Christmas shopping." She raised the bags in the air, then put them on the floor, taking a chair beside his desk. "Sara wanted to get something for her cousins, and Mom and I went around the shops here."

"Ah, Sara didn't need to buy presents for us. What a sweetheart. What did she get me? I can make a list if you want—"

Kenzie laughed. "Actually, I wanted to talk to you about your house."

A veiled look came over Tom's face, and he put his feet flat on the floor as if bracing for an onslaught. "What about it?"

Putting as much of her heart and soul into her voice as possible, Kenzie pleaded, "Isn't there *some* way you could sell the house to me?"

"I told you before, Kenzie—I already accepted Jared's offer. Exactly what part of that don't you understand?"

"But you're a realtor! Isn't there some way you can get around that? I mean it was just an offer . . ."

"A legally binding offer." Tom pronounced each word distinctly.

"But surely there's some loophole—"

"You mean something only real estate agents know about? Secret tricks of the trade on how to get out of an agreement?"

Now they were getting someplace. Kenzie nodded eagerly.

"Well, why didn't you say so?" Tom leaned forward, then peered toward the reception area to make sure no one was within earshot. "I know a number of underhanded strategies we can use to double-cross Jared and break our legal agreement."

"Very funny. That isn't exactly what I meant."

"Really? It sounded like that to me. Look, the only way this sale wouldn't go through is if Jared doesn't sell his home by the twenty-fourth. When he made the offer, it was contingent on selling his home by then so he could qualify for a loan."

This was exciting news. "And if he hasn't sold his house by then, would you sell your house to your loving sister?"

"I suppose." There was a lot of doubt in Tom's voice. "But it's a slow time of year—Jared might ask for more time."

"You're the one who told me you had a legally binding offer. If he asks for more time, tell him your hands are tied and you have to abide by the terms of the offer," Kenzie said sweetly. "He'll understand you can't give him more time when you explain you have another buyer."

"My dear sister, who is waiting in the wings."

"Right." Kenzie's spirits soared. She still had a chance to get the house. Jared only had a little more than a week and a half left.

"Don't get your hopes too high," her brother warned. "Jared just reduced the price on his house, and I've had a few people call. I've got a couple of showings lined up, and Carlos and Tracy Perez, who own the travel agency down the street, are very interested in it."

Her brother was right; she had to be realistic. "All right, all right. If you're set on stiffing your sister, you'd better show me what other homes you have available." Kenzie pulled out her cell phone. "Would you be able to take me home afterwards? I told Sara and Mom I'd meet them for ice cream, but I'm going to be here longer than I thought."

"Sure. No problem." Tom started tapping on his keyboard.

Then Kenzie had an idea. A brilliant idea. "Jared said he saw a lot of homes before he put an offer on your house."

"Yes—"

"Have any new homes come on the market since he made his offer?"

"A few."

"If there are any similar to your house, I'd like to see those first."

Tom looked at her suspiciously. "Any particular reason? Or should I say 'motive'?"

"Not really." Except there might be a newly listed home Jared would like better than her brother's. But Kenzie wasn't going to tell Tom that. "Jared and I have similar tastes in homes. So could you print those out?"

"Okay, but it'll take a few minutes."

While she waited, Kenzie texted her mother, saying to go ahead without her and that Tom would take her home.

Once she had the papers in hand, Kenzie ruffled through them. "These are nice, but can you also show me some that are a little newer and have a master bathroom off the bedroom?"

Tom frowned. "Why didn't you say so before?"

If she had, Kenzie wouldn't have a list of homes to present to Jared. Instead she said, "I'm new at house hunting."

With a groan, her brother asked, "Are there any other parameters you want to change?"

"Maybe the price range and the area. And a few amenities.

Tom frowned as he typed. "So essentially, we're starting over." When he was done, he asked, "Do you want me to print these out?"

"Let me see them first."

Tom had two monitors, and Kenzie pulled her chair around. When Kenzie saw one she liked, Tom printed it out.

"This is a nice home except for the flooring," Tom said, pointing at the monitor. "The linoleum is peeling up in the kitchen, but they've priced it to allow the buyer to put in new flooring."

"At least I'd get to pick flooring I like."

Tom printed out a few more. Then he said, "Here's a nice one." As Kenzie looked at it, he added, "That's Jared's house."

Grimacing, she sat back. "Very funny."

Tom chuckled, and they continued. He dissuaded her from a rambler she liked. "I'd avoid that one. The area has a high water table, and the people have to keep the sump pump on all the time."

He pulled up interior shots of one house, then said, "Oops, didn't mean to show you this one. There's a question of mold."

When they were through. Kenzie slid her chair back and rubbed the back of her neck. "Tonight I'm going to dream about basements, fireplaces, and kitchen islands."

"Could be worse—you could dream about peeling linoleum, flooding, and mold." Tom rolled his chair away from the computer. "We made a good start."

"Yes, we did." Kenzie stood. "Have I got time to run a quick errand before you take me home?"

Tom glanced at his phone for the time. "If you make it fast. I need to leave in fifteen minutes to have time to take you home and meet some people for a showing."

Hurrying out, Kenzie jaywalked across the street to Jared's Café. She bypassed the order station and strode to the sandwich bar, earning her a few looks from people in line. She asked the young man there if she could talk to Jared. He went to the back.

When Jared came out, he looked surprised. "Hungry again?"

She waved the papers in her hand. "I have something for you."

He walked over, and Kenzie handed him the papers.

"What's this?"

"Homes you might be interested in."

Casually, Jared flipped through them. "I don't think so. I've already found the home I want."

Kenzie nailed a smile to her face. "I know you saw a lot of homes before making an offer on Tom's, but these are *new* listings—you might like one of them."

He thrust the papers toward Kenzie, but she pleaded, "Take a look at them. What could it hurt? There are some really great homes." She pointed at the top paper. "This one has huge trees, a big backyard, and an oversized garage. And the price is about the same as Tom's house. And there are a couple of homes that are zoned for animals. You could even have sheep if you wanted. Wouldn't Corey love that?"

"Unfair," Jared said, but there was amusement in his voice.

"I've got to run, but look through them. Please?"

From the grimace on his face, what Jared really wanted was to throw the papers in the garbage. But when Kenzie gave him a hopeful smile, his expression softened.

"All right. But like I said, I've already found the house I want."

CHAPTER TWELVE

IT WAS PAINFULLY EVIDENT JARED had said the wrong thing. Ever since he'd mentioned his son's race-car bed might not fit in the bedroom Corey wanted, his son had been pestering him to go to Tom's house and measure the room. Since there were other things he wanted to measure, Jared called Mandy and arranged to stop by after school. Corey was eager to go, and it would be helpful to have someone hold the other end of the tape measure.

As they walked up the sidewalk, a thrill went through Jared to think this would soon be his house. Mandy invited them in, and they went to the bedroom where Brian was feverishly picking up clothes, Legos, and assorted toys—probably under orders from his mother. Corey stood at one end of the room, and Jared stepped over shoes, pajamas, a helicopter, and some cars to get to the other. Hillary came in to watch, grinning at her brother, who stuck his tongue out at her.

The doorbell rang, and Jared overheard Mandy talking to someone as he gave his son the good news that his bed *would* fit. "Okay, Corey, let's go check out the basement."

Brian and Hillary went with them, but Jared stopped in the hallway when he saw Kenzie and Sara by the front door.

"Why, hello, Jared. Hi, Corey." Surprise colored Kenzie's voice. "What are you doing?"

"We had to measure a few things," Jared replied. "Corey has an unusual bed, and we wanted to make sure it would fit."

"It's a race car!" Corey spoke proudly. "My grandpa made it for me."

"Wow! Sounds pretty special." Kenzie smiled at him.

Sara was impressed but also a little confused. "A car?"

"Yeah, want to see where we're going to put it?"

"Sure!" Sara was as excited as if she'd never seen the house before. The four children raced down the hall.

Jared turned to Mandy. "If it's all right, I'd like to do some measuring in the basement."

"Go right ahead."

Half the basement had been roughed in, and Jared jotted down measurements on a notepad. He was pleased with the dimensions of the large, open area but decided he'd make it even bigger by taking down a wall. He'd build a large closet at one end with shelves for smaller tools and supplies. All he needed to do was put up sheetrock and tape and mud it, and the walls would be ready to paint.

When he went upstairs, Mandy and Kenzie were in the kitchen.

"It seems like my equipment will fit fine; although, I'll probably take out a wall."

Kenzie blurted out, "What equipment?"

"I'm going to put in a workshop."

"A *workshop*? In the *basement*?" she sounded horrified.

"You make it sound like I'm going to be operating a still." Jared grinned good-naturedly. "It beats working in a cold garage; plus I'll be in the house with Corey." He studied the entryway between the dining room and kitchen, and walked closer. "I may take this wall out too."

This prompted another outburst from Kenzie. "You can't do that."

Jared raised his eyebrows. "Why not?"

Wearing an amused expression, Mandy also waited for Kenzie's response.

"Because . . . well, that wall has always been there."

A pretty lame answer. Jared disguised his smile and put on a thoughtful expression. Actually, he had no plans to take down the wall, but it was awfully fun to mess with Kenzie.

As a final touch, he added, "Time for it to come down." He wasn't surprised that Kenzie had more objections.

"But if you have visitors, they'll be able to see into the kitchen!"

"So?"

"What if it's messy? You don't want visitors seeing a messy kitchen."

"Why would I care if they saw?" Then Jared added dryly, "Besides, I have been known to wash dishes before I invite people over." He stepped into the front room and looked around. What else could he find to rile Kenzie?

"Hmm, I might take out the fireplace and put in a wood stove insert." Jared had to work hard not to laugh when Kenzie's jaw dropped.

"But everyone loves the fireplace! It's one of the great features of the house."

"A wood stove is much more efficient at heating. With fireplaces, most of the heat goes up the chimney." He watched Kenzie, amused at how he could almost see the gears churning in her brain, trying to come up with a rebuttal. Her eye lit on the stockings hanging on the mantle.

She turned to him triumphantly. "Santa can't come down the chimney unless you have a fireplace."

Mandy giggled, and Jared didn't bother to hide his grin. "I don't think that's ever been documented."

This was fun. Jared strode back to the kitchen, knowing Kenzie would follow him like he was the Pied Piper. "Another thing. I'd like to take out this floor and put in tile." He swiveled round to Kenzie. "Any objections?"

"I guess tile would be all right."

"I have some leftover boxes from when I remodeled the café."

Kenzie gasped. "You want to use black-and-white tile?"

"There may not be quite enough, but I could put something different by the back door."

When Kenzie threw Mandy an appalled look, Jared turned so she didn't see him grin. Then he went into the dining room. "I'll use this as my office. I've got a big desk, and it'll go great in the corner." He waited.

"Where will you eat?" Kenzie's voice was feeble.

"If I squeeze, I can make room for a small table, but we'll probably eat at the counter most of the time."

"What if you have guests?"

He rubbed his chin as if considering. "Guess I could pick up a couple more bar stools." When Kenzie closed her eyes in pain, Jared figured he'd tortured her enough.

"Corey!" he called. "Time to go." As the children came running, Jared thanked Mandy for letting him come over. Mandy walked him to the door, and he glanced over her shoulder at Kenzie, who still stood in the kitchen, looking shell-shocked. "See you later, Kenzie."

He told the children good-bye, and although they responded cheerily, Kenzie's good-bye sounded like she had a fish bone caught in her throat.

On the way home, Jared chuckled—remembering the pained expression on Kenzie's face when he'd mentioned the bar stools. Despite her ferocious frowns, she was still a very pretty lady.

"Why are you laughing?" Corey wanted to know.

"Oh, I was teasing Kenzie. When I told Kenzie I was going to put in a wood stove and take out the fireplace, do you know what she told me?" Corey shook his head. "She said I shouldn't do that because Santa wouldn't be able to come. She didn't know Santa can come down anywhere."

Being very patient, Corey told his father, "Dad, I know there's no Santa Claus."

"You do?"

"I'm too big for that. Only little kids believe in Santa."

Jared blinked. Only yesterday Corey *had* been a little kid—and he'd had a mother. After Robin died, Christmas became one of the hardest times of the year. Even decorating the tree was difficult, since his wife had always taken charge of that. Robin always put on the lights herself except for the last year, when she'd been too frail. Still, he'd carried her out and laid her on the couch so she could direct him and point out if he'd put the lights too close or too far apart.

His first Christmas without Robin would have been impossible if not for her parents. They'd had him and Corey sleep over on Christmas Eve. Corey feared Santa wouldn't know where to bring his toys, but he relaxed once Jared helped him write a note, which they'd left at their own house giving his present whereabouts. Corey had placed the letter beside a saucer of cookies and an empty glass, explaining that since he liked his milk cold, he figured Santa did too, and Santa could find it in the fridge.

Jared's thoughts went back to Kenzie, and he smiled inside at the agitation she'd displayed over his remodeling plans. Once he and Corey arrived home, Jared started Corey on his homework, then got out a box of Hamburger Helper and a jar of salsa. Adding a cup of salsa at the end made all the difference.

As they worked, Corey piped up. "Say Dad, when we were at the house, Sara told me she likes to walk in the woods, just like me."

"That's nice, but thinking about the woods isn't going to get your homework done."

While the noodles simmered, Jared set out saucers, doled out pears, then put a dollop of cottage cheese on top. So Sara liked the woods. Interesting. She was about the same age as Izzy when he'd met her in the woods shortly after he and his mom had moved to West Lake Forest. They'd become fast friends, and most long summer days had found them in the woods near their homes. Only rarely had they ventured into Lake Forest or West Lake Forest. He remembered being surprised when his mother told him he and Izzy lived in two different towns.

As he stirred the sizzling noodles, Jared smiled at Kenzie's reaction to the black-and-white tile. He had no intention of using that, but it sure had been fun to tease her and see those big eyes widen and those long lashes blink rapidly. Tom had said Kenzie was divorced. Then Jared shook himself. He had to stop thinking about that woman.

He thought about Pam, but really, there wasn't much joy there. Jared was well aware Pam wanted more than an occasional date. Why didn't he ask her out more? He liked her all right. After all, what was there not to like? Pam was smart and fun to be with. In fact, she had a whole list of good qualities. And whenever they did go out, he always had fun—though she teased him because he had a tendency to talk too much about the café.

"Nearly done?" Jared asked Corey as he set out plates and utensils.

"Two more problems."

Jared poured milk into glasses and carried them to the table. Pam was good company, but he was content to take things slow. At first he'd thought it meant he wasn't over Robin, but after a few years, gradually he came to the realization that something was missing. He'd been content with their employer/employee relationship and had been surprised when, a couple of years ago, Pam had asked him to a concert. They'd had a good time, but weeks went by before they went out again, since most of his time was taken up with launching his new business.

Corey slapped his book shut.

"Great timing," Jared said. "Go wash up, and I'll put dinner on." He dished up their plates. There was no doubt the café had required all of his time and attention at the beginning, but now he was at the point where he could take things a little easier. Now that the café was doing well, he needed to get out of the mindset of working 24/7. In fact, maybe he ought to ask Pam to a movie this weekend.

CHAPTER THIRTEEN

WHEN THE DOOR SHUT BEHIND Jared and Corey, the three children ran off, and Kenzie took the opportunity to vent.

Throwing out her arms in a theatrical gesture of amazement, she asked Mandy, "Did you *hear* him?" She pointed at the front room window. "He'll probably board that up. It'll save on heat and be more efficient, you know."

"Oh, Kenzie!" Mandy laughed. "I think Jared said half of those things to get a rise out of you."

Kenzie wasn't so sure. It was hard to explain her feelings. It was like Jared was trespassing on her personal territory as he went through the house *she* wanted, listing all the changes *he* wanted to make.

"Jared sounded pretty serious about the workshop, but who puts something like that in their *house?*" Kenzie said. "Is he crazy? Think of the sawdust and the grease. And what *kind* of a workshop is he planning on anyway?"

"Hey, I don't pry into a man's religion or his workshop," Mandy deadpanned. "But I agree with you—it's a horrible, low-down kind of a man who would build a workshop in the basement so he can be close to his son."

Rolling her eyes, Kenzie stalked into the front room and plopped onto the couch. "The man's a demolishing maniac. Just *think* what he's going to do to this house."

"I hate to break it to you, but people *do* remodel." Mandy settled into the easy chair. "Tom wants to put crown molding in the Steadman home and build shelves in the closets before we move in. *And* I'm going to paint, and *you* get to help me."

"I'd hoped you'd forgotten about that."

"Nope, you're stuck." Then Mandy's expression changed, and she looked at Kenzie with sparkling eyes. "I think someone likes you," she said in a sing-songy voice.

"What are you talking about?"

"Jared. He likes you. I can tell."

"You can? Gee, I don't know why I can't see it. It must be the animosity that fooled me."

"Take it from me. He likes you."

"Mandy, the man gave me an extra pickle!"

Throwing back her head, Mandy peeled with laughter. "See, that *proves* it! He's acting like a little boy—you know how boys like to pull pigtails and swipe pencils from someone they like."

"Jared is hardly a boy, and all it proves is that he likes to provoke me."

"Because, my dear, you're so easy to provoke." When Kenzie made a rude sound, Mandy went on. "I wouldn't dismiss it so easily. I caught a lot of vibes coming from both of you after the Christmas play. *Strong* vibes. If I'd gotten caught between you two, I would have ended up fried." Kenzie glared at her, and Mandy changed course. "Okay, forget Jared. There are plenty of other men. All they have to do is take one look at you, and they'll be hooked. But first, we need to set you up with some dates."

"We? So you're planning on coming with me?" Mandy eyes narrowed, but Kenzie went on, "I know what you mean. Anyway, thanks for the offer, but no thanks. I've dated too many sleazeballs who only wanted a one-night stand. So you can stop with the matchmaking."

"Listen, your moving back is more than a coincidence. There's a reason. I think it's because your subconscious wants to fall in love."

"Fine," Kenzie retorted. "My subconscious can fall in love. In fact, it can do whatever it wants—as long as it leaves me out of it."

"You're leaving your home in Chicago, coming here, and buying a house—all of that means you're ready to settle down." Mandy leaned her head to the side pensively. "I can set you up with a lot of guys, but first I need to know what kind of a guy you're looking for."

"I am *not* looking." Well, perhaps that wasn't strictly the case. She'd kept her eyes open. But something in her rebelled at the idea of "looking." It was too close to "hunting," and it wasn't as if she wanted to track and capture some prey.

"For someone who can be so impulsive, you're being very cautious about dating."

"Shouldn't I be?" Kenzie replied primly.

"Of course you need to be careful, but you didn't answer my question. What *do* you want in a man?"

Kenzie sighed hugely. Mandy wasn't going to let it go. Okay. What was she looking for? "I guess I'd like someone warm, thoughtful, and funny. He needs to be confident, great with kids, and I'd really like it if he was a Mormon." Her last preference created more problems than all of the rest put together. It was difficult finding a single LDS man.

Mandy raised an eyebrow. "Do you realize you've just described Jared?"

"Except for the Mormon part."

"He's a member of the Church."

Her words took Kenzie back. "Really? I didn't see him at church on Sunday.

"Aha! See, you *are* interested." Mandy was delighted. "I don't recall seeing him either, but he's usually there. Maybe Corey was sick. Anyway, Tom told me that when Jared was little, he had a friend who was LDS and invited him to Primary activities. Then, after he got married, some missionaries knocked at his door, and he let them in. He and his wife were both baptized."

Kenzie stretched her legs. "Jared seems nice except for when he's tormenting me, but I don't even know him."

"Well, I do. He's a good man." Mandy sounded firm. "The only thing is you'd have lots of competition. Half the single female population of Lake Forest is drooling over him, although he doesn't seem to notice."

"I'll find someone when the time is right. Contrary to your belief, I *do* put myself out there and date once in a while. I'm also praying that one day I'll meet someone special. That's all I can do. Now, let's change the subject."

Kenzie looked around the front room. Every inch was familiar. "Tom told me if Jared doesn't sell his house by the twenty-fourth, he won't be able to get a loan and then I can buy this house."

"Really?" Mandy sounded surprised. "Tom mentioned some kind of time limit, but I didn't know it was coming up so soon." Her brow wrinkled. "Jared is really counting on getting this house."

"This house means a lot more to me than it does to him," Kenzie burst out. "How many birthday parties did *Jared* have growing up here? Did he help his mom and dad plant the apple and peach trees in the backyard? Did he help dig out sod to make the garden bigger?" Stung, Kenzie pointed to an imperfection in the wall. "Did he put a hole in the wall while wrestling with his brother?"

"Okay, okay, I get the picture." Mandy held up her hands as if to ward Kenzie off. "I know it holds a lot of memories and means a lot to you. All I'm saying is that it also means a lot to Jared."

But her desire to buy this house came from the very deepest part of her. For the last two years, her world had been upside down and inside out. From her husband leaving, to the estrangement with her father, to desperate problems at work—everything had combined and sent Kenzie into a downward spiral. In a world where so many things were out of her control, she needed something solid to hang onto— something stable in her life. This house, where she had spent the first years of her life, was not just a house—it was a return to a time when life was simpler and kinder, a time when the world was not spinning out of control. Perhaps subconsciously she was trying to return to a time when her greatest worry had been getting a passing grade on her book report or finishing dinner in time to watch *Full House.*

Emotion tightened her throat as Kenzie gazed around the room. "I'm just so tired. I want a place where I can come home, shut out the world, and catch my breath. I've always considered this place home. It's comfortable; it's familiar. I want to curl up and be at peace in a place I know—in a place that knows me."

Tears stood in Mandy's eyes. "I didn't realize this home meant that much to you. And I understand you wanting a place where you feel comfortable, especially after all you've been through. It's been hard, I know."

Unbidden tears stung Kenzie eyes. Mandy did know. She'd been one of Kenzie's lifelines. Three years before, when Kenzie found out her husband was having an affair, she'd called her mother and Mandy. Because Kenzie hoped she and Larry might be able to work things out, she hadn't told them the full story, saying only that they were having serious problems. Larry was still her husband, and if their marriage was going to work, she couldn't talk about what had happened and have her mother and Mandy looking at Larry with distrust in the future.

That all changed after one dark night. She and Larry had gotten into a particularly brutal argument when he got home at three in the morning. All hopes of working things out seemed gone when Larry packed a bag and left. Feeling numb and shocked, like she'd walked straight into a plate-glass window, Kenzie called Mandy in tears.

However, after a separation of a few weeks, Larry ended the affair and begged forgiveness. Over time and with counseling, their marriage got back on track. Then, a year later, Larry had another affair. This time, he didn't ask Kenzie to take him back. Larry wanted a divorce. In that harrowing, sinister time when earth had fallen from beneath her feet, Mandy was there for her. And when Kenzie hit rock bottom, took sick leave, and felt like a soul passing out from life, her sister-in-law came to stay with her for a week. Mandy made her eat, took her to see a doctor, then a therapist, and went with her to fill her prescription for an antidepressant. For months, Mandy took her late-night phone calls, helping her through a dark time and proving herself one of Kenzie's truest friends. One of her favorite quotes described Mandy perfectly: "A friend is one that knows you as you are, understands where you have been, accepts what you have become, and still, gently allows you to grow."

Mandy came to sit by Kenzie on the couch. Her voice broke as she said, "I'm really sorry we didn't know you wanted the house before Jared made an offer on it."

"It's not too late—" There was naked hope in Kenzie's voice.

"I'm going to have to let Tom handle this. I'm sorry."

"It's all right," Kenzie whispered through the knives in her throat. After a few moments of recovery and in a stronger voice, she said, "Well, I'd better get back. My parents are going to wonder where we are." They stood and hugged tightly. Then Kenzie called for Sara.

"Everything will turn out all right. You'll see," Mandy said as they waited for Sara. "You just have to plan what you're going to do next. You've always been one for meticulous planning, so do that now; plan, then take steps to get what you want."

Her sister-in-law was right, of course. It was time to take action. She had to do something to get this house, and even though she wasn't sure what that would be, her resolve was strong. And heaven help anyone who stood in her way. Right now, that someone was Jared.

Sara and Hillary came in. "Time to go, honey," Kenzie told her daughter. Then she patted Mandy's arm. "You're right. A big part of my job involves solving problems. So I need to apply what I know to my own personal life and come up with a plan and take steps to get what I want. I'll work things out one way or another."

"Why does it sound so different when you say it?" Mandy's eyes were worried. "Oh dear. I've unleashed a monster."

CHAPTER FOURTEEN

KENZIE LOVED HER FAMILY, BUT it was good to have time alone to do Christmas shopping. She drove downtown, parked, and walked along Main Street, stopping at a few stores. Nothing caught her eye, though, and she went on, mostly window shopping, until bright travel posters caught her attention. There was something so compelling about the exotic locations that Kenzie stopped, gazing in admiration at the turquoise waters of Cancun, the Eiffel Tower towering above the sparkling Seine River, and the soaring Cathedral of Santa Eulalia in Barcelona. The posters looked like screensavers. How incredible it would be to go to a sun-drenched village in Italy! Perhaps someday.

A woman with long, straight black hair and loaded down with multiple bags stopped beside Kenzie. She carried a large box tucked awkwardly under her arm. Eyeing the sandy beach, she said, "The Bahamas are fabulous!" The woman was about Kenzie's age. A cheerful smile showed full lips colored with exquisite red lipstick.

Kenzie studied another poster, this one of Cancun with its jewel-blue sea, pristine white beaches, and palm trees. "Standing here in my parka, I have to admit those beaches look irresistible."

"Oh, they are, believe me. I've been there, and those pictures don't lie." The box under the woman's arm shifted and started to fall.

Reacting quickly, Kenzie grabbed it before it hit the sidewalk.

"Thanks! Would you mind bringing it inside?" She moved a few feet down to a glass-fronted door, which Kenzie pushed open.

"You're a lifesaver," the woman said, going to a desk in the corner of the small but neat office. The walls were lined with more glorious posters. The woman set her bags down then glanced through an open door into a back room.

"Hi, sweetheart. I'm back," she called, waving gaily at a lean, dark-haired man who was working on a computer.

The man acknowledged her with a pleasant expression, and after a friendly nod toward Kenzie, he returned to his work.

The woman flashed a dazzling white smile. "Now, were you actually interested in Cancun or the Bahamas, or were you just window shopping?"

"Window shopping, I'm afraid. You must be Tracy Perez."

A finely groomed eyebrow raised. "Yes, how did you know?"

"My brother, Tom Dahlquist, is a realtor. He was showing me some houses—I'm moving here from Chicago—and he mentioned your name."

"You're Tom's sister?" Tracy squealed. "What a small world! Well, you're much better looking than he is."

Kenzie laughed. "I'll tell him you said so."

"So you're searching for a house too? What a break to have a brother in real estate. He can give you all the good inside information." Tracy indicated a chair. "Go ahead and sit down if you've got a minute."

Tracy was so friendly that Kenzie sat without hesitation. She eyed the office. "So you and your husband run this?"

"That's right." Tracy nodded toward the back. "Carlos is the good-looking guy in the back office. We're both travel freaks and decided to put our love of exotic places to practical use." She studied Kenzie. "So what brings you to Lake Forest?"

"A new job. I'm going to work at Reliance Software in Mundelein."

"Wonderful! Mundelein's only a few minutes away. I hope you got a promotion."

"Not really. It's more of a lateral move, but I was glad to take it."

Tracy appeared sympathetic. "Laid off?"

"Actually, I quit. A guy at work was being a real jerk."

"Ah—too bad."

"But I'm excited to come back. I grew up here."

"So you know all about Lake Forest."

"It's changed some, but basically, yeah."

"I'm *so* glad we bumped into each other. Knowing about Lake Forest and having a brother in the real estate market, you can give me lots of great advice."

It wasn't as if her brother couldn't do that. "Tom will tell you anything you want to know. He really knows his stuff."

"Oh, he's been great, but I believe the old saying that two heads are better than one." Tracy used a manicured hand to fling her shiny hair over her shoulder. "We could pool our information. My time is limited, and I don't want to waste it seeing houses that aren't what I want. So tell me, when you talked with Tom, did you find any homes you liked?"

"He showed me some on his computer that looked interesting." Kenzie opened her cavernous purse and pulled out extra copies of the printouts.

Tracy's eyes brightened. "Oh goodie! Let's see what you have. And you even took notes!"

"How many bedrooms do you want?" Kenzie asked as Tracy took the papers and began skimming them avidly.

"Doesn't really matter. We don't have any children. Yet."

"If a baby is in the plans, you ought to get at least three. You can use one for an office and have a spare in case a baby comes along. You don't want to move again in a year or two."

"You're right about that," Tracy said emphatically. "This house hunting business has been exhausting. It's not something I'd want to do again anytime soon." She peered closer and pointed a red-tipped finger at the second paper. "Have you seen this one?"

"I haven't looked at any yet." That's because Kenzie was only interested in one—Tom's. "It does sound great though—three bedrooms, not too old. Walk-in closet and two fireplaces."

"Oh, I love fireplaces," Tracy exclaimed.

"*And* it has a garage—always a plus in winter!" It was then that Kenzie remembered Tracy and her husband were going to see Jared's home. Did it have a garage? She couldn't recall, only having seen it for a few seconds on Tom's computer.

"Carlos doesn't mind a carport."

"I'm sure, since he's not the one wearing a skirt and high heels when it's freezing."

Tracy laughed. "I guess that's true."

"I want a big yard. What about you?"

"The smaller the better. We're not really into yard work. What's important is the living room, family room, and kitchen. My husband and I host a lot of small dinner parties."

"Then you wouldn't want an older home," Kenzie exclaimed with only a twinge of guilt. "They're notorious for having small kitchens." What was that old saying? All's fair in love, war, and buying a house?

Tracy's face fell. "Carlos and I thought we could save money by buying an older home and remodeling."

An incredulous expression bloomed on Kenzie's face. "Don't believe it. Remodeling is very expensive, unless you do it yourself. Either way, you have to put up with a big mess and having your house torn up. I had a close friend in Chicago hire a contractor to remodel their older house, and she said it was a nightmare. Someone told her later, when it was too late, that a contractor always takes twice as long and costs three times as much as they tell you up front. It was true. My friend said she'd never do it again."

The look of undisguised horror on Tracy's face gave Kenzie pause. It dawned on her that she sounded opposed to older homes, but she rambled on in one of those rambling blue streaks that hit her now and then. "Just be sure you know what you're getting into if you buy an older home—have a professional check it out to make sure it's structurally sound. Tom mentioned that one house had foundation problems, but I can't remember which one."

Looking troubled, Tracy said pensively, "Maybe we ought to avoid older homes altogether. Carlos and I thought it might be fun to fix one up."

"It's hard work and takes a lot of time. And unless you have a lot of experience, things never turn out the way you want. You'd be better off hiring the work done. Or just buy a newer home—it might cost a little more, but then you don't have to worry about outdated wiring, plumbing, or heating, which can all cost a fortune to replace." There she was, talking too much again! But Tracy was so interested—she was soaking up every word like a sponge. "Building codes back then were a lot looser—they allowed all sorts of things that aren't permitted now. I'd hate to wake up in the middle of the night to an electrical fire."

Okay, she'd gone too far. Tracy's eyes widened in alarm. Kenzie flipped through the pages. "Are you into townhouses?"

"We've seen a few."

"If you want someone else to pull the weeds and mow the grass, this one would be perfect. It's only four years old, and the owners just reduced the price."

Tracy's pencil scratched furiously as she wrote down the address. She flipped through the papers again, reading Kenzie's notes and writing down any that caught her eye.

As she looked, Kenzie threw in all kinds of helpful information. "This one's in a good part of town, and that one has a nice grocery store a few blocks away."

When they finished, Tracy sat back with a satisfied air. "I'm *so* glad you stopped by. You've been so helpful. I'll talk to Tom about these homes, unless, of course, you want to see them first."

Kenzie stood, and they shook hands. "Don't worry. Actually, I'm looking for something a little different."

CHAPTER FIFTEEN

SOUNDS WERE COMING FROM THE family room, so Kenzie went in and saw her father kneeling by the fireplace. Her mother had gone to run errands, and Sara was playing at a friend's house.

"Building a fire?" Kenzie asked. She was going to offer to bring in firewood until she saw the tall stack against the wall.

"Nothing like a fire on a cold winter day," Allen said, stacking small pieces of wood on top of crumpled-up newspaper. He added a few bigger logs then twisted some newspaper. Lighting one end of the newspaper, he held it inside the box near the flue to force the heavier, cold air up and out of the chimney. That way, the smoke would go up the chimney instead of out into the room. Allen lit two corners of the crumbled newspaper inside the wooden teepee on the bottom of the fireplace and shut the door.

He rose a little stiffly, then took a chair by the fireplace so he could keep an eye on it. "There we go. We'll have this room toasty in no time."

"Dad, I wanted to ask you about the offer Tom got on his house." She sat nearby on the couch.

"What about it? Are you still upset Jared bought the house before you did?"

Something in his tone or words—maybe both—irritated Kenzie, and she ignored the question. "Is there any way Tom could get out of it? I mean, I know he signed the offer, but I'm wondering if there was any way around it."

"I don't know of any."

Her father didn't seem to be trying very hard to be helpful. "I thought that since it was only an *offer*, there might be some kind of loophole somewhere. Surely there's something I could do!"

"Talk with Tom—he'd know if anybody would."

"I did, and he says there's nothing."

"There's your answer, then. Besides, Tom lives up to his agreements. He has integrity."

Kenzie's spine stiffened until she was sitting ramrod straight. "And I *don't*. Is that what you're saying?"

Her father ran a hand through his silver hair. "I swear! You're touchier than a bear with hangnails. I only meant that Tom signed an agreement, and he's living up to it."

"But it was just an offer. I thought the house would always stay in the family. And I'm Tom's sister. Shouldn't family come first?" Kenzie threw out her hands palms up to make her case.

"Integrity comes first," her father said.

She should have known better than to ask him! Kenzie huffed. He was no help at all. Not only didn't he understand how badly she wanted the house, he didn't even to *try* to understand. "So you'd rather have Tom sell the old family home to a stranger than to me."

"Not at all, but if you had used the brains God gave you, you'd have spoken up a long time ago. You knew the house was for sale—what were you waiting for?"

"I had a lot going on," she shot back. "For one thing, I had to make sure I had a new job before I said anything to Tom. If I'd told him I wanted the house before I got hired at Reliance, you'd say I was irresponsible."

"There you go again, being defensive. I was simply asking a question—a reasonable one, I might add." Allen went to the fireplace, poked at the logs, and threw on another one. The flames crackled and danced.

He settled back in his chair. "I couldn't help notice that you decided to move back to Lake Forest when you thought your mom and I were leaving."

"I didn't plan it that way—it just happened."

"Like the way you just happened to be too busy the last couple of years to come and visit?"

"Look, I brought Sara down for two weeks just last summer."

"Dropped her off and hightailed it home. Oh, I know you were busy at work and it was hard when Larry left, but what I don't understand is why you cut us out of your life. Your mom and I wanted to be there for you—but you didn't want anything to do with us. Most people rely on family during hard times, but not you. Why?"

Was he really asking her that? Her father couldn't possibly be that clueless. There was no way he could he have forgotten saying such outrageous and hurtful things about her and Larry. Kenzie's chest hurt just thinking about it. Working hard to control herself, Kenzie stated flatly, "You know why."

Allen's head jerked back a little. "I wouldn't be asking if I did."

"It was all those horrible accusations you made."

Her father sat very still, brows knit together in puzzlement. The only sound in the room was the crackling of the fire. Kenzie dared not say any more—else the volcano inside her erupt.

The side door opened, and Elaine walked in, carrying sacks of groceries, which she set on the counter. "Sorry I'm late." Then she frowned at them. "You two look cozy, but do you realize what time it is? We've got to get going."

Glancing at the clock above the fireplace, Kenzie remembered. Tonight was the Relief Society activity where they were taking Christmas baskets to needy families. She'd totally forgotten—what with the tense conversation. Since it would be dark when delivering the baskets, the Relief Society president had asked to have at least one priesthood holder go with each group of two or three sisters.

Kenzie pulled out her cell phone. "I'll call Sara and tell her to come home. She wanted to go."

Going into the kitchen, Allen started putting groceries away. "What time do you need me to come over?" he asked, pulling out a bunch of bananas from a sack.

"Why don't you drive over with us." Elaine put the milk in the fridge. "It won't take long to assemble the baskets."

Her father threw a regretful glance toward the fire and his chair, then put apples and oranges in the vegetable bins. Kenzie was putting on her coat when Sara burst through the door with Kaylee, a pink-cheeked little cherub with long brown hair.

"Can Kaylee go with us?" Sara begged her grandmother. "You said I would see some Christmas magic tonight."

"I suppose so," Elaine replied, "but we'll need to check with her mother to make sure it's all right."

"I already asked my mom, and she said it was fine," Kaylee burst out.

Kenzie had been caught in similar situations before, only to find out later the mother was unaware of her child's plan. She called Kaylee's mother to confirm, and they were soon on their way.

At the ward house in Gurnee, tables had been set up in a long line in the cultural hall. Women and men formed assembly lines on either side of the tables with each person adding cookies, fruit, or canned goods to a basket and sliding it along to the next person. On other tables were blankets, quilts, coats, and other items tagged for certain families. There were also brightly colored gift bags that contained items for specific families, such as diapers, formula, school supplies, clothes, and other things chosen based on home and visiting teachers' suggestions. As the baskets were completed, men carried them out. Supervisors made sure each group had the correct gift bags and specialty items for the families on their list.

Tom arrived late, and Kenzie was surprised to see Jared and Corey with him. She busied herself packing apples and oranges, and when the apples gave out, she went to the kitchen to see if there were any more. While there, Esther, a friendly older woman with a reddened face and wearing wire-rimmed glasses, asked about Kenzie's family. Esther could have talked all night, and it took a while before Kenzie could break away. Returning to the cultural hall, she saw that quite a number of people had already left. She went over to her mother, who was packing the leftovers into boxes. Kaylee and Sara were helping.

"Where did Tom go?"

Waving a hand around vaguely, Elaine said, "I don't know. He must have left with one of the groups."

Rats. She'd hoped to go with him.

"Sara and Kaylee wanted to go with Sister Taylor, me, and your dad, but Melanie and Becky could use someone else in their group." Kenzie looked toward the doorway where the two ladies were waiting, coats on. She knew them well.

Although in her late fifties, Melanie had retained the slender figure of a young woman. She saw Kenzie looking in their direction and waved her over. "Come with us, Kenzie," As they went outside, Melanie checked her list and directed them toward an SUV. "Over here. Jared Rawlins is going to be our driver."

Oh no! Kenzie glanced around, hoping to see some other group she could join, but it was too late. Many vehicles had left, and others were backing out, red lights shining in the darkness.

Melanie and Becky, a handsome woman with coffee-colored skin, beat Kenzie to the backseat. "Go on and sit up front with Jared," Becky directed. "We'll sit by this handsome young man." They slid in beside Corey.

"Nice to see you, Kenzie." Jared sounded amused as she clicked her seat belt. "Glad you decided to come with me."

His teasing rankled a bit, and Kenzie turned her head so she could roll her eyes without him seeing. She didn't look forward to the ride, but Melanie and Becky were bright and chatty, and soon all of them were laughing on their way to the first of three stops they would make in Gurnee.

When Jared parked in front of a small square-brick home, the five of them poured out of the Ford Explorer. The women pulled their scarves tighter against the cold wind as they arranged themselves in a semicircle around the front door and sang, "Hark! The Herald Angels Sing."

Mr. Keeler, an elderly man wearing suspenders, opened the door. He had an expression of utter delight on his wrinkled face as he called in a reedy voice for his wife to come. Mrs. Keeler, a frail-looking woman with thin hair, shuffled to the door in worn slippers. She clutched at her sweater with one hand and held onto the door frame with the other as the group sang another carol. The elderly couple exchanged rapturous looks with one another, and to Kenzie, their smiles seemed brighter than the stars. She no longer felt the cold. There was only a warming inner glow. When they finished, Mr. and Mrs. Keeler eagerly invited them in. They oohed and aahed over their gift basket, then unpacked the gift bag, which held new sweaters for both of them.

Tears shone in Mr. Keeler's rheumy eyes. "I'll make good use of this!" he said, taking off his own worn sweater, which was missing a button. He put on his new blue sweater and smoothed down the front. "How did you know I needed one?".

"Santa must have got your letter," Jared told him with a smile.

Becky handed a blanket to Mrs. Keeler, who rubbed it against her cheek in wonder. "It's as soft as a kitten," she exclaimed.

"Oh my gosh, I nearly forgot," Jared cried. Hurrying outside, he returned with a large sack of dry cat food.

"You thought of everything," Mrs. Keeler said. "I'd ask Mittens to come and thank you, but she always hides when we have visitors." They chatted for a while, and when it was time to go, the Keelers reluctantly bid them good night.

As Jared headed for the Nesrin home, Melanie and Becky filled Kenzie in on the family's circumstances. The father had been laid off. While trying to land a new job, he worked nights at a warehouse. They pulled up in front of a modest white stucco home. Kenzie and the others stood at the bottom of the porch, and as they started to sing, four bright-eyed children of assorted sizes came to stand on the porch, their faces wreathed in smiles. Their mother joined them in wide-eyed wonder. After several carols, Mrs. Nesrin invited them in. Tears sprang to her eyes when she saw them carry in gift bags, coats, and an overflowing basket.

The children could hardly contain themselves, eying the basket and trying to peek past the tissue paper into the holiday bags. Standing close to the mother, Becky told her in a low voice, "There are a few presents for each of the children in the bags. You can open them now or on Christmas, whichever you'd rather."

Mrs. Nesrin appeared torn, but finally she whispered, "I think we'll wait—Billy and I don't have a whole lot for them." She told the children, "Put the bags under the tree; they're for Christmas. But you can have the coats and the basket now."

There were only a few groans before the children started trying on coats. Two of the boys dug into the basket, taking out candy, fruit, and cookies and holding them up to show the others. A shaggy-haired boy of ten pulled out a canned ham, looking thoroughly puzzled.

Mrs. Nesrin took it from him with a laugh. "This is for Christmas dinner. Then she reached for a package of cookies while asking the group, "Would you like to have some?"

"That's very nice of you, but we're good," Melanie said warmly, sitting on the blanket-covered couch. "We'll just visit a minute before we head to our next stop."

Kenzie's chest tightened as she viewed the tree, a tall version of Charlie Brown's Christmas tree. A little girl around Sara's age zipped up her coat then spun in a circle for all to admire the pretty pink fabric.

"It's beautiful!" Kenzie said, making the girl beam. She wished they didn't have to go. A tiny girl with black braids toddled over to an orange that had fallen out. Picking it up with great effort, she handed it to Kenzie before wobbling off toward the basket.

Kenzie's heart melted when Jared took time to speak to each child, asking them their name, age, and what they wanted for Christmas. When he put the littlest girl on his lap, her dark eyes peered up at him trustingly as if he were Santa Claus himself. Kenzie yearned to leave more than a basket, coats, and a few presents, yet the Nesrins acted as though they had received the world.

When they got up to leave, Kenzie reached into her pocket, where she had tucked a twenty-dollar bill a few days ago. Wishing she had more, she slipped it into the basket to be discovered later.

Their last stop was at a neat little clapboard house. Mr. Rodriguez, a cheerful elderly man with wispy white hair, opened the door and shouted, "You can't sing out there! It's too cold! Come on in here where it's warm."

Backing up his walker to make room, Mr. Rodriguez watched as they filed into the small cluttered room. With some difficulty, he maneuvered himself into a chair then watched cheerily as they sang. Kenzie stood by Jared, listening to his deep voice ring out. When they finished one carol, Mr. Rodriguez's asked for another, then another, his face beaming. Then he asked them to sit and visit.

A blanket hung from the ceiling, closing off the tiny room from the rest of the house. Noticing Becky's curious glance, Mr. Rodriguez explained, "During winter, I close off the heat vents in the rest of the house except for my bedroom. A friend of mine put up the blanket to help keep the cold out."

Jared nodded toward the fireplace. "Do you have any wood?"

"My neighbor usually chops some for me, but I ran out a couple of days ago."

"I used to chop wood a lot," Jared said. "Nothing gives your muscles a better workout." He nodded toward Corey. "I was telling my son the other day that I needed to get more exercise. Would you mind if I came here once in a while and chopped wood? It would be a lot cheaper than me going to the gym."

Mr. Rodriguez accepted graciously. "That would be very nice, thank you."

Melanie handed the elderly man a gift bag and a colorful quilt the Relief Society had tied. "Why, this is exactly what I asked Santa for!" Mr. Rodriguez exclaimed happily, his gnarled hands clutching the quilt. His eyes went to the gift basket Becky had set on a table. "It's sure nice of you people to remember me like this."

Kenzie was glad for the envelope she'd seen tucked in his basket, which would help Mr. Rodriguez afford simple necessities. They visited for a time then gave him a hug before wishing him a Merry Christmas.

As Jared drove to Becky's home in Gurnee, they talked in soft, emotional voices about the evening. Melanie said she would check to make sure each family was being visited regularly by home and visiting teachers. After dropping Becky off, they headed for Lake Forest.

During the evening, Kenzie had been very aware of Jared. As he drove now, Kenzie glanced over just as a passing streetlight lit up Jared's face. She liked what she saw. When they'd first met, there had been an immediate connection, but Kenzie had pushed her interest aside once she'd discovered he was buying her brother's house. Still, sheer magnetism kept drawing her to him. The attraction she'd always felt had been amplified by the tender emotions of the evening, and it came as a jolt to realize that Jared Rawlins had claimed a piece of her heart. Just how much, she wasn't sure. It came as a surprise—Kenzie had been fiercely independent ever since her divorce. Although she dated, Kenzie had not met anyone she wanted a long-term relationship with—and here Jared had crept into her heart without even trying.

Melanie cheerily bid them good night, and Jared headed for Kenzie's house. She stole another glance at him, wondering at the strange, fluttery sensation in her stomach. How could she be charmed by a man who was taking her house away from her? It was unanswerable. And yet on this night, there was a special and undeniable camaraderie between them as they chatted quietly. Even when they fell momentarily silent, driving past houses festooned with Christmas lights, the very air was full of warmth and tenderness. And when Jared gave her one of his special smiles, Kenzie's heart began beating faster.

Too soon, Jared pulled in the driveway of her parents' home. She turned to see that Corey had fallen asleep, his head lolling against the side of the SUV.

"Thanks for taking us around," Kenzie said softly.

"I'm glad Tom asked me. Tonight made me remember what Christmas is all about. I hope the Relief Society decides to do this every year."

"I hope so too." For Kenzie, it had been a life-changing experience— one she would always remember. The evening had brought back all the special emotions and excitement she used to feel as a child at Christmastime.

"All the families were so appreciative, but seeing how little they had made me feel guilty," Jared admitted. "I have so much, and I don't appreciate it enough."

"I thought the same thing. I need to count my blessings more often." Her head felt light with Jared looking at her like that.

"I'm really glad you came with me," he said.

"Me too. Earlier tonight, my mom told Sara that if she came, she would see some Christmas magic." She smiled gently when he reached over and took her hand in his warm fingers. "She was right," she said, gazing into Jared's eyes. "There was a lot of magic tonight."

CHAPTER SIXTEEN

THE SNOW WAS CRUSTY, THE trail through the woods, well worn. A raw breeze caused Sara to zip her puffy coat up to her chin. The day was softly gray, and Sara tilted her chin up at the sky, trying to gauge if the heavy clouds contained snow. She hoped it would snow for Christmas—soft fluffy snow. It would be fun to come here after a snowstorm and be the first one to walk through it.

While ambling along, Sara kept her eyes open for animals. If only she could see a fox. She'd never seen one except in the zoo, but their tails were unbelievably thick and bushy, and she was anxious to see one in the wild.

A crackling sound from behind made Sara turn. A boy about her size in a blue parka and black knit cap came toward her on the trail. Soon, he was close enough to recognize.

"Hi, Corey!"

He waved a black-gloved hand. How nice that he'd remembered her saying she walked in the woods by her grandparents' home nearly every day.

"I'm glad you came today," Sara said a bit shyly when he caught up to her.

"I like the woods," Corey said as if that explained everything, and they walked on together. Once, her sharp eyes caught a line of tracks crossing the cushion of snow, and they left the trail to examine them.

Corey studied them knowingly. "Deer," he pronounced, then looked around as if some might be skulking behind the thick oak and hickory trees.

Smaller tracks skittered over the frozen top layer of snow. "Are these rabbit tracks?" Sara pointed at the tracks.

"Could be."

"Do you think it could be a fox?" Sara clasped her hands in rapture to think a glorious animal such as a fox might be close by. "Or maybe it was a raccoon."

"I think raccoons sleep during the winter, like bears."

"Do they ever come out to eat?"

"I think so." Corey didn't sound as sure as Sara would have liked.

When they returned to the trail, she asked, "Have you ever been here before?"

"Yeah, I come here a lot with my dad."

"Have you seen the pond?"

"My dad and I go ice skating there, but we haven't been yet this year."

Although Sara always enjoyed her solitary walks, it was fun to have someone with her and point out different things. They came to a bend, and after rounding it Sara took the right fork, which led to the pond. The path was almost as well used as the main trail.

"A lot of people must come here," Sara remarked.

When they reached the frozen, bluish-gray pond, Corey took a few steps onto the ice. Alarmed, Sara cried out, "Don't go out there! It might crack, and you'd fall in."

"Don't worry. I won't go any farther. My dad always tests the ice before we skate to make sure it's safe. But look, people have already been skating." Corey pointed at the multitude of grooves and scratches on the pond's surface.

"Do you like to ice skate?" Sara asked.

"Yeah. My dad and I go a lot. Have you ever skated here?"

"Not for a long time. I used to come with my mom and dad." It seemed like forever since the three of them had held hands and skated here.

"Do you want to go skating?" Corey asked eagerly. "I have ice skates. Do you?"

Sara was thrilled with the idea but unsure about skates. "I outgrew mine years ago. But my grandma has a box of skates in her garage. They're pretty old, but I can see if any fit me."

Chatting enthusiastically, they followed the trail as it circled around the pond, making plans. They could see their breath when their laughter echoed in the clear, bright air. Corey talked about how his car-bed would have to be dismantled when they moved.

"Are you excited about moving?" Sara asked.

"Yeah." Corey's voice was soft, and he looked at her out of the corner of his eye. "I know your mom wanted to buy the house we're moving to."

"She *really* wanted it." Sara's voice turned mournful. Her mother had been *so* disappointed. "Mom was really excited about moving back here, but now she's kind of sad." Sara didn't want to tell Corey that her mom still hoped to buy the house—especially since Sara didn't understand how that could happen. Grandpa and Aunt Mandy both said Corey's father had bought it.

As if trying to keep up with Sara's confidences, Corey offered, "My dad's sad sometimes."

Why would he be sad? He was getting the house, wasn't he? But then, maybe he was sad about other things too, like her mom. "My mom's been sad a lot, ever since she and my dad got divorced. She doesn't want me to know, but I can tell." At least her mom didn't have red eyes as often as she used to. Now she only got quiet and had a solemn look on her face when Sara left for weekend visits, carrying her bulging backpack. Her mother tried to hide it, talking all bright and shining as if everything was wonderful, but it wasn't. Her mom would stand at the door, her smile too big, while she waved too energetically— as though nothing was better than watching Sara walk to her dad's car.

Corey digested that in silence. "That's kinda like my dad, only he didn't get divorced. My mom died."

Inhaling sharply, Sara stopped in her tracks. Having your mom die was the very worst possible thing in the whole world. She felt so bad for Corey that she didn't know what to say. Finally she murmured, "I'm sorry. It must have been awful."

Corey acknowledged Sara's condolences with a nod, and they walked on. "I think my dad's lonely."

"Me too—I mean my mom is too." Sara's scarf came undone, and she fumbled with it, throwing one end over her shoulder.

Corey had an idea. "Maybe your mom and my dad can be friends." Peering at Sara out of bright, dark eyes, he added, "Dad told me once that it's hard for him to talk with girls, but he talks to your mom all right."

Sara didn't want to dampen his enthusiasm because on the surface it *did* sound like a good plan—but there were all those bits and pieces she'd overheard. Her mom didn't sound like she liked Corey's dad very much. "Maybe." Her voice was doubtful. "But my mom isn't very happy that he's buying my uncle's house."

Her words put Corey on the defensive. "My dad bought it before you and your mom even got here." Then he stopped, unsure. "Well, I think he bought it. He signed a bunch of papers."

That sounded pretty final to Sara.

"If your mom wanted it, she should have said so," Corey added.

Sara frowned. Corey's statement sounded like he was repeating something he'd heard his dad say. Annoyance on her mother's behalf sprang up, and she blurted, "Mom *did* say something! She wanted it to be a surprise for Uncle Tom and Aunt Mandy. Like a Christmas present." Her eyes flashed with blue fire at what she perceived as an affront to her mother.

"Oh. I didn't know that." Corey sounded apologetic.

"Mom thought it would make Uncle Tom and Aunt Mandy happy. Mom wanted the house because it's where she grew up." Sara kicked at the snow as they went along. She looked up at Corey, whose cheeks were flushed from the cold.

He nodded deeply, assuring her it all made sense. Then they smiled, the tension melted away, and they were all right again.

"Does your dad go out on dates?" Sara was curious about the process and glad to have someone she could ask.

"Sometimes. What about your mom?"

"She goes out once in a while, but I don't think she likes it very much." Sara didn't understand it. If you went out with someone, didn't that mean you wanted to? Yet her mother often came back tight-lipped about the whole thing.

Then Corey said something that took her breath away. "I think my dad likes your mom."

Sara couldn't help it. She blurted out the first thing that came to her mind. "She's taken. Mom likes a boy she used to know when she was little." Her mother's face lit up whenever she talked about Tyrone.

It was something Sara wanted to see all the time. "I think he lives here. They used to meet here in the woods all the time, but then he moved away."

Corey was confused. "How can your mom find him if he moved away?" It was a natural question.

"I think he moved back." It sounded dumb when she said it out loud. But it hadn't sounded like that when she'd said the same thing to Grandma. She didn't know for sure that Tyrone had moved back— it was just something Sara really hoped for—sure it would erase the sadness she saw at times in her mother. More than anything else, Sara wanted her mother to be happy and laughing, without all of that awful pretending. Sara hated seeing the emptiness behind her mother's smile. She'd gotten good at spotting forced cheerfulness. She wanted the real thing—the way her mother used to be before her dad left.

They came to a fork, and Corey examined the sky as if gauging the time. "We'd better turn back."

They turned around as one and walked along in comfortable silence. The tip of Sara's nose was cold and most likely red. Sometimes in her prayers, Sara asked Heavenly Father to bless her mother. And she knew God had listened because things were a lot better than they used to be. But things could be better still. That was part of why her mother had moved here. Whenever her mom talked about living in Lake Forest, her voice got all soft just like when she talked about Tyrone. Her mother *needed* something—someone. And that had to be the boy with the dumb name—Tyrone. He just *had* to be here. Sara picked up the conversation as if it had never ended.

"I know Tyrone could have moved a long way away, but I still think he came back." Then Sara played her trump card. "Besides, my grandma said there's magic at Christmastime. So he really could be here."

"How could magic make him come back?" Corey was skeptical.

His question made Sara feel foolish—and defensive. When she'd talked with her grandma, magic was the perfect explanation for how and why Tyrone had returned to Lake Forest. She tried to explain. "Magic *can* happen if you want it to. I read a book about it. It's pretty good. I'll lend it to you if you want."

Corey was agreeable. "Okay."

"If you want, we can go to my grandma's house, and I'll get it for you. Grandma said that if I believe in magic, it can happen."

"Magic is for kids."

"Grandma says we're *all* kids at Christmas."

CHAPTER SEVENTEEN

COREY WAS USUALLY SUCH A bouncing, running bundle of energy that Jared was surprised to see him curled up in a chair with a book in the living room. "What are you reading?"

"Sara let me borrow some books." There was a pile on the end table beside Corey.

"When did you see her?"

"I went for a walk in the woods, and she was there. We went to the pond."

Talk about déjà vu. Boy meets girl in the woods. A glistening pond provides a backdrop to a delightful playground in a forest. Then Jared's parental instincts kicked in. "Wait a minute. You didn't go out onto the pond, did you?"

"Just a step or two. I knew you didn't want me to go any farther."

"That's right." A wave of relief washed over him. When Corey asked if he could go to the woods, Jared hadn't even *thought* about the pond. He lifted Corey up and settled into the chair, putting him on his lap.

"Sara and I want to go ice skating. Can we?"

"Not until I check the ice. Do you remember what to look for?"

"It needs to be thick."

"At least four inches, and the ice should be blue or clear. If it's gray, white, or opaque, the ice is weak. What did it look like today?"

"Um, I think it was kinda blue."

"Why don't you and I go skating and check it out. If it's safe, then you and Sara can go. How about it?"

"Yeah!"

Corey's elbow was digging into his side, so Jared shifted him. "So what did you do in the woods?"

"We saw some deer tracks. And a bunch of other tracks. Sara said they might be a fox or a rabbit. Maybe even a raccoon. Do raccoons sleep during the winter, Dad?"

"Mostly. They're kind of like bears, but they wake up sometimes and come out for food. Then they go back to sleep. Unless it's really cold—then they stay put. I think bears sleep more soundly than raccoons."

"I wanted to see some deer, but there weren't any. We walked around the pond."

Something he and Izzy had done many times. "It's pretty there, isn't it?" From the expression on Corey's face, Jared could tell his son wasn't sure about the "pretty" part.

"I liked it," he offered, trying to find common ground. "Did you go skating there when you were little?"

"Yep."

"How long did you live here, Dad?"

"A couple of years. And actually I lived in West Lake Forest." Jared had almost lost track of all the places he had lived. Life without a father had been difficult, and it was only when he was an adult that he realized how his mother must have struggled. Now that he was older and wiser, Jared had a better appreciation for all she had done.

"Oh, yeah. And Izzy lived here."

"She lived on the south end of Lake Forest, and I lived on the north end of West Lake Forest with only the woods in between us. So I'd ride my bike and meet her there."

"Where did you lock up your bike?"

Oh, the simpler times of years past! "We didn't lock them—we never even thought someone might take them." Corey looked astonished. What a sad commentary that was on the state of the world.

"What did you do there?"

How to even start? Jared told him how their days had been filled with wandering through the woods, skipping stones on the pond, gathering leaves, and climbing trees. Sometimes he and Izzy pulled long lush grass in open meadows, stuffed it in sacks, then went to a nearby pasture to feed it to the horses. Once, Izzy brought an old tarp, and they'd made a tent.

Corey looked envious.

"One day, Izzy and I decided to become trappers. We made our own trap out of an old wooden box and propped up one end with a stick. We baited it with lunchmeat from our sandwiches, then tied a long rope to the stick and backed off, waiting for an animal to smell the meat and go inside. Once it did, we'd pull the rope, and the box would fall and trap the animal." Jared chuckled. "For a while, my mom wondered why I didn't want peanut butter and jelly sandwiches anymore."

"Did you catch anything?"

"Nothing but ants. Once a magpie flew in, but by the time I pulled the rope, it had flown off. Sometimes we'd take jars to the pond to catch polliwogs. I wanted to take mine home, but Izzy couldn't stand to see the polliwogs cooped up in a jar. So when my back was turned, she dumped them back into the pond."

When he paused, Corey looked at him expectantly. "What else did you do?"

"Let's see . . ." Jared scratched his chin as he tried to remember. "Well, we brought sack lunches every day. Most of the time we'd trade—except for when Izzy's mom made hers out of homemade bread. Then Izzy wouldn't trade—not unless I threw in my cookie along with my sandwich." Izzy had been smart as well as shrewd.

Corey was disapproving. "That wasn't fair."

"Ah, but if you'd tasted that bread, you'd know it was worth it. Besides, Izzy always broke the cookie in half and shared it with me along with whatever treat she'd brought that day." Izzy had always been generous. Jared had liked her tremendously and had been amazed at how he could talk to her all day long. He was never tongue-tied like he was around other people.

Those were the days! Each afternoon when it was time to go home, Jared would marvel at how the day had passed so quickly. He'd been heartbroken when his mother told him they were moving—again. He and Izzy promised each other they'd write faithfully. And yet she hadn't. He still had a sore spot about that. Why hadn't she written? He'd checked the mailbox so many times, his heart dropping to his shoes each time he turned away. They'd been such good friends—he thought. Perhaps their friendship had been one-sided on his part.

Corey squirmed a little, ready to talk about something else. "Dad, are we still going to buy that house?"

"We sure are."

"Oh good. I told Sara you'd signed some papers. She said her mom really wanted it. Because she grew up there."

A pang shot through Jared, but he pushed it aside. "Kenzie could have bought the house. It had been up for sale for a while before I bought it."

"That's what I told Sara." Corey sounded very firm.

Great. And Sara would tell Kenzie all about that. But then, why did he even care? He didn't.

Corey went on, a veritable fount of information. "Sara said her mom's sad a lot since she got divorced. Maybe you and Sara's mom could be friends."

When pigs fly! But Corey stared at him so earnestly that fatherhood compelled him to say something encouraging. "Sure. I guess so." Actually, when he'd first met McKenzie Forsberg, Jared had wanted very much to be friends—perhaps more than friends. But Kenzie's one-track mind had put an end to that.

"Maybe you could ask her out to dinner."

Jared frowned at his son. "I thought you didn't like it when I went on dates. You always get a stomachache."

"Oh, Dad! That's when I was little. I'm okay when you go out with Pam."

True. But then, they hadn't gone out *that* much. Jared liked Pam, but he wasn't sure he wanted to pursue a relationship. She was always dropping hints about going to the movies or dinner, but somehow his heart wasn't in it.

Then there had been the night he'd spent with Kenzie—taking those baskets around. There had been something special between them that night. The look in Kenzie's eyes told him she was interested. He hated to admit it, but he'd felt a stirring that night—something warm in his chest. Then Jared caught himself and pushed all thoughts of Kenzie out of his mind. He was definitely *not* going to go there.

CHAPTER EIGHTEEN

SATURDAY MORNING, KENZIE'S MOM ASKED her to run a few errands. After picking up a prescription and stopping downtown at the dry cleaner's, Kenzie headed for the bookstore on Main Street. As she walked along the sidewalk, warmth flooded her as she thought about taking the baskets around Thursday night—the grateful Mr. and Mrs. Keeler, the excited Nesrin children, and the jolly Mr. Rodriguez. All of them were struggling financially, and some physically, yet they were all cheerful and upbeat.

With a jolt, Kenzie realized she was just coming to Jared's Café. She stopped to look in the display window, where the exhibit was being changed. There were pieces of brown and blue material, fluffy batting, and tinfoil scattered about. It would be interesting to see the final results. Suddenly, a disembodied head peered at her from above the back wall of the display. Startled, Kenzie jumped, and Jared grinned at her mischievously. Raising an arm, he beckoned her in, then disappeared.

A warmth came to Kenzie's cheeks, fueled by the memory of two nights ago when she'd felt so attracted to Jared. Then she shook herself. Nothing could come of that, so it would probably be best to act cool and distant. Perhaps she shouldn't even go in. But, no, she didn't want to be rude.

Jared was waiting. "You looked cold out there. How about a hot chocolate—on the house?"

It did sound good, and it was doubly hard to resist when he looked at her that way. There was something about Jared that seemed to naturally draw her to him.

Before she could respond, Jared added, "I just have one request. No talking about the house."

She grinned. "I can live with that. And I do want to buy some more chocolate-walnut fudge before I leave. It's sinfully delicious."

"It *is* awesome—it's one of my specialties."

"*You* make the fudge?"

"Don't act so surprised." As Kenzie wiped the shock off her face, Jared told her, "Go ahead and sit down. I'll be right over." She picked a booth in the corner and laid her father's suit, in its thin plastic covering, over the bench.

Scott came from the back room, holding a broom. He looked around as if uncertain what to do. Jared, carrying two mugs, stopped to talk to him and nodded toward some empty tables and booths. Although Kenzie couldn't hear the words, Jared's tone sounded encouraging. The young man responded with a trusting smile then set to work.

Kenzie watched as Scott carefully swept under a booth.

Sliding a bright red mug toward her, Jared said, "Scott usually just cleans tables, but I'm having him take on a little more responsibility."

"He has Down syndrome, doesn't he?" When Jared nodded, she asked, "How long has he been working here?"

"About a month. Scott came in with his mother, searching for work. She told me that Scott wanted to work at the grocery store, but the manager was reluctant to hire him."

"Wasn't sure he could handle the job?"

"Yeah. He's a little old-fashioned. When I told Scott I didn't have a position open, he thanked me anyway even though I could tell he was really disappointed." Jared shrugged. "What could I do? I gave him a job anyway. His mother was as happy as Scott was. She said the guy at the grocery store didn't know that a lot of stores hire people with Down syndrome—they can be good workers. Anyway, the manager told her if Scott worked someplace for six months and brought back a reference, they'd hire him."

Kenzie was impressed. Not too many people with a new business would hire and train an employee they didn't need. "That was really nice of you."

"Not really. For six months I'm off KP duty."

"How's he getting along?"

"Really well. The other employees are good to help him. As you saw, he sometimes gets a little confused, but once I show him how to do something, he's good to go."

Kenzie stirred her chocolate. "Yay! Real marshmallows!"

"I don't allow any of those itty-bitty crunchy imposters on the premises."

He beckoned to Scott. "Hey, buddy, would you ask Pam for two packages of Oreo cookies and bring them over here?"

Scott nodded and in his hurry leaned the broom against a chair. It slid to the side and fell with a loud thunk. The young man looked worried, but Jared waved it off. "Don't worry about it."

When he returned, Kenzie thanked him for the cookies. Scott smiled, then went back to work.

Tearing open his packet, Jared took a cookie and dunked it in his hot chocolate.

Kenzie frowned. "Figures. You're a dunker."

"And I bet you're a twister."

Snatching up a cookie, Kenzie twisted it open and took a bite of the creamy middle. "Ummm."

Jared shuddered. "That's wrong in so many ways."

Picking up her mug and warming her fingers, Kenzie sipped her chocolate. "This is really good!"

"It's a secret recipe—been in my family for generations."

"Really?"

"No, but it sounds good, doesn't it?"

She giggled and studied the small, cozy restaurant. "You've got a really nice place here. It seems to be doing well."

There were a number of people eating at booths and tables, and Jared looked at them appreciatively. "I'm thankful for that. The first year was slow going, but things have picked up since then."

"I like your decor. The colors are great, and I like the baskets and green plants."

"Thanks. A friend of mine who owns a restaurant, Michael Burkinshaw, told me it was really important to have the right decor— said it could mean the difference between a one-time customer or one that keeps coming back."

"Who did your decorating?"

"I hired a decorator to make recommendations. Since I was on a strict budget, I asked my sister and Pam to find the recommended items—from paint to baskets to tile. My sister's really good at this stuff. And Pam helped a lot."

Kenzie glanced toward the dessert display case, where Pam was waiting on a customer. Pam's eye flicked toward Jared, then Kenzie, before going back to her customer, who had settled on the lemon tarts.

"What made you decide to open a café?"

"I blame Michael. He's got a restaurant in Rockford, where I used to live. I started working for him and eventually worked my way up and bought out his partner." Jared dunked another cookie. "He taught me all about the business and said the secret of success was to create something different or unique—something people don't normally cook in their own homes. I go along with that to a point, but I also wanted to offer familiar foods, something nutritious and healthy. So I decided to specialize in soups and sandwiches, although we have a few other dishes."

"What made you decide to move to Lake Forest?"

"I've always loved it here. It's a beautiful area, and there's a special atmosphere here. People are so friendly. I guess part of the reason I came is because I needed to go someplace new and kind of start over, you know?"

Kenzie did know. That was exactly what she was doing now. She'd gotten over Larry, but she also needed to go someplace new—even if was her hometown—and reinvent herself and her life. Trying something different was a sign she was putting the past behind and showing the world—and herself—that she was ready to move forward.

"Now let me ask you," Jared said. "What made you decide to come back?"

"A lot of reasons. I need a fresh start too. I'm tired of the hectic pace in Chicago. And I want Sara to have the same kind of childhood I had." Impulsively she added, "Also, I had to get away from my job at Midwest. A guy was causing some real problems for me—so I started searching and applied for a position at Reliance Software." She took a sip. "I'm glad to be back. Even though Lake Forest has grown, it still has a real, small-town feeling about it. I loved growing up here and think it'll be good for Sara. How did Corey react to moving here?"

"It was hard for him to leave Rockport, but he settled in quickly, and now he loves it."

Kenzie debated with herself over asking about his wife, but since their conversation had been so easy and comfortable, she went ahead. "It must have been hard after your wife died."

"The hardest thing I've ever been through." Jared looked somber. "It's difficult being a single parent, as I'm sure you know. I knew Robin stayed busy, but it wasn't until after she was gone that I began to understand how much she did. Especially with Corey! Taking him to the library, soccer practices, the dentist, outfitting him for school in the fall. Boy, that last one's a killer." He grinned, then said, "But then, you know what it's like."

She wondered if Tom had told him the reason behind her divorce. Oh well, no matter. It was nice to be at the point where she could talk freely about her past.

"I'm lucky because Larry is still very involved with Sara. But it's the little things I miss. Like if I had an important meeting and Sara got sick, Larry would take time off and step in. If I had to work late, he'd make dinner and help Sara with her homework. That's not an option anymore. Then, there's losing Sara every other weekend and holiday. I'm not sure I'll ever get used to that."

"I'm sorry—that must be very hard." Their eyes met and lingered. His words, so simply said, carried a mountain of sympathy. Jared's compassion was palpable, and the expression on his face was kind. She felt so comfortable talking with him—as if they were kindred spirits. Something in her heart softened into a spreading pool, and she smiled at him. Then Kenzie caught herself and looked down. Picking up her mug, she took a drink, steeling herself. "How are you and Corey doing?"

"It was an uphill battle the first couple of years, but now I think we're in a good place. Corey had to work through his grief. When he started having nightmares, I talked to a friend who's a child psychologist. She saw Corey for a while and told me a few things to do and not to do, and soon the nightmares stopped. Corey used to be kind of shy, like me, but since we moved here, I've encouraged him to be more outgoing, and he has. So we're doing good."

What a good father. So much of Jared's focus was on his child. Obviously it was second nature for him to think that if Corey was doing good, then he was. Surely, Jared had to have heartaches and worries of his own. Yet all of his concern was for his son. She wanted to know *his* feelings. "You've talked about Corey, but what about *you*?"

The question seemed to stump him. "Well, I guess I've adjusted too. For a long time, I didn't think I ever would. There are a lot of things I miss—like having someone I can go home to and tell about my day. Someone to sit by me on the couch at night, holding my hand and watching TV."

Pam approached their booth, stopping a few respectful feet away. "Jared?"

There were a number of people waiting in line. Jared took in the situation immediately. "I'll be right there," he said, and Pam hurried back to her station.

"Thanks for the chocolate." Standing, Kenzie picked up the wrappers.

"We have a couple of different flavors. You ought to try the candy cane one next time."

Next time—that sounded good.

Jared paused before slipping around the counter and giving her an endearing little wave. Mesmerized, Kenzie watched as he slipped on his apron. It seemed like some cosmic joke that when she finally met someone she could fall for, it had to be the man who stood between her and the house she wanted so badly. For the past six months, the one thing Kenzie had clung to—like a life preserver—was settling down in the home she had grown up in. Just thinking about living there was like putting on a pair of slippers after a day of high heels. She needed an anchor for her life, one that her brother's house alone could provide. Kenzie slipped on her coat, picked up her father's suit, then waved good-bye to Jared.

Kenzie crossed the road and was on her way to the parking lot when she peered in the front windows of Dahlquist Realty. Her brother was at the front counter. She'd pop in and say hi. The chimes tinkled as she opened the door. "Hi, Tom!" she called out cheerily.

Her brother rose, his face set like granite as he came around the counter. "I want to talk to you." He took her arm and pulled her into his office.

Perplexed at the harsh edge in his voice, Kenzie asked, "What's going on?"

"I'm the one who should be asking that." Tom glowered at her as she laid the dry cleaning aside and sat down. Taking a seat behind his desk, Tom ran a hand over his short, bristly hair. "I was supposed to show Jared's home yesterday to Carlos and Tracy Perez. Imagine my surprise when they told me they didn't want to see it anymore. Tracy had a list of other houses that sounded more interesting to her. Homes *you* suggested would be much better for them."

"I'm not sure I would put it that way, but Tracy and I did talk about homes."

"I can't believe you deliberately went to the travel agency to talk Tracy out of seeing Jared's house."

Kenzie's cheeks flamed. "That's not what happened!"

"Tracy said she talked with you at the agency."

"Well, yes, but it's not what you think"—"

"Did you or didn't you talk to Tracy about seeing other houses?"

"She asked me about some of the houses you showed me."

"Tracy said you advised her against buying a two-bedroom home."

"Well, yeah. They're a young couple with a business, and I assumed they did some work at home. I thought a three-bedroom home would probably be better."

"And you knew Jared's house only had two bedrooms. Tracy and Carlos were *very* interested in it. They'd seen it once already, and I'd arranged for them to see it again." The blood drained from her face, and Tom went on. "I just find it very interesting that you went to talk to them *after* I told you I was going to show them Jared's house."

"I had no idea they were that interested in Jared's house. We didn't even talk about *his* house. We talked about—"

Tom broke in. "Yeah, yeah. She told me you just *happened* to have all of the notes you'd taken when I showed you houses."

Kenzie wanted to stamp her foot. "Of course I had them. They were in my purse, which I happen to take everywhere."

"And you had to scare Tracy away from Jared's home by talking about how out-of-date building codes were for older homes."

"Well, they *are* out-of-date! Look, I'm really sorry, but we were just talking about house hunting and what we wanted in a house."

"Don't play innocent. You need to take some personal responsibility and own up to what you did." Tom's voice was cold. "I know you run off at the mouth at times, but how could you tell Tracy all those negative things about older homes and about how expensive it is to remodel?"

Her temper flared. "Oh, is that something you're trying to hide? I have a friend who had a really bad experience, and—and I told Tracy about it. She needed to know what she could be getting into. Honestly, she was like a kid—hadn't thought anything through."

"Such as lack of insulation, possible mold, cracked foundations, having room for future children, needing a garage for winter—oh, yes, Tracy had a whole list of ideas she got from you." Tom went on, "In fact, Tracy told me you were so helpful that I ought to hire you. So now what? You want to start selling real estate on the side? Maybe you want to take over my job?"

Okay, he was going overboard here. He must be pretty mad since it wasn't like him to talk like this. How could she make Tom understand?

"We were just talking. Okay, I admit I may have gotten carried away with the old houses, but I wasn't talking specifically about Jared's house!" But as soon as the words left her mouth, Kenzie winced and ducked her head. All right. That wasn't absolutely true. She *had* thought of Jared's home, and while she hadn't said anything against it specifically, it might have caused her to say more against older homes than she would have. At the time, talking with Tracy had seemed like a heaven-sent opportunity to persuade her to look elsewhere, but that hadn't been her intent—not really. And she certainly didn't know Jared's house only had two bedrooms. "Will you stop and let me explain?" she implored.

But Tom was not in a mood to listen. "I really thought Tracy and Carlos might buy Jared's house," he said angrily. "Mandy told me how badly you wanted our house and that you were going to think of some way to get it. Well, you did. You talked Tracy out of it and blew the sale for Jared."

"That's going a little far, isn't it? You don't *know* they would have bought it. Okay, I should have curbed my big fat mouth, but was it wrong to point out the pitfalls of older homes when my friend had such a terrible experience? Maybe I shouldn't have pulled out the homes you'd printed out for me, but I can't see why it was wrong to show them to Tracy. Why shouldn't she look at whatever house she wants to see? And if all it boils down to is Jared not being able to buy your house, well, he can always find another one."

When Tom glanced over her shoulder, Kenzie whipped around. Jared stood stiffly in the doorway. His eyes were dark circles of shock and anger. The air turned thin as she looked at him, stricken. How had he come in without her hearing the chimes?

Moving very carefully, Jared set a small white box on the desk. In a lifeless monotone, he told Kenzie, "You left without your fudge. Scott saw you leave and told me you came here." Without another word, Jared turned and strode out. The chimes on the door tinkled the way they always did, but this time, they sounded macabre.

CHAPTER NINETEEN

A FEW BLOCKS PAST THE Dalquist home, Jared turned into a small parking lot at the end of the road. Most people in Lake Forest, at one time or another, parked here to go hiking in the woods. Jared and Corey got out their skates, tied the laces together, and draped them around their necks. Then Jared grabbed his backpack out of the Ford, and the pair went to the opening in the rail fence where the trailhead began. Boots crunched in the snow as they headed down the trail. Corey was bursting with what he and Sara had seen during their walk, and as his son talked, Jared looked east. The woods were so thick he couldn't make out the Dalquist home even though he knew it was there.

Farther along the trail, Corey pointed out a spot. "That's where I saw deer tracks, Dad."

Jared went closer. "Yep, you were right. Those *are* deer tracks. Maybe we'll see some today." Corey's face brightened, and Jared knew his son would be thrilled if they happened upon some deer. And frankly, he'd get a kick out of it himself. There was something so noble and majestic about the large-eyed animals. He couldn't imagine how anyone could shoot such a beautiful animal.

When they reached the large pond, Jared unzipped the backpack and pulled out a small blue tarp, which he spread on the ground. Corey sat on it and began taking off his boots.

"Hold up, son. I've got to check out the ice, remember?"

Corey objected. "But people had been skating on it."

"They might be *lucky* people; we're going to make sure it's safe."

Although the weather had been below freezing for some time, Jared wanted to be sure. Robin had often accused him of being overly cautious, but there were worse traits.

It had snowed a little the night before, and a few feet from shore Jared brushed the snow away so he could see the ice. Corey stood at his shoulder.

"See the color, son? How it's kind of a bluish-white? And there's no slush, cracks, or holes." He stood. "You stay here. I'm going to check it a little farther out."

Carrying his auger, Jared went out, visually inspected the ice, then went near the middle of the pond. Using the auger, he drilled down, then measured. The past month of cold weather had frozen the pond to a little over four inches. Perfect. He gave his son a thumb's up.

With a loud whoop, Corey ran to the tarp to change into skates. He was on the ice before Jared even had his boots off. When he finished lacing up, Jared joined his son.

Snow draped the pine trees and frosted the bare branches of the oak, maple, and hickory trees. The stillness of the air was broken only by an occasional chickadee, sparrow, or the honk of a goose flying overhead. Not many people had a winter paradise like this to play in. This pond and these woods were a magical place indeed. In fact, all of Lake Forest was magical. It was a place where Jared could hum, sing, and shout if he wanted—a place where he could be himself and be at ease without the discomfort and awkwardness that so often claimed him around other people.

As a child, Jared had been different from other boys his age. Most families back then had a mother and a father. Plus other families stayed put, while he and his mom were constantly on the move. Jared despised being the new kid, and he always was.

Although he always made new friends, Jared fought feelings of inadequacy. He was perpetually on the outside looking in. The one place Jared felt comfortable was when he'd lived in West Lake Forest and played with Izzy in these woods. It seemed strange now, how they'd spent most of their time here and that he'd never gone to Izzy's house. Although once, her parents had driven him home from the carnival, and Izzy had pointed out her house. But it had been dark, and all the houses looked alike.

What a friend he'd had in Izzy! When he was with her, Jared shed his feelings of inadequacy and felt like he was the same as anyone else. If only he and his mom didn't have to move each time she couldn't pay the rent. So many times he'd longed with all of his being to stay in one place. And the place he'd loved the best was Lake Forest. He made a vow that when he grew up, he would come back and live there.

But life did get better, especially after his mother met and married Bill Rawlins. Bill had been a kindly stepfather, and over the next ten years, they had welcomed the arrival of three babies. Before he knew it, Jared had two sisters and a brother. Although all of them were married now, they had stayed close.

He and Corey skated around the pond, the cold air icy on his face. Why didn't they come more often? The exhilaration of speeding around the pond got Jared's blood pumping. When Corey bent to peer at something, Jared did a hockey stop, spraying fine bits of ice all over him.

"Hey!" Corey yelled. Then he asked, "Show me how to do that!"

"It's easier with hockey skates," Jared told him, then went over it patiently again and again until Corey got the hang of it.

Tiring of that, they skated around the pond's perimeter, with Corey doing his best to keep up with his dad. When he and Corey had moved to Lake Forest, Jared was no longer a shy boy. Strangers were no longer strangers, and he walked with a light step. It was as if he had slipped into his team's colors. He joked with customers and made easy conversation with everyone he met. For once, Jared truly belonged—a heady feeling he hadn't experienced while growing up.

Although his cautious nature made him buy a small house, Jared had been more excited than he cared to admit when the café began doing well enough for him to afford something larger. Tom's big red brick house and yard had everything Jared had been searching for. It was the stuff of his boyhood dreams. There was a big front porch, tall sturdy trees, and large rooms. It was exactly what he wanted—a well-built home in an established neighborhood. The house had a sense of permanence that appealed to him. As a boy, Jared and his mother had always lived on the fringes—temporary interlopers—and Jared had always longed to have this kind of stability. He was eager to establish roots—to be in one place long enough for people to know his name and wave as they went by.

Corey caught up with him and, with a burst of speed, zoomed past. Jared grinned and let his son enjoy his victory. As he glided over the ice, he thought of Kenzie's treachery. Now his dreams were in jeopardy. It disturbed him to realize how misguided he'd been to be drawn to a person as deceitful as McKenzie Forsberg. He hated to remember how attracted he'd been her when they'd sat and talked at the café. It had been a long time since he'd responded so deeply to a woman. He'd been taken in by her outward charm and false warmth. And on the inside, she'd been plotting against him. Jared grimaced. Usually he was an excellent judge of character, and this lapse bothered him. He'd let himself be taken in by a pretty face.

Yet it hadn't been just her face that had drawn him. He'd truly enjoyed talking with her, being with her. Kenzie had seemed like a warm, sensitive, and caring person, and to discover the truth had been a jolt. He couldn't believe her duplicity. Kenzie was a regular Dr. Jekyll and Mr. Hyde. At least he'd found out the truth before—before—he refused to finish the thought.

Suddenly, Corey swatted at him from behind, laughed, and sped away.

Jared shook off his doldrums. "You want to race, do you?" he called. "I'm going to get you!"

Corey's legs churned, but with Jared's long legs it didn't take long to catch up. Jared slapped his son lightly on the shoulder as he passed. Tag. Then he slowed. Corey caught up, and then it was Jared's turn to chase his son. Round and round they went. Jared's blades made whirring sounds as his feet crossed each other on curves. When Corey slipped and fell, laughing as he slid on the ice, Jared decided to take a break.

"Let's have some hot cider," Jared suggested, and they made their way to the tarp and pulled out the thermos. As Jared poured, steam rose from their foam cups.

"So it's okay if I come here with Sara?" Corey wanted to be sure.

"Just be careful. Don't be showing off." But of course it was a lost cause. He was speaking as a parent rather than from what he had done himself as a young boy. It seemed the natural order of things for boys to show off for girls.

"I don't want you falling and breaking your nose," he teased, making Corey grin. "I say that because I had a lot of bumps and bruises when I tried to show off for Izzy."

"Did you come here a lot?"

"Almost every day in the summer, and in the winter—every chance we could. Izzy was a really good skater," Jared recalled. "She had these beautiful white skates her parents had bought for her. I was embarrassed by mine. They were way too big, and I kept tripping." He'd stuffed the toes with pieces of rags, which often made them uncomfortable. Jared recalled how he'd begged his mother for ice skates and his disappointment when she couldn't afford them. She explained that Jared needed other things more—a coat, pants, and shoes—but Jared continued to beg. He stopped, though, when he saw tears in his mother's eyes and felt ashamed for causing her pain.

"And then Izzy gave you some skates." Corey had heard his father tell this story before.

It was one of Jared's fondest memories. "We met here in the woods, and she had this huge box for me, tied up with green ribbon—her favorite color. It was a couple of weeks before Christmas, but Izzy said she wanted to give me my present early so I could use them as long as possible. You see, I'd already told her my mom and I were moving in February."

"And you didn't know what was in the box?" Corey could hardly believe his father had been so slow.

"Nope. I don't think I've ever been as excited over a present as I was over that one." Jared poured a little more cider. "We skated for hours, although it seemed like minutes. I had terrible blisters but never even realized it until I took off those skates."

After such a magnificent present, Jared had been determined to find something equally stunning for Izzy. Trouble was, nothing he thought of could equal such an incredible gift. Another difficulty was that he had no money. Unwilling to give up, Jared went door to door, asking neighbors if they had any odd jobs he could do to earn money. He'd struck the jackpot when he knocked on Mr. Manzano's door a few houses down.

The big man in worn overalls nearly filled the doorway. He stroked his huge mustache contemplatively as Jared asked for a job.

"What do you need the money for?" Mr. Manzano asked gruffly.

"A Christmas present."

"For who?"

"A friend." Somehow, he found himself telling about the wondrous gift he'd received.

"Got something in mind?"

Jared shook his head. "I just want to get her something nice."

"Come on in." Mr. Manzano led him to two straight-backed chairs in a small, musty front room with heavy curtains. A bookshelf held wooden animals, and a cuckoo clock on the wall ticked loudly. "What about your mom? You doing something nice for her too?"

"I already bought her present." Jared explained that he occasionally went without lunch so he could save his lunch money. He'd also collected empty pop bottles during the summer so he could buy his mother a pair of soft slippers. "She's a waitress," he explained, "and her feet hurt a lot."

"Good boy." Mr. Manzano rubbed his whiskery chin. "Now, about this friend—did you ever think about making her something?"

Jared had, but making a picture frame out of popsicle sticks seemed lame as did everything else he'd thought of. "Not really, sir."

Mr. Manzano pointed at the bookshelf, and Jared took a closer look at the astonishing array of wooden animals. "Any of those strike your fancy?"

As if drawn by a magnet, Jared rose and went over. He touched a German shepherd, running a finger over the satiny finish. He jumped when Mr. Manzano spoke from directly behind him. He hadn't heard the big man get up.

"Nice, eh? I made them. Every one."

Jared could hardly believe it. He peered at the man with wide eyes, then studied the rows of giraffes, elephants, dogs, monkeys, and kangaroos. "You made all of these?"

"Every last one. Got a woodworking shop." The old man picked up a wooden reindeer. "Now, this'd be just the ticket for Christmas." He handed it to Jared, who examined it closely. It was perfect. The antlers and hooves were painted white, and it had a red nose and blue eyes. It stood on an oval pedestal with one front leg raised as if ready to paw the ground.

A deal was struck. Nearly every day, Jared showed up to do whatever job Mr. Manzano had lined up for him that day. When he was done, they'd head for the workshop.

The old man cut out the reindeer himself. "Don't want you to lose a finger, now do we?"

Under the light of a single dangling bulb that illuminated the workbench in the garage, the old man showed Jared how to sand the wood to a smooth finish. When he was done, Mr. Manzano explained two thin coats of shellac were better than one thick coat. When the reindeer was done, it rivaled any of the old man's animals.

After packing it in a box with wadded-up newspaper, Jared wrapped it carefully and tied it with the green ribbon he'd saved from his present. When he gave it to Izzy, she was thrilled beyond measure. You'd have thought he had plucked a star down from heaven and given it to her.

Jared was brought out of his memories by the noise of Corey tearing his foam cup into pieces. "You're making a mess, son," he admonished, then put the thermos in his backpack. "I treasured those skates. Don't believe I've ever had a better present."

"Is that why you put them in the café window each year?"

"They bring back some wonderful memories—even if they do have green laces." For some reason that was fathomable only to her girlish mind, Izzy had taken out the black laces and put Kelly-green ones in. The first time Jared put on the skates, he felt embarrassed and was about to ask for the original laces, but before he could get a word out, Izzy told him about all the trouble she'd had getting those awful green ones. When Izzy explained she'd gotten them because she wanted something special for him, he'd clamped his mouth shut and never mentioned it again. Still, Jared had been awfully glad his pants covered up most of those embarrassing laces.

"Dad, look!" Corey's voice was an urgent whisper as he pointed at a pair of deer emerging from the wintry woods at the far end of the pond. They were nosing the snow-blanketed bushes. From time to time, one of them stretched its neck and glanced quietly in their direction. Clearly, the deer were aware of them but appeared unafraid. Finally, the animals meandered away, and Jared and Corey packed up and headed back down the trail amidst the bare-limbed trees.

There was one thing Jared hadn't mentioned to Corey about Izzy's gift. Mostly because it came from something so deep he couldn't put it into words. But it was there inside him nonetheless. Each year, when he decorated the store window and put his childhood skates in the display, Jared felt a deep longing—a hope—that Izzy would pass by his café and see the skates with those green laces. Then she would walk inside, all grown up and beautiful, and ask to see him. Tears would be in her eyes as she explained that she'd seen the skates. They would sit and talk for hours—like they used to.

Jared shook himself as they reached the car. He popped the trunk and set his backpack and tarp inside. He'd let time get away from him this year, but tomorrow for sure he'd finish the window display.

CHAPTER TWENTY

WAITING FOR SACRAMENT MEETING TO begin, Kenzie turned around, hoping to spot Tom and Mandy. She was saving a spot for them on the blue upholstered pew beside Sara and her parents. But instead of her brother, Kenzie saw Jared and Corey shaking hands with the door greeter. She couldn't take her eyes away. Jared *did* look fine in a suit! When he came up the carpeted aisle, Jared noticed her and nodded. Kenzie smiled back. A few minutes later, Tom, Mandy, and their children came in.

After the meeting, Sara went off with Brian and Hillary while Kenzie followed Tom and her parents to Sunday School. Ahead of them, Jared stood at the library door. The librarian handed him a picture of John the Baptist.

Tom and her parents said hello and went on, but Kenzie stopped. "You must be a teacher."

"Fourteen-year-olds." Jared rolled his eyes, then grinned. "They can be a handful at times."

This wasn't the ideal place or time, but Kenzie had to say something. "I know this isn't a good time, but sometime I'd like to explain what happened with Tracy Perez."

Instantly, Jared's face changed—hardened. "You're right; it isn't a good time."

"I didn't mean now, but maybe we could talk sometime soon?"

He shrugged. "It's over. What's done is done."

When Jared made a motion as if to go, Kenzie put a timid hand on his arm. "I'm really sorry about what happened. Please, I'd like to explain—I think you and Tom took it a lot worse than it was."

"We did, huh?" Jared's words were scornful. "And now you want to whitewash it?"

Despite the sting, Kenzie replied slowly, "No, I only want to explain."

"I've heard all I need to. Now, I really have to go."

Kenzie felt a great ache as he walked away.

After church, Allen, Elaine, Kenzie, and Sara went home and had a light snack. Tom and Mandy were coming over later for dinner. There was a roast in the slow cooker and potatoes, ready to be baked, wrapped in tinfoil on the counter. Her mother lay down for a nap, and her father did the same, sitting in the recliner, holding a drooping newspaper as he snored. Restless, Kenzie wandered through the house then stopped beside Sara, who was reading.

"Feel like going for a walk?"

Sara looked up with an eager expression. "Sure!"

It took a few minutes to bundle themselves in coats, hats, boots, and gloves, but finally they were set. Almost.

"Wait a minute!" Sara clumped into the kitchen, took off her gloves to grab a baggie, then filled it with birdseed from a sack in the pantry.

"I think Grandma filled the bird feeders the other day," Kenzie told her.

"I want to take some to the woods and feed the birds there."

They went through the backyard gate and along the trail, which was dusted with new snow. For a while, the trail was wide enough for them to hold gloved hands as they walked along side by side. When they reached an open area, Sara pulled off a glove, dug into her baggie, and threw a handful of seed—which promptly went through the inch of new snow.

Disappointed the seed was hidden, Sara frowned, but Kenzie told her, "When the sun melts the snow, the birds will be able to see it."

Sara went off the trail, her boots punching through the top crust. "Maybe we could make a snowman and put birdseed over him."

"Wouldn't the birds be frightened of a snowman?" Kenzie teased.

"They'd know it wasn't real," Sara patiently explained.

They tried to roll up a ball, but the snow didn't pack together.

"Maybe we could make a baby snowman," Kenzie suggested. This was met with approval. With much effort, they got the requisite three balls of snow and stacked them precariously on top of each other.

Digging down to the ground, Kenzie found some small rocks for eyes and a mouth while Sara fetched twigs for the arms. Sara sprinkled what was left of the birdseed on the snowman, and they stood back and admired their mini-creation. Then they went back to the trail and moved farther into the woods.

Sara went off the trail to explore. Finding a clump of small pine trees weighed down with snow, she pushed aside some pine boughs and exclaimed, "Look! It's like a room. This can be our home!"

Kenzie smiled at her daughter's enthusiasm. When they went in, the branches snapped back into place, enclosing them in a snug little hollow. "What a great idea! A home of our own."

"Let's clear it out," Sara said. "We've got to have a clean house."

Industriously, Kenzie picked up branches and leaves, remembering how, shortly after she and Larry became engaged, they had looked at a little house to rent. The yard needed cleaning up, but they were so excited about the discounted rent and the idea of getting a home of their own that they wanted to start working on the yard immediately. They'd had so many plans and dreams. Deeply in love, they'd held hands while sitting on the tiny patio, looking over the yard and talking about their future. They'd discussed religion a few times, and that evening they sat on the porch steps of the home they'd just rented and talked about their future life. When Larry told her he wanted to be baptized so he could share that part of her life, tears came to Kenzie's eyes.

Larry started taking the missionary discussions, but as their wedding date approached, he told Kenzie that he felt pressured because there was so much going on. He wanted to put off his baptism and focus on the wedding. After they were married, his church attendance became sporadic, and after a year he stopped going altogether.

Their plans for children also changed. In the beginning they both wanted at least four, but Larry became so involved with his work—and Kenzie was busy as well—that he thought it best to wait until they were more established in their careers. Kenzie accepted it but, after a few years, began longing for a baby so much that Larry gave in. Then after Sara was born—faced with sleepless nights and round-the-clock care—Larry decided one child was plenty. Kenzie's heart ached, but she immersed herself in taking care of Sara and attending to work, rising rapidly up the corporate ladder.

When Larry began spending more and more time working, Kenzie didn't give it much thought until she happened to read a text on Larry's phone from Nichole about their plans for Thursday night—the night Larry had told her he had to oversee a focus group.

Kenzie's world imploded. But Larry begged for forgiveness. They went to counseling, and slowly she began to heal.

Then Larry began working extra-long hours once again. Kenzie had no inkling until he sat her down at the dining-room table and explained he'd fallen in love with someone else. There was no begging for forgiveness this time. Larry wanted a divorce.

A small clump of snow fell on Kenzie's head as she worked, pulling her back to the present. When they had cleared the thicket sufficiently, Sara looked over their "house" with a satisfied expression.

"This is great! Maybe we can bring some boxes to sit on," Sara suggested. When they went out the "door," a misty gray fog had descended, making the skeletal branches of the oak and hickory trees stand out.

They continued along the trail, Sara scuffing her boots and kicking up clumps of snow. Kenzie picked up a small piece and lobbed it gently at Sara.

"Hey!" Her daughter took up the challenge, moving off the trail where the snow wasn't so hard and trying to scrape up enough to make a snowball. Kenzie did the same, but they had to settle for bits of frozen crust. Back and forth. Kenzie ducked, then hit Sara on the shoulder. Her laughter made Sara launch a barrage, forcing Kenzie to cover her head with her arms as she ran. They laughed and threw more with most of the bits and pieces of snow disintegrating before they ever reached their target.

Finally, they brushed snow and ice from their coats and pants and returned to the trail. Taking the right fork to the pond, they saw fresh footprints.

"See that?" Sara said, peering at them. "Someone's been here."

"Two people." Kenzie pointed out the larger footprints and a smaller set.

Sara put her feet in the smaller ones. "This one's about my size," she cried. "Let's follow them!"

"All right. But what if they turn out to be Big Foot and his kid, and they're waiting for us?"

"They wouldn't be wearing boots," Sara explained in a withering tone of voice.

"Maybe they're trying to trick us."

Sara giggled. At the pond, they found a place where the snow had been well trampled. Sara pointed at the pond. "Look, Mom! They were skating!"

There were tracks all over, most of them following the outer curve of the pond.

"Maybe it's that boy you liked—Tyrone—and he came skating here!" Sara sounded excited. "You have to meet him and find out if he still likes you."

"You're getting carried away. Tyrone moved away a long time ago. A lot of people come here to skate. Nearly everyone in town knows about this pond."

"Like Tyrone!" Sara was insistent. "He *could* have moved back."

Wouldn't that be something? Then Kenzie shook herself. No good indulging herself in Sara's make-believe. Tyrone *had* said more than once that he wanted to live in Lake Forest when he grew up—but back then Kenzie had planned on becoming a ballerina. They were just childish dreams.

Kenzie gave Sara a stern look. "You, my dear, have a one-track mind." She turned her back on the pond. "Ready to go home? Uncle Tom and Aunt Mandy are coming for dinner, remember?"

"You don't believe me," Sara said, "but it could happen. Grandma says magical things happen at Christmastime."

CHAPTER TWENTY-ONE

OPENING THE BACK DOOR AND going into the utility room, Kenzie could hear the pleasant murmur of conversation coming from the kitchen. Mandy, Tom, and their children must have arrived. In a flash, Sara shed her boots and coat, and ran off to find her cousins.

On her way to the kitchen, Kenzie paused to gaze at the small wooden reindeer standing amidst the greenery on the table. She scooped it up, running her fingers over the smooth surface. She remembered how cute Tyrone had been as he explained in great detail how he'd made the reindeer with the help of a neighbor. He'd even described the different grits of sandpaper he'd used and how he'd painted the hooves and antlers white. He'd added spots to the reindeer's back—making it look a fawn. The nose was red, of course, and Tyrone had given the reindeer a crooked but happy smile.

What Tyrone hadn't told her, but she'd learned later from his mother, was that he had worked hard to pay for the wood and his neighbor's help. A soft smile curved Kenzie's lips. He had been the most wonderful, extraordinary friend she'd ever had.

When Tom wandered in, he stopped short. "Why are you smiling?"

She blinked. "I'm not smiling."

"The ends of your mouth are pointed up. I almost didn't recognize you." He came closer, looking at the reindeer. "I remember when you got that. You acted like it was made of gold. Wouldn't even let me touch it."

"You were so clumsy I knew you'd break it."

"Let me see it."

"Not on your life."

Mandy walked in. "I thought I heard you. What are you guys doing?"

Tom complained in a little-boy whine, "Kenzie won't let me hold her reindeer."

Smiling, Mandy came over. "That's because she's smart." She asked her husband, "Did you make this?"

"No, Kenzie's boyfriend did. He was madly in love with her and vice versa."

With lifted eyebrows, Mandy asked Kenzie, "Why haven't you ever told me about this mystery man?"

"I was eight years old, for goodness sake."

"And the flame has never died," Tom pronounced in a melodramatic voice.

"Okay, you have to tell me." Mandy went to the closest chair in the family room and threw herself in it, settling herself for a good story.

Tom broke in before Kenzie could say a word. "That's old news. Let's talk about something interesting—like football. The Forty-Niners are playing the Broncos tonight. Who looks good to you?"

His wife brushed a dismissive hand toward Tom as if he was a pesky mosquito. "Go away."

"Hmph. I'm going. But if you change your mind and want me, I'll be out in the backyard, eating worms."

He started toward the kitchen, but Kenzie stopped him. "Tom, can I talk to you later?"

His brown eyes looked at her speculatively. "Is this about Tracy Perez?" Kenzie nodded. "Look, I told you when you stopped by the office that I'd sell you the house if Jared's house hasn't sold by the deadline. What more do you want?"

"We talked for five minutes. You got a phone call, and I didn't have a chance to explain what happened with Tracy."

His brow furrowed, remembering. "Yeah, but why get into it again? You talked the Perezes out of seeing Jared's home—a home they might have bought. I really don't want to get into it tonight."

Kenzie fumed. How typical of Tom to say all he wanted but refuse to listen to her side. The quintessential big brother.

"What's this about Tracy Perez?" Mandy asked as Tom went into the kitchen. "Tom hasn't told me about it."

"Oh, I'll explain later." Kenzie put the reindeer inside the top drawer of the side table so it would be safe in case her nephews started roughhousing after dinner, as they usually did. Then she sat by Mandy.

"Don't forget. Now, tell me all about that boy who loved you so much."

"He didn't love me! We were just friends. And he made me a reindeer."

"If that's not love, I don't know what is. So come on—tell me." Mandy cupped her chin in her hands, happily expectant.

Kenzie went over everything, and at the end Mandy dramatically put a hand over her heart. "Star-crossed childhood sweethearts." Then she sighed. "It was so sweet of you to give him a pair of ice skates."

"He loved skating so much, and my parents helped pay for them. On the bottom of one of the skates I wrote, 'Best friends are forever.'"

"That's just the cutest thing *ever*! And he made the reindeer for you in return." Mandy sighed. "Sounds like he went to a lot of work. Tyrone must have been crazy about you."

A smile fluttered on Kenzie's mouth as she thought about their shared laughter and the ease of talking with a really good friend. "We were very close—for a while anyway. I wonder where he is now." Kenzie crossed her legs and smiled indulgently. "Sara is convinced he came back to Lake Forest. She's an incurable romantic—like you—and she's only eight."

"You were eight when you met Tyrone," Mandy said with portent. "Coincidence? I think not."

Kenzie laughed. "Actually, he and his mom lived in an apartment in West Lake Forest. She was a single mom. A friend of hers said her manager intended on hiring someone in a few months. So the friend told him about Tyrone's mom, and he hired her."

"Did you and Tyrone keep in touch?"

"We meant to, but we were both moving, and I didn't know my new address. Tyrone told me not to worry about it and said he'd write me. He gave me his address, but I lost the paper."

"*Kenzie*! How could you?"

Even after all these years, Kenzie was bummed that she'd lost that precious piece of paper. She'd always been so responsible and organized, even as a child, but somehow the paper had disappeared. "On the day

Tyrone left, he gave me a little piece of paper with his new address on it while we were in the woods. I was sure I'd brought it home and put it in my jewelry box—you know, the kind that has a little ballerina that dances when you open it. Anyway, I looked in the box, but the paper wasn't there. I searched the house, the backyard, and the woods for days—sometimes on my hands and knees—but I never found it."

"Oh, that's awful." Mandy was quiet a few moments then went on. "What if Sara *is* right and this guy is in Lake Forest?"

Kenzie scoffed. "Sara's eight. She still believes in Santa Claus and the Easter Bunny."

This didn't dissuade Mandy. "But wouldn't it be cool if Tyrone *was* here and you met him again?"

"He's probably married and has five kids."

"What was his last name?"

"I think it was Hatch. It's hard to remember, and we really didn't talk about our last names." Kenzie then admitted, "And, yes, I've checked the telephone book and Facebook."

Mandy squealed with delight. "I knew it! You want to see him again! You were hoping he'd be here in Lake Forest."

"But he's not."

With a sigh, her sister-in-law gave in. "Okay, but there are plenty of other eligible men around. Let me set you up with someone. You know you're ready to date and get serious."

"Give me some time."

"You've *had* time. Come on, you can't stay at home night after night."

"I *like* being home."

Allen walked in. "Hate to interrupt the gab-fest, but dinner's ready. Your mother wants everybody up to the table, pronto. I'll get the kids."

Mandy shook an accusing finger at Kenzie. "I'm not done with you."

After a blessing on the food, Allen carved the roast, while side dishes of baked potatoes, peas, and a basket of soft rolls were passed around.

"Kenzie made the rolls this morning," Elaine announced. "She also put the roast in and got the potatoes ready to bake."

"Ah, but what has she been doing *tonight*?" Tom asked. "Lollygagging!"

Elaine laughed. "I don't think Kenzie knows the meaning of the word. Since she got here, she's taken over all of the housework and cooked most of the meals. I've become a lady of leisure."

The children finished first and rushed off to play while Tom and Mandy cleared the table.

When Allen rolled up his sleeves and started filling the sink with hot, soapy water, Kenzie asked, "What's that for?"

"I'm going to wash the pans." He then started filling the sink with utensils, plates, and glasses. Allen noticed her watching. "It won't take long to wash these things up."

"But you have a dishwasher."

"This way they'll all be done and put away. Don't be such a fuss-budget."

Elaine shrugged. "You'll never believe this, but I've known him to actually take dishes *out* of the dishwasher and wash them." She held up her hand, palm out. "True story."

When the kitchen was clean, Mandy and her parents went to check on the children. Kenzie and Tom went to the family room and settled on the couch.

"Mandy told me you offered to help her paint," Tom said, propping his long legs on the ottoman.

Kenzie replied in a monotone, "I'm real excited."

Her brother laughed—the hearty laugh of a big man. Then he said, "Thanks for helping her. I don't want Mandy overdoing it."

"Glad to help."

"Say it once again, but this time with feeling." Tom chuckled. "So when do you start your new job?"

"January 5 is the big day."

He studied her. "Do I detect some anxiety?"

It was not something Kenzie wanted to admit. People always complimented her on how calm she appeared, and she hated not being able to live up to that image. "Who wouldn't be nervous starting a new job?"

"Hey, no need to be defensive." Tom held up his hands. "I'm not Dad."

"Sorry to be defensive. I'd been at Midwest for so many years that it's hard to have to start all over. Everything's going to be new and different. And challenging. I hope I can handle it."

"It's normal to feel anxious starting a new job. You'll be the new kid on the block, but you'll do great. You're smart, talented, and great with people."

"Tell me more."

"I would, but I don't want to give you a swollen head." Tom patted her hand.

Kenzie tried to talk herself out of her anxiety. "A lot of the responsibilities will be the same, so I shouldn't be nervous."

"You wouldn't be human if you weren't a little anxious."

"But I'm there on a trial basis! If I screw up, I'm history. And what then?"

"Stop worrying. You'll do fine. You did amazing at Midwest—getting promotion after promotion. You're very good at what you do."

The praise helped. But Kenzie still had concerns. What if she hated her new boss? What if *he* hated her? And worst of all, what if she was put into the same situation that had caused her to leave Midwest?

CHAPTER TWENTY-TWO

With her hands weighed down with sacks full of groceries, Elaine's efforts to turn the doorknob were fruitless. The sacks banged against the door until, finally, someone inside heard the noise and opened the door. Kenzie grabbed some sacks to lighten her mother's load.

"Thanks," Elaine said. "I shouldn't have tried to bring everything in one load." Setting the bags on the counter, she saw three baking sheets covered with towels, which meant Kenzie had once again made rolls. They would go along perfectly with the clam chowder she planned for dinner. And her daughter had cleaned up the kitchen to boot. There was a large plastic container beside the trays of rolls.

"What's that?" Elaine asked.

"I made some Gingersnap Cookies[3]," Kenzie said. "And, yes, I made enough to freeze a few for your get-together on Christmas Eve."

"You *have* been busy. Thanks to you, I'll have a nice assortment of cookies to serve at the party and to take to the rest home." Every year, Elaine volunteered to take cookies for the residents after the holiday program. She'd never missed except for the year she'd had shoulder surgery.

Putting the celery and onions away, Elaine asked, "Where's Sara? I got some of those little oranges she likes. Cuties."

"She's not back from skating yet."

Elaine checked the clock. "Oh dear, I thought they'd be back by now. She and Corey must be having a good time." She looked around. "Where's Dad?"

---

3 The recipe for Gingersnap Cookies can be found at the end of the book.

"I don't know." Kenzie put the milk in the fridge, then a hand on her hip as if thinking. "Let's see, it's not the day before Christmas, so he can't be doing his Christmas shopping."

"Oh, I remember. He went to get some replacement bulbs—some of the Christmas lights over the garage are out." She folded the reusable grocery sacks and stored them in the pantry. Reusing bags and helping the planet was something Kenzie had talked her into a few years ago. Unfortunately, she sometimes forgot and left the bags in the pantry.

The house was unusually quiet. As Elaine washed the carrots, it seemed like the perfect time to broach a delicate subject. Heaven knew she rarely had Kenzie all to herself. "I guess there hasn't been a good time for you to talk to your father yet." Kenzie groaned loudly, but Elaine pressed on. "I hoped the two of you could work things out while you're here. Actually, what would have been better was for the two of you to talk long ago."

"Right. Blame it all on me," Kenzie said with some bitterness. She scrubbed the potatoes at the sink. "Forget about what Dad said."

Chagrined, Elaine pulled out a cutting board and the grater, and began grating the carrots. "Oh, sweetheart, that's not what I meant. It's just that, well, it's best to clear the air immediately instead of letting it go on for years. And after that day, you stopped coming here. And talking about things like this is best done in person—not over the phone." She picked up another carrot. "We did come to visit you in Chicago, but you had so many activities lined up—going out to dinner or a show or an exhibit—that there was never any time to sit and talk."

"So now you're upset because I made plans for you and Dad? That I tried to entertain you?"

Elaine sighed. Her daughter's defenses were up—deflecting the conversation. It would do no good to take offense, especially since Kenzie was doing such a good job of that herself. And she had a pretty good idea Kenzie had purposely set a frenetic pace during their visits to Chicago to avoid any chance of an intimate chat.

"Not at all," Elaine replied. "I only wish you and your father had time to sit down and work things out. And you've been here for a week and a half, and the two of you still haven't talked." She washed the celery as Kenzie began dicing the potatoes.

"I plan on talking with him, but I've had a lot to do. And Dad never asked to talk to me about what happened." This was said in an aggrieved tone.

"Oh, he approached you, but only in roundabout ways. You know your father—when it comes to sensitive topics, he likes to beat around the bush. Besides, most men aren't too big on talking about feelings."

"Of course not. Step on them, trample them, crush them, but let's not *talk* about feelings." Kenzie waved her knife around wildly—and a bit theatrically, Elaine thought.

"That about sums it up," Elaine replied good-naturedly as she slid sliced celery into a large glass measuring cup. "I know he hurt you and said some terrible things, but sometime you've got to put it behind you and forgive."

Her words apparently riled Kenzie, whose cheeks showed two spots of pink. "Why am *I* the one who's supposed to forgive? I'm the one that got trampled! Boy, Dad's got it pretty easy. He can say all the horrible things he wants, and I'm supposed to take it and turn the other cheek. Seems like he should take a little responsibility—"

"I can't disagree with you there. But you can't change other people— only yourself, and you're the one I'm thinking of." Elaine stopped slicing so she could look her daughter in the eye. "You can't be at peace while holding a grudge. No one can be truly happy until they can let go of old wounds. Forgiving is something we all need to do for our own sake."

"You make it sound easy, and it's not."

Oh, how the young could judge! You'd think Kenzie would understand that maybe Elaine had learned a little wisdom over the sixty-four years she'd spent on earth. "I *know* it's not easy. You forget, dear, that although you've had problems with your father now and then, I'm the one who's lived with him day in and day out for forty-one years." Had that been the right thing to say? Elaine didn't especially like the expression of pity and horror that splashed across Kenzie's face. She hadn't meant to disparage Allen. Sure, he was a rascal of the highest order at times, but he was also loving, kind, and thoughtful, and she loved him dearly.

Putting the diced potatoes in the sink, Elaine turned on the tap and covered them with water. Then she put her arm through Kenzie's and drew her into the family room, where a cheery fire was burning.

They sat next to each other on the tan couch. "I know you don't understand how your father could have said such things, but you *do* know he's always been outspoken. Speaking first and thinking second—that's his motto. If you could try to accept him for who he is and throw in a bit of forgiveness once in a while, it would help."

"It would also help if Dad thought about other people once in a while and realized his words can hurt."

"You're right of course. He has things he needs to work on, just like everybody else. I guess what I'm trying to say is that it's easier to forgive if we realize everybody—ourselves included—has their own faults." It was hard to know what to say. Elaine prayed Heavenly Father would give her the words to help her daughter. She went on, "You've gone through such a rough time these past couple of years. Your father and I have ached for you. We've always been here for you although I know it hasn't seemed like that to you." Moving closer, Elaine clasped her daughter's hands. "Your father regrets what he said. He is so sorry."

"That's nice of you to say, but I haven't seen any signs of Dad being sorry. If he was, he'd say so."

"I think it's difficult for a lot of men to admit when they're wrong. But your father did feel terrible about it. He told me once that he wished he could wrap you up and bring you home, and that if he could, he'd take your pain and bear it himself so you didn't have to hurt so much."

Kenzie sat so still, her eyes downcast, that Elaine began to hope she had reached her.

Then Kenzie's head came up, and she asked sharply, "You didn't tell him about Larry?"

"No." Elaine spoke quietly. She'd kept her promise not to tell Allen about Larry's affairs, but it had been hard. She wasn't used to keeping secrets from her husband. When Kenzie had called late one night, sobbing so hard she couldn't catch her breath, Elaine had been frantic with worry. She knew Kenzie desperately needed to talk, but she said she wouldn't unless her mother promised not to repeat anything she said to her father. Unhappily, Elaine agreed, knowing Kenzie needed her. It was shocking to find out Larry was having an affair and doubly so to learn he'd had another one years before. How on earth had Kenzie gotten past it and remained a loving mother and confident career woman? Elaine doubted she could have done it.

Kenzie went on. "I was going to tell Dad, but then he started blaming me for the divorce."

"I don't think your father meant that—he misspoke. Sometimes he means one thing and says something else." Elaine reached over and stroked Kenzie's hair. "All your father and I want is for you to be happy. He loves you very much—and so do I."

They hugged each other for a long time. When they pulled back, Elaine saw a few tears shining on Kenzie's cheeks. "Let's hope a little Christmas magic will help mend things," she said to her daughter. "Just remember, each day you have a choice to make, and that choice can either make for a brighter tomorrow or not."

"Once again, you make it sound so easy."

Elaine laughed. "I wish it was!"

The side door opened, and Allen came in carrying a bulging sack.

"Looks like you got more than a few Christmas lights," Elaine exclaimed, going into the kitchen to see. Kenzie followed.

Elaine pulled a large box out of a sack. "What's this?" She turned it over. "Oh, what a pretty doll!"

"It's for Sara," Allen said gruffly.

"Dad, really—*a doll?*" Kenzie said. "She's eight years old."

A confused expression appeared on her father's face. "I thought girls liked dolls." Then he glanced around. "Put it back in the sack. I don't want Sara to see it."

"She's not back from skating yet," Elaine said.

As one, the three of them looked at the clock.

"She really should have been back by now," Kenzie said. "I'll go see if her coat's here. She might have slipped in."

When Kenzie came back and shook her head, Elaine glanced out the window. "What time was she supposed to be back?"

"I didn't give her a time. I figured they'd come back when they were tired." Kenzie turned to her father. "Dad, the pond's safe for ice skating, isn't it?"

"It's a little late to be asking that."

Kenzie stood stock still.

"Allen! Will you *think* and stop blurting out the first thing that comes to your mind?" Elaine went to Kenzie, who looked numb, and put a hand on her arm. "Don't pay him any mind."

"Sorry, that came out badly." Allen was contrite. "I'm sure the ice is plenty thick—it's been real cold lately."

Without a word, Kenzie went to the utility room and yanked her coat off the hook.

Elaine followed. "Sara told me Corey and Jared went skating at the pond the other day. Jared would have made sure the ice was safe."

"That's right." Kenzie took a breath. "I remember that now." But her face remained pale. "I'm going to walk over, though, and make sure they're okay."

"They might have gone to Jared's house. Why don't you call him before you go."

A pause, then Kenzie hurried to the kitchen. Allen looked up Jared's number on his phone, dialed, then handed the phone to Kenzie. It rang once, twice, then Jared picked up. She punched the speakerphone.

"Hi, Jared. This is Kenzie. Are Sara and Corey there?"

"No, I thought they were at your house."

"They haven't come back from skating yet, and it's getting late." Anxiety was in Kenzie's voice.

"I'm sure they're fine. Probably just lost track of time."

"Sara told me you'd gone skating with Corey. Was the pond frozen hard?"

"Yeah. I drilled down, and it was plenty thick."

A pause of relief. Then Kenzie said, "I think I'll head on over there anyway—to make sure."

"Wait a minute, and I'll go with you. I'll be right over."

CHAPTER TWENTY-THREE

AT THE INTERSECTION OF SHERIDAN and Walnut, Jared went through a light that had been yellow a while. It turned red before he made it through. The alarm in Kenzie's voice had made him uneasy.

Why weren't Corey and Sara back?

Had they simply lost track of time? A distinct possibility. Or had something happened?

Jared swung into the driveway, but before he even turned off the engine, the front door opened, and Kenzie and Allen came out. They must have been watching from the window.

Kenzie's face looked pale and strained as she told him, "Dad insisted on coming."

"Thought you could use another pair of eyes," Allen said somberly. He held several flashlights, and when Jared glanced at them, said, "Just in case."

Not the most reassuring thought that it might be dark before they found them. And yet, a glance at the pink-stained western horizon showed the sun was lowering fast. Darkness wasn't that far away. Initially, he'd told himself Corey and Sara must have been having so much fun they hadn't noticed the sun beginning to set, but now he wasn't sure of that. They went around the house and crossed the backyard. As they started down the trail, Allen handed him a flashlight, which Jared stowed in a coat pocket. Leading the way, he glanced back to see Kenzie searching the woods anxiously.

"Don't worry," Jared said. "They probably lost track of the time."

She nodded, but her brown eyes were clouded with worry. "Yeah, I'm sure that's it. But it's not like Sara to be gone so long."

Nor was it like his son. What could Corey be thinking to stay out so late? Jared fought to control his anger. Yet in the next instant, fear rose. Was Corey hurt? Or Sara? Caught in a tight cage of fear, he fought to hold off the wave of sick terror that threatened to swamp him.

As they hurried toward the pond, Jared said, "They're probably still skating." Kenzie didn't answer but gave a small nod, her gaze searching the woods.

They rounded the bend and took the right fork. Their sudden appearance surprised a flock of crows and set them to cawing as they rose in a dark cloud. When they reached the pond, it was a shot to his chest when Jared saw the tarp, skates, and Corey's backpack. But no Corey and no Sara. Kenzie knelt, touching the skates. When she glanced up at Jared, her eyes were large with fear and asking the same question he wanted to know—where could they be?

Allen started around the pond. "Corey!" he shouted. "Sara!" Kenzie and Jared joined him. They circled the pond and came back to the folded tarp.

"They must have walked farther into the woods," Jared concluded.

In silence, they backtracked to the main trail, calling loudly as they went. A feeling of panic left him lightheaded when Jared saw how quickly the darkness was starting to gather. Already he had to strain to see in the gloom. He and Allen pulled out their flashlights and shone the beams on the trail. Fresh footprints in yesterday's snow.

"They look like the right size," Kenzie murmured.

"You were right," Allen told Jared. "They decided to go exploring."

They hurried on, calling, "Corey! Sara!"

Suddenly Jared stopped. The prints ended. His light shone on the path ahead, white, smooth, and unbroken. Allen swung his light left then right. There was a quick intake of breath from Kenzie when they finally saw two pairs of footprints leading off the main trail.

The going was more difficult now because of the uneven surface under the snow. Kenzie tripped once and would have fallen if Jared hadn't grabbed her arm. They hurried along, calling as they went. There was a thrumming in Jared's mind as he swung his flashlight around, hoping with all his heart to see Corey and Sara.

Why on earth had they left the trail and gone out in the middle of nowhere?

CHAPTER TWENTY-FOUR

"It was a good idea to bring that," Sara said as Corey pulled a small tarp out of his backpack and spread it on the snow. They smoothed it out and sat to put on their ice skates.

Corey had to give credit where it was due. "My dad always brings one. I also brought some hot chocolate."

"And I brought some cookies. My grandma is making like a million of them." Sara set the zippered baggie of cookies on the tarp. When Corey looked at them longingly, she told him, "Go ahead and have one. They're Apple Cider Cookies.[4]"

"Apple cider?" Corey looked unsure, but after a bite his expression changed to rapture. He took another before resealing the bag.

Sara went on to more important matters. "Are you sure the ice is thick enough?" The uneasiness in the pit of her stomach went away when Corey explained how his father drilled a hole to make sure it was safe.

Sara's ankles wobbled as she walked unsteadily to the pond. Once she was on the ice, she started out slow. Afraid Corey might think she was a baby, Sara explained, "I haven't skated since last year." It didn't take long, though, for her to feel more comfortable, and she skated faster. Although glad Corey's dad had checked the ice, Sara still avoided the middle. And whenever Corey ventured there, she kept a watchful eye on him in case the ice cracked and he fell in.

Sara tried a circular turn that came out so gracefully she threw her arms out exuberantly—like she'd seen skaters do on TV. Then she waved her arms gracefully up and down. "Maybe I'll start taking lessons and go to the Olympics," she called out.

---

4 The recipe for Apple Cider Cookies can be found at the end of the book.

"You're too old," Corey said, skating up to her. "I saw on TV that gymnasts start really young. I bet it's the same for skaters."

Her lips pressed thin. Privately, Sara thought she could still be in the Olympics if she really wanted to, but she let it drop. "Do you go skating a lot with your dad?"

"Yeah. He likes to skate. Dad used to go a lot when he was little. Does your mom skate?"

"Not too much."

They went round and round. Corey fell a lot, but then he skated a lot faster and made sharper turns than she did. When he began skating backwards, Sara stood still, watching in open admiration.

"Can you teach me how to do that?"

"Sure," Corey said. "The easiest way to learn is to hold on to my hands so you can keep your balance. That's how my dad taught me. But watch first, and I'll show you how to move your feet." He gracefully weaved his feet in and out.

It looked easy. "Okay. Let me try."

Corey held her hands, steadying her as she tried to make her feet obey. Awkward and frowning in concentration, she watched her feet, willing them to move like Corey's had. One trip around the pond, and Sara was already steadier. It was a great help to have Corey hold her hands and give her momentum.

Another two times around, and Sara said, "Let me try it on my own now." She skated backwards, proud of how well she was doing. But when she glanced over to see if Corey was watching, she straightened her knees too much and fell. Corey raced over to help her up. Sara's cheeks flushed from cold and embarrassment.

"You'll catch on," Corey said kindly. "It took me a while before I got it."

But she'd had enough and started skating forward. At least she felt competent at this. They skated for a long time, then Sara said, "My ankles are tired."

"Mine aren't."

"That's because you turn them out all floppy-like. You should keep them straight." When Corey frowned, looking like he was about to disagree, Sara said quickly, "Let's have some hot chocolate and then go for a walk."

"Okay." After they put their boots on, Sara held the cups while Corey poured. Then he got another cookie out. "I'm glad you're going to move here. When are you coming?"

"I don't know. I guess when Mom finds a house. Uncle Tom said we could live with him for a while, but my mom hasn't decided. She said we might stay in Chicago and she'd drive to work until she finds a house. But it's a long drive. I'd like to stay with my grandma and grandpa, but I don't think we will."

Corey gazed at her, puzzled. "Why not?"

She shouldn't have said anything. It was too hard and too embarrassing to talk about. But she had to say something. Corey was waiting. Finally she said, "My mom's mad at my grandpa." She sipped her hot chocolate then added, "He said something that hurt her feelings." Sara got a cookie for herself and handed another to Corey.

"Do you ever see your dad?" he asked hesitantly.

"Oh yeah, every other week. But I don't like leaving my mom alone. It makes her sad." Corey nodded as if he knew all about it. His sympathetic expression made her go on. "She was sad for a long time when my daddy left."

"Why did he go?"

"He liked someone else better." Even now, Sara couldn't understand it. Sometimes it made her chest ache to think her dad liked someone else so much that he didn't want to live with her and her mom.

"Did they fight a lot? Corey asked munching on his cookie. "One of my friends told me his parents are getting a divorce, and he says they fight all the time."

"Not too much, but sometimes I'd hear them at night."

"What did they fight about?" Corey was curious.

"Lots of different things." Sara shrugged. It was impossible to keep track of them all. "Mom didn't like him being gone so much. And they'd fight about having a baby. Mom wanted to have one, but he didn't." Sara sighed. "It would have been fun to have a baby sister."

"Is your mom still sad?"

"No. Well, sometimes. She used to come home from work grumpy. There was a man there who was mean to her. I think that's why she quit. She got a new job, but I think she's scared."

"Why?"

"I don't know."

Corey put his head to one side. "Maybe it's like going to a new school. When we moved here, I didn't like that." He put the thermos away, and when they stood Sara shook the tarp so crumbs went flying.

"The mice can come and eat the crumbs," Sara said, then folded it into a neat square.

Corey put the backpack on top of the folded tarp. "Let's leave our skates here too, so we don't have to carry them. We can pick them up on our way back."

It was a good idea. They set off and turned right at the main trail. The trail wasn't as well-trodden as the path to the pond had been. "I guess not too many people come this way."

When they came to a fork, Corey pointed to the left at an unbroken path. You could only tell it was a trail by the shallow indentation of snow. "Let's go that way."

Sara hesitated, eyeing the thick trees all around. "Do you think there are any bears around here?"

"Nah." But Corey glanced around as if making sure. "Come on. Let's go this way, and at the next fork you can pick which way to go."

"What if we get lost?"

"We can't get lost; we can follow our footprints."

"Oh, yeah."

They went on, with Sara following Corey as he plunged ahead. It was fun at first. And Corey seemed to be having such a good time that Sara didn't want to tell him that her legs were tired. But he went on and on, and finally she had to say something.

"Corey, stop! Let's go back."

"Just a little farther. Come on, Sara, I want to show you a neat place. If I can find it. At least it looked neat in the summer."

That reminded Sara of the little hut she'd found. "Me and my mom found a cool place. I'll show it to you on our way back."

They came to a large tree that had fallen across their path. Putting their hands on the trunk to keep their balance, they stepped between the branches, which were partially covered by snow. Corey tripped on a branch after climbing over the trunk, and tumbled to the ground. Then Sara lost her balance and fell. Laughing, they got up and brushed the snow off themselves.

They went on, zigzagging around bushes and trees and tripping over hidden obstacles. Finally Sara planted her feet. She'd had enough. "Come on. Let's go back."

Corey turned yearning eyes at the untrammeled woods before him but apparently heard the note of finality in her voice.

When she added, "It's getting late too," he sighed deeply and turned around.

They started back. When they reached the fallen tree, Sara stepped between two branches and reached out to put her hands on the trunk as she moved forward. But her left foot became wedged at the crotch of the branches. Unable to stop because of her momentum, Sara tumbled awkwardly—falling to the side—her ankle twisting as the branches held it firmly in place. Crying out as she fell, Sara twisted her body around to relieve the pressure on her ankle.

Corey rushed to help. Seeing her leg at such an odd angle, he tried to turn it, which made Sara cry out even more. Finally, with Corey's help, she lifted herself enough to ease her foot out. Tears rolled down her face as Sara clutched her ankle.

After a few minutes of anxious waiting, Corey asked, "Can you stand?"

She rose with Corey's help, but the pain made her dizzy. White lipped, Sara sat abruptly. Fear fluttered up inside. "I—I don't think I can walk."

"I bet you sprained your ankle. We'll wait until it feels better."

Sara nodded and wiped her cheeks. After ten minutes, she was ready to try again.

"Put your arm around my neck and lean on me," Corey said.

She stood on one leg but after a minute shook her head. "I feel dizzy. I need to sit down."

Corey's worried expression as he looked around made Sara fearful he was watching for bears.

"If I had a sled, you could sit on it and I could pull you out."

Sara wished they had one. Then after her head felt clear for a while, Sara asked Corey to help her stand again. This time, she was hopeful. "I'm not dizzy anymore, and it doesn't hurt as bad as it did before."

However, when she put weight on it, the sharp pain caused her to cry out. "What am I going to do?" Sara asked fearfully. "I can't walk."

"Put your arm around my neck. I'll help."

They took a few steps. Sara bit her lip and tried hard to be brave but stopped. "I can't do it—it hurts too much!" She looked around at the deepening shadows, fear rising and making a hard knot in her chest. "What are we going to do?"

"I'll go back to your grandma's house and get help."

The idea of staying behind alone in the woods where there could be bears threw Sara into a panic. "No! You can't leave me!"

"I won't be gone long. I'll run all the way!" Corey spoke urgently, trying to convince her to let him go.

"No, no, don't leave me," Sara begged. Although Corey told her there weren't bears around, he could be wrong. And this part of the woods looked like the kind of place bears might like. No, she couldn't stay here alone. If an animal came, she couldn't even run. But what could she do? Then Sara had an idea.

"Can we say a prayer? Mom says to pray if I'm scared."

"Um, sure. Go ahead."

Sara had hoped he would say it, but she folded her arms, leaned on Corey, and began. "Dear Heavenly Father, I hurt my ankle and can't walk. Will Thou please help us so we can get out of the woods? And that no bears will come? In the name of Jesus Christ, Amen." When she unfolded her arms, Sara gave Corey a confident nod. "Okay, let's try again."

Sara put her left arm around Corey's neck. Leaning on him heavily, they began moving along the trail, a few difficult inches at a time.

CHAPTER TWENTY-FIVE

JARED LED THE WAY DOWN the trail, occasionally slipping as he hurried along with Kenzie close behind. A few minutes later, Jared stopped. "I think I hear something."

Putting a hand on his arm, Kenzie shouted, "Sara! Corey!"

There was a faint sound. It had to be them. They hurried on—faster now. Soon, a faint answer came in response to their cries.

"Dad? Is that you?" It was Corey.

Jared began running—shining his light in front of them. Kenzie kept up with him. In a few moments, their flashlights illuminated two small figures. Reaching them, Jared bent to hug them, and as he did, Corey bumped Sara. Off balance, Sara stumbled and cried out.

Grabbing her so she didn't fall, Kenzie asked urgently, "What's the matter, baby?"

"I hurt my ankle."

"Her leg got stuck in some branches, and she fell," Corey explained.

Allen knelt by his granddaughter. "I bet you sprained your ankle."

"I was going to run back and get help, but Sara didn't want to stay alone." Corey's voice trembled a bit. "I tried to help her walk."

"You were very brave to stay and help her," Kenzie told him.

"It hurts a lot to walk," Sara sniffed, tears beginning to stream down.

Pulling off his glove, Allen wiped her tears away. "I bet it does. We're here now, though, and it's going to be all right now. But you can't cry, or else you'll have icicles hanging from your chin."

His words brought a small smile to Sara's wan face.

There was no sense trying to take Sara's boot off, not here in the cold. Allen handed his flashlight to Kenzie and gathered Sara in his arms. There was a glint of tears on Kenzie's face as she kissed her daughter, then they started back with Allen leading the way.

It was easier going once they reached the main trail. At the turn off to the pond, Allen told them, "You go on and get Sara to the house. I'll get the backpack and skates." Jared held out his arms, and Allen gently handed over his granddaughter.

Holding Corey's hand, Kenzie shone her light on the path ahead of Jared. Two tall figures appeared ahead of them. The bigger one was Tom, followed by his oldest son, Adam.

"Mom called me," Tom explained as he hurried toward them. "What happened?"

"Sara twisted her ankle," Kenzie said.

Rushing to open the gate, Adam held it as they spilled through.

In the house, Elaine and Mandy jumped to their feet when Jared came in carrying Sara. "She's all right," Jared reassured them as he laid the girl on the couch, "but she might have sprained her ankle."

Soon Allen came in, limping.

"You too?" Elaine asked in surprise.

"I tripped and fell, but I'm all right." Allen hobbled to the fireplace and threw on more logs until there was a roaring blaze.

Although Kenzie was careful as she took off her daughter's boots and socks, Sara still cried out. Jared eyed the ankle, which was swollen and blue, while Mandy ran to get ice.

"I think you'd better have that checked out," Tom advised.

Kenzie nodded in agreement as she took a dry pair of socks from her mother. She only put the left sock on partway. "There we go," Kenzie said. "Now your toes won't freeze."

Jared asked Kenzie, "Do you want me to drive you to the hospital?"

"That would be great."

"Dad and I are coming too," Elaine told Kenzie, then looked at Jared. "What about Corey?"

His son had been standing back, watching everything with wide eyes. "Can I come?" he asked his father.

"I don't think so. Trips to the ER can take hours and hours."

Mandy jumped in. "Why don't you come home with us, Corey. Brian and Hilary would love to see you. If you went to the hospital, you wouldn't be able to go back with Sara. All you'd be able to do is sit and wait, and that can get pretty boring." Mandy clinched the deal when she said, "On the way home, we'll stop and get hamburgers and fries for dinner."

Corey's face brightened, and Jared's problem was solved.

Then Mandy said to Jared. "You probably won't get back until late—what about having Corey spend the night at our house? We could stop at your place and get his pajamas and toothbrush."

"That would be great. Thanks."

Tom, Mandy, Adam, and Corey left, and Allen was locking the back door when Kenzie spoke up, "I think we ought to give Sara a blessing before we leave." She turned to her daughter. "Would you like one?"

When Sara nodded, Allen went to get the consecrated oil. Kenzie and her mother stood side by side with folded arms, while Jared anointed. Then Allen gave his granddaughter a blessing. After the *amen*, Kenzie wiped tears from her cheeks.

Elaine tucked a blanket around Sara as Jared scooped her up, and they were off. On the way, Kenzie distracted Sara by pointing out Christmas lights and displays of lighted deer and sleighs.

At the hospital, Jared carried Sara inside, placing her carefully on her grandmother's lap. Kenzie filled out the paperwork, and after a long wait, a cheerful nurse in blue scrubs came with a wheelchair. Kenzie and Elaine went back with Sara.

Time dragged—it felt like a month before Kenzie came out and told them that the X-rays confirmed a bad sprain.

"That's what I thought," Allen said.

Jared asked, "How's she doing?"

"Though she be but little, she is fierce!" Kenzie quoted. Jared stared, and Kenzie quickly explained, "Sorry, I have a thing for Shakespeare quotes. But Sara is amazing. She hasn't complained about anything— she simply grits her teeth when it hurts."

"A real trooper," Allen said.

Kenzie went back, leaving Jared and Allen to settle in their chairs. After a while, Allen fell asleep, snoring like a freight train. Jared watched a tremendously boring TV show and dozed off a few times himself.

When Kenzie tapped him on the shoulder, Jared jumped. "We're all done," she said. Sara sat nearby in a wheelchair—her ankle wrapped securely. A slender young nurse with short brown hair and a friendly expression stood behind her, holding the handles of the wheelchair.

The nurse looked at them brightly. "Whoever wants to drive this pretty young lady home can get your vehicle and bring it around to the ER doors."

"That'll be me." Jared practically ran out to his Ford Explorer.

Once everyone was inside the vehicle and buckled up, Elaine asked Sara, "Are you hungry?"

The answer was affirmative.

"Do you want me to stop and get hamburgers?" Jared asked, glancing over his shoulder at Elaine and Kenzie before he pulled out of the parking lot.

Elaine shook her head. "Not when I've got soup and rolls at home. I finished making the soup and baked the rolls while you were off looking for Sara and Corey."

Allen held the door open for Jared, who laid Sara on the couch. Kenzie got several pillows to go under her leg, reminding Sara the doctor wanted her ankle elevated above her head for a few days. Still limping, Allen put more wood on to revive the fire. Kenzie brought over Poppy the Penguin for Sara and sat with her while Jared helped Elaine butter rolls and reheat the soup. Although he'd called from the hospital to check on Corey, Jared called again. Mandy said he was asleep.

The clam chowder was delicious, easily as good as what they served at the café. The warmth of the house was inviting. They put their food on trays and took it into the front room to be near Sara. Allen brought over the ottoman so Sara could prop up her leg while she ate. As they enjoyed their food, the flames danced, throwing patterns on the walls. Jared asked for a second bowl, glad they hadn't stopped for a burger.

When Sara's eyelids began to droop, Jared took her into the bedroom. He waited in the hall as Kenzie got her ready for bed. Then Kenzie came out, shutting the door softly. Her face looked all teary and fragile.

"Is everything all right?" Jared asked, concerned.

"She's fine." Kenzie's voice was tremulous though, and suddenly her eyes brimmed with tears.

"Hey, she's okay," Jared said, taking a step toward her. "It's all over." Kenzie moved into his arms, and he held her as she cried softly. He rubbed her back, trying not to think about how good it felt to have her body pressed against his.

When Kenzie pulled back, he hated to release her. "Sorry about that," Kenzie said, wiping her eyes. "I don't know why I lost it there."

"Delayed reaction. It's understandable." He looked into her eyes, thinking how easy it would be to get lost in them. She, too, seemed affected and ducked her head shyly. He took her hand and led her back to the family room.

"How's Sara?" Elaine asked.

"Nearly asleep."

"I think I'll look in on her." She rose and moved toward the hall.

"Mom," Kenzie protested, "I just left her. She's fine."

"I just want to peek at her." As Elaine slipped from the room, Allen smiled then went to the fireplace. Grabbing the poker, he pushed the logs around to settle them.

Jared and Kenzie sat close together on the couch. He could feel the warmth of her body and wished they were alone.

"I can't thank you enough for all you've done," Kenzie told him softly.

"I didn't really do anything."

"You did a lot. I don't know what I'd have done without you."

She looked so beautiful sitting there in the firelight that if Allen hadn't been there, Jared would have kissed her. Then he came back to himself. What was he thinking? This was the woman who had gone to talk Carlos and Tracy Perez out of seeing his house. He turned his head so Kenzie couldn't see the anger and bitterness he knew was in his eyes. How could she have done that? Tell the Perezes to avoid older homes and not to buy one that only had two bedrooms? This was the woman who had torpedoed the sale of his house. He had to get out of there, before he said something he'd regret.

Jared rose suddenly, avoiding Kenzie's eye, as Elaine came down the hall. "Thank you so much for dinner," he told her. "It was wonderful."

"Thank you for all you did tonight." Elaine came over and gave him a hug as Kenzie stood.

"Glad to help."

Jared went over, shook Allen's hand firmly, then walked to the door. He'd studiously avoided looking at Kenzie, but once he opened the door, he couldn't stop himself from glancing at where she stood by the couch, watching him with those big eyes. He turned quickly but not before he saw the hurt that was stamped all over her face.

CHAPTER TWENTY-SIX

THE NEXT MORNING, THE PAIN medication made Sara sleepy, and after she'd dozed off, Kenzie drove to the medical supply store to pick up a walking boot. Then she headed for Tom's office, walking briskly down the sidewalk. She had never had a chance to fully explain what had gone on with Tracy Perez, but she was determined to make Tom listen to her today.

As she neared Jared's Café, her footsteps slowed. Normally, Kenzie wouldn't have thought twice about going in and thanking Jared again for his help, but she hesitated. Why had he acted so strange just before leaving last night? She'd felt so attracted to him and knew the feeling was mutual, so she was puzzled by Jared's sudden cool distance as he left.

As she neared the display window, tears came to her eyes as Kenzie remembered how Jared had swept up her little daughter and carried her out of the woods. And she'd been so touched when Jared had driven them to the hospital.

All evening he had been so solicitous of Sara that Kenzie had been genuinely moved. And when they'd come home from the hospital, there had been a genuine camaraderie—a special warm connection—between them, especially when Jared held her as she cried. She remembered the comfort of his strong arms. But his abrupt departure made her wonder.

Had she only imagined there had been something more than friendship between them? She could have sworn Jared was interested in her. And yet, without warning, some switch had flipped—leaving Jared stiff and silent before leaving so suddenly.

With a sigh, Kenzie looked through the window. Jared had finished the display. There were poofy billows of snow surrounding a great shining lake of tinfoil. Delicate snowflakes hung from threads. To the side were several pairs of children's ice skates—one white pair and one black. Kenzie was impressed—Jared had done a really good job. Then Kenzie's breathing became rapid and shallow as she looked closer.

The black pair of skates had green laces.

It was impossible! Kenzie's hand went to her mouth, and she stepped closer, her nose nearly touching the window.

Could it be?

Her head told her to walk away, give herself time to think, but impulsively Kenzie forced her unsteady legs to carry her to the door and pushed it open. In a haze, she searched for Jared, but he was either gone or in the back. She hurried past Scott, who was busily wiping down a booth, and went to the window, where she stopped with a groan. The heavy corrugated cardboard which provided the backdrop completely hid the display from view inside the café. Unless she stood on a chair, it would be impossible to reach the skates.

But she *couldn't* leave without knowing for sure.

Kenzie glanced behind her and saw Pam, who smiled a hello. She didn't recognize the young man making sandwiches but realized it was a major stroke of luck that Jared wasn't there. His absence would make things so much easier. As discreetly as possible, Kenzie took a chair from a table and put it next to the back of the display.

Scott had been eyeing her curiously and finally walked over, an inquisitive expression on his innocent face. "What are you doing?"

"Oh, hi, Scott!"

Expressionless, he stood waiting for her answer.

"I, uh, there are some ice skates in the window, and I need to look at them."

"I've been helping Jared with the display. Why do you want to see the skates?" Scott tilted his head, and soft brown hair fell over his forehead.

"To see if there's writing on the bottom of one of them."

This explanation seemed to satisfy Scott, and he nodded as if her words made sense.

"Could you hold the chair so it doesn't tip when I reach over and get the skates?"

He nodded. Wearing a look of deep concentration, Scott gripped the chair tightly as though it was making a break for it. A customer came in, and Kenzie waited until Pam was engaged in taking his order before making her move. She leapt on the chair, leaned over the backdrop, and grabbed the skates. She ran a hand over the worn black leather and touched the long green laces before turning one of the skates over.

Nothing.

A weird sense of disappointment flooded her. Still, it would have been a one in a million coincidence for these to be the same skates she had given Tyrone. She turned over the second skate and caught her breath.

There it was.

The words she had painstakingly scratched into the bottom of Tyrone's skates so many years ago. The spidery handwriting read, "Best friends are forever." Kenzie still remembered how long it had taken to scratch the letters—her hand had ached as she went over them again and again until she was sure the writing would last. Scott looked up at her, still clinging to the chair in case it decided to make any sudden moves.

Kenzie whispered, "The writing's still there." Of course that would make no sense to Scott, but it was the best she could do. It was difficult for her to wrap her head around her discovery. These were Tyrone's skates. For real. Suddenly, her legs weakened, and she had to put out a hand to steady herself. But how had they come to be here? Were they Jared's? Or had he possibly gotten them from a secondhand store? Her stomached lurched at the possibility. For some reason she wanted them to be Jared's. But how could they be? Kenzie shook her head. His name was Jared Rawlins. Yes, Tyrone had said he wanted to change his first name, but that didn't explain his last name.

"Are you okay?" Scott watched her anxiously.

"Yes, I—I'm fine. I'll put these back." Then she stopped. "Scott, you said you helped Jared with the display—did he tell you where he got the skates?"

The man nodded. "He said a girl gave them to him when he was a boy."

Numbness went through her body like a shock, and she closed her eyes briefly. Scott said nothing, waiting stoically until Kenzie pulled herself together. As she stood on the chair, leaned over, and carefully replaced the skates, Scott held onto the seat for all he was worth. When she hopped down, he picked up his basin while Kenzie returned the chair to its table.

"Hey! What are you doing?" The loud voice came from a husky man in a grubby T-shirt.

"I cleared the table, but I didn't wipe it," Scott explained. "I stopped to help Kenzie." He bent over the table with his cloth.

"You can't wipe the table while I'm sitting here!" The man's face turned red as he glowered at Scott. People turned to stare.

Scott's brows drew together, and he looked confused. "But it's dirty. I'm supposed to wipe the tables before people sit down."

"You're not going to wipe it with that dirty cloth when I'm sitting here. I don't know why they hire people like you to work with the public. Get out of here, will ya?"

Hurrying over, Kenzie put a hand on Scott's shoulder. He turned, his troubled eyes looking up at her. "It's all right, Scott. You can wipe the table when he's done. Why don't you go wipe that table over there." She pointed at a recently vacated booth.

"Okay." Scott seemed relieved at being told what to do and left.

Bending over, Kenzie hissed at the man, "Scott was just trying to do his job."

"He was gonna wipe the table while I was sitting here," the man blustered.

"And you could have told him *nicely* that it was all right and he could wipe it later. But no, you had to be a bully and shout at him."

Aware that everyone nearby was listening, the man tried to save himself. "Who are you? A manager? All I did was try to stop that moron from wiping the table while I was sitting here. If this is the way you treat customers, I'll leave, and I won't be back."

"If this is the way you treat young men who are simply doing their job, I'd say that was an excellent idea."

The man glared at Kenzie then stood, shoving his chair back with a scraping noise. He took a couple of steps, then came back, grabbed his sandwich, and with a defiant sneer, strode out.

Kenzie's face was flushed as she headed for the door. On her way, a woman reached out and touched her arm. "Good for you, dearie."

Her hand was on the door when someone called, "Kenzie!" She turned. Jared was walking toward the display case, carrying a tray of fudge nestled in ruffled white papers. Apparently he'd been in the back room.

"You're not leaving without getting some fudge, are you?"

The front door began to open, startling Kenzie, who still had her hand on it. She stumbled, then recovered as a young couple walked in. The young man apologized profusely, as did Kenzie. Then she went to the display case.

"Have you been here long?" Jared asked. "I was in the back, cutting fudge." His black eyes, set beneath straight, dark brows, watched her intently.

Thank goodness he'd missed her little scene with the redneck. Kenzie couldn't take her eyes from his face. His expression was so different from the cool, distant expression he'd worn last night.

"No, not too long," she said faintly, putting a hand on the case to steady herself.

He gazed at her curiously, his brow furrowed. "You're kind of pale. Are you all right? Do you want something to eat?"

Kenzie blinked. Food. He thought she needed food. She glanced around. Where was an escape hatch when you needed one? "Thanks, but I'm fine." Kenzie couldn't help herself. She studied Jared's face, trying to picture Tyrone's dark-brown hair. Jared's hair was cut fairly short, but it was about the same color. And his eyes. So dark. They definitely could be Tyrone's eyes.

Setting down the tray, Jared asked, "You're staring. Have I got something on my face?"

"No, I was just—" Her words trailed off.

"Are you sure you're okay? Sara's all right, isn't she?"

"Oh, yes, she's fine." Still Kenzie gazed into those eyes—trying to uncover the face of a little boy.

Turning, Jared glanced behind him, then back at Kenzie. "Are you looking at me, or something else? You look like you've seen a ghost."

A faint smile crossed her face. "I think I have."

CHAPTER TWENTY-SEVEN

SOMETHING HAD HAPPENED; JARED WAS sure of it. He watched Kenzie through the glass doors. She stopped on the sidewalk and turned back toward the café, her face looking strangely anguished. He raised an arm to wave, but just then she turned away. She probably hadn't seen him.

What was up? Kenzie had acted so peculiar—flustered even. And she was mighty pretty when flustered. The blue blouse she wore did amazing things to her eyes, making them shine a little deeper and transform his thoughts. But he had to stop thinking that way. He stared out the window again.

Was Kenzie having some sort of mild, post-traumatic breakdown after her scare with Sara? She'd seemed fine last night except for those few minutes in the hallway. Jared recalled the way she'd looked at him—almost as if she were attracted to him.

Then it hit him. She was acting this way because of the way he'd left. He'd definitely hurt her by acting so cool. Last night, he'd let himself become upset at Kenzie's duplicity, yet today he'd acted all warm and friendly. Jared sighed. He'd thought Kenzie was a regular Jekyll and Hyde, but actually he was the one that deserved that title. He wasn't sure how he could feel angry one moment then mesmerized another. No wonder she was flustered and puzzled. He couldn't understand his behavior himself.

Jared slid open the doors of the display case and started arranging the fudge. Last night at Kenzie's house had been great—at least, after they'd gotten back from the hospital. He couldn't remember when he'd felt so at home. While he worked, Jared recalled something humorous

Kenzie had said and smiled to himself. She really was fun and witty. He could really have been interested in her if she hadn't been so devious.

Finished, Jared closed the case and took the tray to the back, mentally shaking his head at himself. *He could have been interested in Kenzie?* Who was he trying to kid? He would have asked Kenzie out in a heartbeat if he hadn't found out what she was really like. It bothered him that he'd let himself get so carried away last night. For most of the evening, Jared had forgotten her underhanded machinations. Once they'd left the hospital and returned to the house, he'd let himself get caught up in the sound of Kenzie's voice, the sparkle in her eyes, and the curve of her lips.

And yet . . . When they were at church, Kenzie had asked him for a chance to explain, and what had he done? Cut her off. He should have given her a chance. That would have been the fair thing to do.

Jared took over at the sandwich counter, glad to be busy. He had to stop thinking "what if" and quit imagining there was some explanation that would reconcile Kenzie's treachery with the person he had seen last night—someone warm, pretty, and personable. It would be best to put all thoughts of McKenzie Forsberg out of his head.

A few hours later, Jared went to the back. He was taking off his hat and apron when Pam walked in and pulled out a box of white paper sacks.

"Lucky you to be leaving early," she said, grabbing a large stack of the bags.

"Tom asked if I'd help him put up some crown molding."

"Sounds like fun!" she teased, pushing the box back. "Well, have a good time."

After Pam left, Jared looked after her. Pam was fun. Nice too. And she got along with Corey. He wasn't sure why he didn't date her more often than the once-in-a-while dinner and an occasional movie. He pulled on his coat.

Once outside, he called Corey, who was at a friend's house, to let his son know he'd be there soon. Tom came out of Dahlquist Realty, saw him, and waved.

Jared crossed the street. "I'm on my way to pick up Corey."

"Great. I'm on my way home myself. Say, I have some news on your house."

"I hope it's not more bad news." Jared's voice sounded bleak even to himself.

Tom was consoling. "I know you've been anxious, but I have been working on it."

"So has Kenzie." Jared's voice was bitter. "I'm sorry—I shouldn't have said that. I guess I'm just frustrated."

"I understand."

Jared went on, "I don't know how she could have done what she did." He was about to add a few choice words like *underhanded* and *devious*, but this was Tom's sister. He might rise to Kenzie's defense even if her position was indefensible. "It wasn't right, you know—for her to deliberately talk Tracy and Carlos out of seeing my home—killing any chance I had of selling it." Jared spread out his hands to underscore his words. "And then to give them addresses and descriptions of other homes!"

Tom neatly sidestepped the issue. "Let me tell you my news. I have a couple who'd like to see your house tomorrow—and I have another couple who might want to see it."

That sounded hopeful. "I'll keep my fingers crossed." Then he said, "So I'll meet you at the Steadman house after I take Corey home and get him a snack."

"Sounds good."

Jared honked when he pulled into the driveway.

Corey came out and hopped in the backseat. "Hi, Dad!"

"Have a good time?"

"Yeah!"

"Did you play video games the whole time?"

"Not *all* of the time."

"Most of it, I bet. Sounds like you'd better bring your homework and finish it while I'm helping Tom."

"Oh, Dad—"

"Don't 'Oh, Dad' me. You could have been done."

At the house, they changed clothes, and both of them ate some apple slices with peanut butter. As Corey crunched away, Jared reached over and ruffled his son's hair. "You gave me quite a scare last night."

"I was scared when Sara couldn't walk."

"You did the right thing by staying with her. Do you like Sara?"

Corey turned bashful. "She's all right. She talks a lot though."

It was hard not to laugh. "What did you guys talk about?"

"Sara talked about her mom and how excited she was about moving here until she found out you'd bought the house she wanted."

Jared rubbed his chin.

"Sara said her dad left because he liked someone better than her mom."

Ouch. That had to hurt. Jared was curious. "What else did she tell you?"

"Um." He thought a moment. "Oh, she said her grandpa hurt her mom's feelings."

Not exactly a surprise. Jared was well enough acquainted with Allen to know he'd been born without the tact filter that most people employed when talking to others. Allen always spoke off the top of his head, spouting whatever he happened to be thinking—no matter how inappropriate or hurtful.

Although Jared tried to convince himself he wasn't interested, he asked, "Anything else?"

Corey bit his lip, thinking. "Sara says her mom sometimes came home from work all grumpy and that she quit her job because a man was mean to her."

What was that about? Still, if you worked in the business world, you had to expect that sort of thing. And yet Kenzie didn't seem the kind of person to back down just because someone didn't treat her right.

His son, the fountain of knowledge, went on. "And Sara's mom got a new job, but she's scared." Corey wrinkled his nose. "I guess it's like when we moved here and I had to go to a new school. I didn't like that."

"It's hard to be the new kid on the block." As he spoke, Jared's heart softened toward Kenzie a little.

Telling Corey to grab whatever he wanted to bring, Jared put their plates in the sink and put the peanut butter away. The cupboard was overflowing with cans and boxes of cereal. He sure would be glad when they could move. There was scarcely room to turn around here. Jared shut the door. He'd blamed Kenzie for advising the Perezes to get a bigger place, but here he was thinking the same thing. He shook off the thought. He hoped the people Tom mentioned would like the house and make an offer. He only had until the end of the week. Then, like a yo-yo, his resentment at Kenzie returned. Tracy and Carlos Perez had been interested in the house—so interested they'd asked to see it a second time. They might even have bought it.

Corey came in with a bulging backpack, and they went out to the Explorer. As he drove, Jared regretted pressing his son for details. He didn't want to feel sorry for Kenzie. Being angry made it much easier to steel himself against her.

At a red stoplight, Jared glanced at his son, who was reading. "What book is that?" Corey held it up so his father could see the cover. "Ah, *The Magic of Christmas.*"

"I like this book."

"Why don't you read it to me?"

So Corey read about a girl who woke up on Christmas to find her pets singing and presents flying around the Christmas tree. When he was finished, Corey closed the book. "Sara's grandmother told her that Christmas is a time of magic. Do you believe in magic, Dad?"

"I sure do."

Corey tilted his head and studied him. "You don't really, do you?"

"Hey, what part of 'sure' don't you understand?"

"You have to believe, Dad."

They pulled into the driveway. "Okay, I'll put that on my to-do list."

CHAPTER TWENTY-EIGHT

The day—long-dreaded—finally arrived.

Painting day.

Kenzie borrowed an old shirt and pair of pants from her mother. Since she was taller than her mother, her ankles showed, but no one would see except Mandy.

Her sister-in-law's car was parked in front of the Steadman home when she arrived, so Kenzie went in without knocking. Mandy was in a back bedroom, stirring paint with a wooden stick. Barrettes kept her dark hair away from her face.

Mandy grinned when she saw her outfit. "Love your style. Can I take a picture of you in your 'mom jeans' and post it on Facebook?"

"Only if you want that paint dumped on your head. Then *I'll* take a picture."

"How's Sara?"

"Taking another nap." That morning Mandy had called, suggesting they paint another day, but Kenzie's parents urged her to go ahead. "Sara's been sleeping so much she won't even miss me. Mom and Dad are thrilled at the idea of playing nursemaid, and it's good for them to have some one-on-one time with Sara."

Kenzie looked around the bare room. The carpet was covered with thin plastic sheeting. "So are you painting the ceiling too?"

"Nope—it's fine. I like it white—makes the room look bigger, you know." She showed Kenzie a two-foot-long metal strip which was about five inches tall. It had a cut-out area for a handle. "I got this doohickey so we don't have to tape as much. You hold it in the corner between the ceiling and the wall, so when you paint the top part of the wall, you don't get any paint on the ceiling. Eliminates taping."

"That'll save a lot of time."

Mandy poured paint into a paint tray. "Don't worry about getting paint on the baseboards or door or window frames. Tom's going to paint them with enamel next week."

While Kenzie got on the ladder and used the metal edger to paint the upper edges, Mandy used a roller on the rest of the walls.

"Say," Mandy said after a few minutes, "you never filled me in on why you quit your job at Midwest. I thought you loved it there."

"I told you about Matt."

"You said he was ogling you and making life miserable, but I had no idea it had gotten to the point where you were going to quit."

"The last six months have been impossible." Kenzie used a rag to wipe the edger clean. "I don't get it. I dress conservatively, but he was always making suggestive comments."

"Doesn't Midwest train employees about sexual harassment?"

"They do, but it didn't sink in with him." Kenzie dipped her small roller in the paint tray atop her ladder. It got to the point where even passing Matt in the hall made her want to cringe—not that she ever showed it.

"This guy sounds like a grade-A creep. Couldn't you talk to your supervisor?"

"At first, I tried to handle it myself by talking to Matt—but he played the innocent and said I was imagining things. But I wasn't imagining his comments, so I finally went to my boss."

Mandy peered up at her. "What did he say?"

"He listened, but I could tell he thought I was being too sensitive and exaggerating the situation. I was surprised because he's always been understanding and supportive. Then he admitted that Matt had been in to see him because he was worried about the 'situation.'"

"What?"

"Yeah. Preemptive strike. Matt told my boss I kept flirting with him and that he'd rejected my advances—can you believe it?" She climbed down the ladder and wiped the edger again. "Boy, you have to wipe this off constantly or the paint seeps through. Well, that didn't take long. Do you want me to help with the walls or paint the inside of the closet?"

"The kids' closets are fine. Grab another roller and help me finish these two walls." Mandy poured more paint into Kenzie's tray. "So what happened next?"

"Matt told my supervisor I might try to get back at him because, in his words, he didn't want to play my game."

"Oh, this guy's a real jerk." Mandy was outraged.

"I didn't think it was possible, but Matt got my boss on his side."

"Doesn't your boss know you better than that?"

"I thought so, but when I talked with him, it was so hard to prove what Matt was doing. How do you say someone looked at you the wrong way or stared a little too long at your chest? I told him about the vulgar comments Matt had made. But after I talked with Matt and told him if he didn't stop, I was going to my supervisor, he stopped with the comments though not with his ogling, as you so indelicately put it."

It didn't take long to paint a room when you didn't have to do the closets or ceiling, and they moved on to the next bedroom. Kenzie moved the ladder as Mandy opened one of the cans and poured the paint in clean liners.

As Kenzie began painting the edges, Mandy asked, "So what happened then?"

"My boss agreed to talk to Matt again, but naturally Matt denied everything. When my boss and I talked again, it was clear Matt had convinced him that I was making it all up. I was so mad, I almost quit on the spot." Anger bit at her like the sting of an insect, even now.

"Kenzie, you've got to stop acting first and thinking later—it gets you into trouble."

"I didn't quit; I said I *almost* did." Kenzie wiped the edger. "I decided I wasn't going to let Matt get away with it. I went to human resources and filed a complaint."

"I'm glad you stood up for yourself."

"For all the good it did."

Mandy paused in rolling paint around the window to peer at her in dismay. "What do you mean?"

"Matt decided to make me pay. Oh, he eased up—there was no more staring, no more comments about my figure, and he stopped brushing against me 'accidentally,' but it was open warfare. In meetings, Matt would shoot down my ideas, ridiculing me in front of everyone.

He constantly talked to coworkers behind my back, belittling my work and criticizing me. He complained to superiors, saying I hadn't done this or that I'd done that wrong or that I hadn't followed through with a vendor or that I'd promised something to another department and hadn't followed through. Oh, it was endless."

"You know, this is the kind of thing that makes me glad I'm a stay-at-home mom." Mandy shook her head and went back to the tray for more paint.

When Kenzie finished the edges, she started in on the walls. "Matt was tight with the vice president, and I found myself saddled with the hardest assignments. Sometimes I got assigned tasks that weren't even in my line of responsibility. If I objected, Matt would tell people I couldn't handle the job or that I wanted others to do my work. I tried to be assertive, but he'd make jokes at my expense, make faces, roll his eyes, make disparaging comments, and do everything he could to undermine me. Matt was very good at making me look very bad."

As they started on the last wall, Kenzie asked, "Why is it if a guy is assertive, people see him as a strong, confident leader, but if a woman is assertive, she's called—well, terrible things."

"It's the way of the world," Mandy said in commiseration. "Did your boss ever catch on?"

"I talked with him one more time, pointing out how Matt was undermining my work and all of that, but it sounded like I was whining. He sympathized but on a very superficial level. I gave it another month, but nothing changed except for other employees giving me a wide berth. So I quit."

"I'm so sorry."

They put the used rollers and paint trays in a garbage sack and moved on to the last bedroom. "This room's going to be fun," Mandy said as she pried open a can and showed Kenzie the pale pink paint. "Isn't that a pretty color?"

"So this is Brian's room?"

Mandy laughed. "Oh, Brian would *so* kill me. Hillary went with me and picked it out." Kenzie put her paint tray on top of the ladder, and Mandy resumed their conversation. "I admire you for standing up for yourself, though I'm sorry it came at such a high price. You lost your job and have to move and leave all your friends. What a tough thing to go through."

"Well, as Matt would say, I'm a tough broad and can take it—only he might use different words." Kenzie paused. "Boy, I didn't mean to ramble on about that. Sometimes I don't know when to stop. But it's all right—everything's turning out for the best."

They talked of other things, continuing to paint as they talked. Finally, they moved on to Tom and Mandy's bedroom when the pink room was done.

Mandy was concerned. "This is the last one, but if you're tired, we can do it another day."

"What? And prolong the torture? No, thanks. I'm good as long as you feel up to it. But what about the baby's room?"

"A friend who is a whiz at stencils is going to help me with that." She pried open the can. "I love this color. I even love the name, 'Honey-wheat.'" As Mandy poured the paint into the two roller trays, she said, "I think you're right about everything turning out for the best—like you moving here. I still think you came back for a reason."

Kenzie positioned the ladder. "A very good reason—to put food on the table and a roof over our heads."

"Nah—you came back to meet someone and fall in love."

Kenzie cleaned her doohickey. "You have a one-track mind. I've heard all this before."

"The time is right though." Mandy nodded wisely. "My instincts—which are never wrong, by the way—are screaming that you're going to find someone. Maybe even that Tyrone, who you were in love with when you were little. Sara told me she thinks he's come back to Lake Forest. I like that—it's so romantic."

Stricken, Kenzie's stomach tightened. She held the roller so tight that her knuckles showed white. She couldn't answer because emotion threatened to choke her.

Blithely, Mandy continued to paint. "Or you could fall in love with Jared." A pause. "Well, maybe not Jared—you kind of blew your chance there."

Outraged, Kenzie declared, "I never *wanted* a chance with him. Besides, he thinks I'm a creep who set out to stop the sale of his house."

"Ah, but you know, 'The course of true love never did run smooth.' That's the one and only Shakespeare quote I know."

How cold Jared had been the night before. Kenzie's eyes narrowed. "Well, you can forget Jared."

"I guess it's for the best because I know Pam wants him." Then in a joking voice, Mandy added, "Still, if you wanted him, I think you could take her in a fair fight."

There was the sound of a door opening, and Tom's deep voice boomed out, "We're here, Mandy."

A few seconds later, Corey ran in, said hi, then ran back out as Tom and Jared walked in, wearing torn jeans and old shirts rolled up to the elbow. If only there was a hole where she could hide. Should she rip off her scarf or leave it? She probably had paint on her nose too. Certainly it was all over her hands. And to top it off, she looked like a hobo with high-water pants held up by an oversized belt.

Tom eyed the room then his wife. "It looks great, but I hope you're not overdoing it."

"I'm making Kenzie do all the hard parts." Mandy smiled. "We've already done the other bedrooms."

"You're miracle workers. Well, I guess we'd better get busy."

"What are you going to do?" Kenzie asked, trying to hide behind the ladder.

"Didn't Mandy tell you?" Tom said. "Jared and I are going to put up crown molding in the front room. And new baseboards."

Kenzie shot a look at her sister-in-law. "No, she *didn't* tell me."

"I didn't?" Mandy tried hard to appear innocent. "It must have slipped my mind."

"How's Sara doing?" Jared asked.

"Good. My parents are waiting on her hand and foot. I've been keeping her ankle iced and elevated. I told Sara this was her chance to catch up on her homework, which she's been neglecting, but she didn't like that idea."

"I'm not surprised. Corey brought some homework of his own to do tonight. He can't wait until school's out. Only a few more days." Jared's smile made her weak-kneed. "Well, we'd better get busy."

When they left, Kenzie hissed at Mandy, "Why didn't you tell me they were coming?"

"Does it make a difference?" Mandy asked sweetly.

"Look at me; I'm a mess."

"An attractive mess. Jared couldn't take his eyes away."

"Because I'm hideous."

"Because you're adorable."

"Oh!" Grimacing, Kenzie whirled around. Snatching up the metal edger, she returned to her work. Before the men arrived, she'd been on the verge of telling Mandy that Jared was Tyrone. Good thing she hadn't—Mandy would have said something to the men for sure.

As Kenzie started on the last wall, she could just imagine what Mandy would say when she broke the news. Her sister-in-law's romantic little heartstrings would twang, that's for sure. Kenzie still found it hard to believe Jared was Tyrone, her once-upon-a-time best friend.

After doing the last edge, Kenzie painted alongside Mandy. Last night, Jared seemed to have put the snafu with the house behind him. She'd even thought something might be developing between them— at least until he'd left so abruptly. That had been weird. But Jared probably thought she had acted just as strange this morning—she'd been so discombobulated at the café.

As she and Mandy finished, sounds of the chop saw and the sharp report of a nail gun came from the front room. They cleaned up the mess from painting, and Corey carried the garbage sack to the garage for them. Then, she and Mandy went and picked up pizza.

When they returned to the new house, the group sat cross-legged on the front-room floor to eat except for Mandy. Tom had brought a folding chair for her. As they laughed and chatted, Kenzie occasionally stole a look at Jared. Once in a while, his gaze turned to her. When they finished, Kenzie picked up the empty pizza boxes, cups, and napkins.

Mandy had bought an extra pizza to take home to her kids. She told Tom, "I'd better get this home before the kids start chewing the rug."

"When you get there, sit down and rest," Tom said. "I'll be home later."

Kenzie said her good-byes, and as they walked outside, Mandy said, "Thanks so much for all your help, Kenzie. I couldn't have done it without you."

"No problem. Let me know if you need help with the baby's room. If so, I'll be sure to be out of town that night."

Mandy laughed. Then she said with a mischievous twinkle in her eye, "If you'll come help me, I'll schedule it for a night when Tom and Jared come over to work on shelves."

CHAPTER TWENTY-NINE

THE NEXT MORNING, KENZIE TRIED a positive motivator. If Sara would do a certain amount of math homework, they would watch *How the Grinch Stole Christmas*. After a few groans, Sara agreed. Kenzie helped when needed, and it wasn't long before Sara was lying with her head in her mother's lap, watching the movie. Kenzie smoothed her daughter's long hair. How thankful she was to have Sara here—safe and mostly sound.

All was right with the world.

The overwhelming fear had not only made Kenzie grateful for her daughter—it put other things in perspective. It was time she mended the rift with her father. She glanced over at the wooden reindeer, which had stayed in the drawer until a day ago, when Kenzie put it back in its rightful place. The reindeer served as a reminder that somehow she had to make things right with Jared. For the moment, however, Kenzie was glad to simply be with her daughter.

When Sara giggled, the delightful sound made Kenzie smile. She loved this movie almost as much as Sara did, delighting in Jim Carrey's amazing physical comedy. Kenzie squeezed her daughter. All other troubles were suddenly of far less importance than they had been a day ago.

It had been such a relief to find Sara. And how kind Jared had been to not only carry her home, but to go with them to the hospital. It had been a comfort for Kenzie to know Jared was in the waiting room with her father and that he cared enough to endure the uncomfortable chairs and mindless TV. Each time Kenzie had gone to the waiting room with an update, Jared had seemed interested not only in Sara, but also in how Kenzie was coping. His loving concern had gone above and beyond the call of duty. Kenzie's face softened, remembering how he and her father had given Sara a blessing. The Spirit had been so strong.

Mandy was right—Jared *was* a good man. Too bad she hadn't recognized how special he was before it was too late. Kenzie sensed he liked her, but unfortunately his attraction was similar to how he might be attracted to a tiger—he might be drawn to her, but he'd make sure to stay far away.

Her gaze rested on the Christmas tree, and a warmth spread to her bones—one of gratitude for Jesus Christ and His birth. It had always been amazing to her that Jesus, a God, would condescend to come to earth and be born under such humble circumstances. How grateful she was that He had come to show people how to live by His perfect example and to bring about the Atonement so people could live again and be together as families. Kenzie bent and kissed Sara's forehead. Family. That's what mattered. As Cindy Lou Who said, everything else was superfluous.

Kenzie's eyes teared up as Cindy Lou sang the hauntingly beautiful "Where Are You, Christmas?" She knew exactly how confused, disheartened, and disturbed little Cindy Lou felt. It had been hard for Kenzie to find Christmas the past few years too. There had been broken dreams, a shattered marriage, problems at work, and a major falling out with her father.

A chill of recognition ran down Kenzie's back as Cindy Lou Who sang, "My world is changing—I'm rearranging." Christmas used to be easy for Kenzie too, but no longer. Christmas hadn't changed; she had.

Sara glanced up with a warm, trusting look before turning her attention back to the movie. A surge of hope and determination rose in Kenzie. Yes, she *had* changed. But if she had changed once, she could do it again. Her scare had given her a new perspective. She had her daughter, parents, and siblings and their families. It was time to appreciate the things that mattered most—and to realize that the things that mattered most were not things at all.

When the movie neared its end, the Grinch's heart was not the only one that had grown. A new spirit filled Kenzie. Not only was she buoyed up by the fact that her daughter was safe, but by the movie's message. Filled with a new sense of purpose, Kenzie resolved to move forward. When the Grinch had a change of heart, he didn't just stay in his cave—he went out and *did* something. He took action, and she would do the same.

After lunch, Kenzie asked her mother to watch Sara, who was napping, while she went downtown. After parking, she walked to the travel agency.

Tracy was at her desk and smiled to see her. "Hello there! Come in and sit down."

"Any luck on finding a home?" Kenzie asked, sitting and crossing her boot-clad legs.

"We've found one we really like, but Carlos and I want to see it again to make sure. If we feel the same way, we'll make an offer." Tracy's face was excited and happy. "What about you?"

"I haven't really had time to look. But I found a house that would be perfect for you."

Tracy's eyes lit up. "Tell me about it."

Kenzie told her all about Jared's house.

As she did, the light faded from Tracy's eyes. "That's the home we were going to see, at least until you stopped by. I told Carlos what you said about older homes and how expensive it was to remodel, so we told Tom we wanted something newer." Tracy's brow was furrowed. "You told me there could be a lot of problems with older homes."

"There can be, but not with this one—it's been well-maintained. I know the owner, Jared Rawlins, and you can trust him. You were right when you said you could save a lot of money buying an older home—but it has to be the right house, like this one. And Jared just dropped his price."

"But the house only has two bedrooms." Tracy was bewildered. "You said we ought to get at least a three-bedroom home."

"That's true, but there are options I didn't think about at the time. You could put your computer in the dining room or even in your bedroom. That way, if you did get pregnant, you'd still have room for a baby." Kenzie put all the brightness she could muster into her voice.

"But we decided it would be best if we had a separate room for a home office. After talking with you, Carlos and I realized we'd need filing cabinets, bookshelves, a printer—lots of stuff. You see, we do a lot of work from home."

"Put a work station in the corner of the front room. That way it'd be centrally located."

"But if one of us was working, the other couldn't watch TV." Tracy paused, idly tapping a pencil on her desk. "Look, I know you mean well, but after thinking about what you said, we feel it would be best to get a three-bedroom home."

"But you liked Jared's home. And it would be a great starter home. What about adding on a room? Why don't you go see it again, maybe with a building contractor who could give you some ideas?"

"I think we'll stick with the house we found. We really do like it." Tracy seemed regretful, but her mind was made up.

"Well, if you change your mind, Tom would be glad to show it to you." Kenzie tried not to sound too disappointed. They stood and shook hands.

"If you ever decide to go to the Bahamas, stop by and I'll give you a special rate!"

Outside, a chill wind blew. Her visit to Tracy hadn't turned out like she'd hoped. But Tom *had* showed Jared's house that day. Perhaps that had gone well.

No one was at the front desk at Dahlquist Realty, so Kenzie went to her brother's office. Tom was behind his desk, and her heart gave a jolt when she saw Jared in a chair.

"Well, hello," she said, a bit startled.

Tom's big square face looked tired. "Hi, sis. Jared stopped by to see how the people liked his house."

"Did they?"

"They didn't seem too impressed, so I told Jared not to count on them making an offer."

When Jared stared at Kenzie, his eyes were cool black marbles. "Tom tells me Carlos and Tracy Perez are about ready to make an offer on another home."

"I know," Kenzie said, pulling a chair closer and sitting down. "I just talked with Tracy."

Both men jerked like they'd been shocked with a cattle prod.

"Don't you think you've done enough?" Jared burst out. "They already decided not to buy my house."

Tom was irate. "What were you doing? Checking to see if they'd changed their mind so you could talk them out of it again?"

They caught Kenzie off guard. "For your information, I was trying to talk Tracy into going to *see* Jared's house."

Tom scoffed. "Yeah, right. And some pigs were flying around here a little while ago."

"Why are you being so mean?" Kenzie blurted.

"Just following your example," her brother replied.

Talk about hitting below the belt. And after she'd tried to do a good deed.

Tom rubbed his forehead. "Sorry, I've had a ton of problems today and a bad headache to go along with them. I shouldn't take it out on you. I'm sorry."

Mollified, Kenzie said, "I wanted to tell you what happened when I talked to Tracy that day. You never let me explain."

"I'm really not up for this right now." Jared got to his feet and stood stiffly. "I'm tired and need to get home."

Frustrated, Kenzie asked, "Why won't you let me explain my side?"

"*Your side?*" Tom flared up again. "We've seen the results of that! How about being on the side of being fair and acting decent?"

Stung to the core, Kenzie flung back, "Are you saying I haven't been?"

Moving to the door, Jared waved a hand to indicate he was outta there, but Tom stopped him. "I have another couple who wants to see your house tomorrow afternoon."

"Unless Kenzie talks them out of it."

That hurt. "I don't even know who they are."

"Don't worry, Jared, I'm not going to tell her," Tom said.

It was no fun being ganged up on. And although Kenzie supposed she deserved a lot of it, it still hurt. She tried one more time. "I'm really sorry about the Perezes, but if you would only listen to me, I can explain. It's not what you think."

Jared told Tom, "Let me know how the appointment goes." Then he walked out.

Jumping up, Kenzie hurried after him. He'd just reached the front door when she called, "Jared, wait."

He stopped and scowled, his eyes alert. "What do you want?"

Taken aback by his harsh tone, everything she'd wanted to say melted away, leaving only two words. "I'm sorry."

"Look, I know the house is important to you, but it means a lot to me too." Jared raised his hands, palms up. "This is the home my son and I want to live in, and we would have if you hadn't messed things up. Corey's been through some hard times after losing his mother. How am I supposed to tell him we can't live in the house he's got his heart set on?"

"Even if Tracy and Carlos had seen your home again, you don't know they would have bought it."

"Maybe not, but you made sure they didn't even see it a second time." Jared rubbed the back of his neck. "I made an offer on Tom's house in good faith, and it was accepted. Everything was fine until you started butting in. And now I only have three days left to sell my house or the deal falls through."

"But Tom's going to show it—maybe that couple will buy it. Or maybe someone else will."

Jared pinched the bridge of his nose. The look on his face was painful to see.

"I—I'm truly sorry," Kenzie said softly.

With a sigh, Jared turned and walked off.

CHAPTER THIRTY

When Mandy opened her front door and saw Kenzie, she immediately asked, "What's wrong? Is it Sara?"

"No, Sara's fine." Like a sleepwalker, Kenzie went into the front room and sat heavily on the couch.

Sitting on the other end of the couch, Mandy asked, "What's going on?"

"I've done something terrible." Kenzie pulled her legs up and wrapped her arms around them.

"You?" Mandy scoffed. "What did you do? Roll through a stop sign?"

"I told you how I'd talked with Tracy Perez . . ."

"Yes, but wasn't that last week? Has something else happened?"

"No, but now it looks like Jared isn't going to be able to sell his house before the deadline." When her sister-in-law blinked in confusion, Kenzie added, "Which means he can't buy this one."

"So why aren't you dancing? Or floating on cloud nine?"

"Because I feel sorry for him."

"Well, yeah, I can understand that. But you said Jared could always get another house."

Kenzie closed her eyes briefly. "He wants this one."

"And so do you." Mandy frowned a little. "Look, you need to tell me what's going on because, frankly, I'm a little lost."

"I feel guilty! I might be the reason Jared hasn't sold his home."

"No and no! The worst you did was tell Tracy about other houses. So what if you told her not to buy an older home and that it is expensive to remodel? Basic information that's readily available to anyone with friends or the Internet. Okay, so maybe you did take advantage of the situation, but really in the end it's up to them to decide what house they want."

"But I showed her all those pages of homes! I told her to buy a home with three bedrooms and a garage. If I hadn't said anything, they might have bought Jared's house! I killed the sale on Jared's house."

"I think you're going a little too far there. You didn't help it along, but you and Tracy were simply talking about houses—that's allowed between two women who are looking to buy one."

Kenzie had to be honest. "Part of me was talking about houses, but I think I *was* trying to dissuade Tracy from seeing Jared's house. And I rambled on too much. You know how it is when you're talking with a good friend? When you say anything that comes to mind? That's how it was with me and Tracy—we had an instant connection. But I knew I wasn't doing Jared any favors." She heaved a huge sigh. "I just came from talking with Tom. Jared was there."

"Oh boy. Obviously it didn't go well."

"Jared hates my guts. Tom told him the Perezes were probably going to make an offer on another home, and they both blame me for losing the sale."

"You're beating yourself up over this, but you don't know they would have bought Jared's home even if they had gone to see it again." Mandy propped up her legs on the ottoman. "I think what's eating you is that you like Jared and it bothers you that he sees you as the Wicked Witch of the West."

No use denying it. She'd fallen for him all right, but she'd also messed up big time. "I feel so bad for him and Corey," she said, trying to swallow the sadness in her throat. "They really wanted this house." There was a physical aching in her chest.

"So did you! And you're the one who spent most of your childhood here. Look on the bright side—now you can buy it. You wanted it so much!"

Right, but at what price? When she'd first arrived, Kenzie would have happily killed any sale on Jared's house with few regrets. But now . . . Kenzie wasn't sure what had changed. Had the movie she'd watched with Sara enlarged her heart? Or had the scare with Sara allow her to see more clearly what was important in life? Perhaps delivering baskets to the needy had played a part to help her think more about others. Then again, a large part of it probably had to do with getting to know Jared.

"There's something else I haven't told you," Kenzie said.

"Don't tell me you had Jared's car repossessed." When Kenzie made a face, Mandy went on, "I'm just kidding. Tell me."

"Jared is Tyrone."

Swinging her legs off the ottoman to face Kenzie directly, Mandy squealed in a pitch that would set cats running for cover, *"What?"*

"I found out that Jared is Tyrone."

"Bu—but how can that be? He has a different name."

"I know. I don't get that part."

"How did you find out?"

"You know that display window that Jared has at his café? He'd put his old ice skates in the window—the ones I gave him when he was little."

"I saw them. So *you* gave him those skates? What's up with the ugly green laces?"

"They're *not* ugly! They're distinctive."

"Are you sure they're the same skates?" Mandy asked.

Kenzie gave her a withering look. "Who else would put green laces on a boy's ice skates? Also, Scott said Jared told him the skates were his and that a girl had given them to him. I went inside for a closer look—I'd scratched an inscription on the bottom of one the skates."

"Really? What did it say?"

Kenzie was loath to say.

"Oh, come on. You *have* to tell me," Mandy demanded. "If you don't, I'll go down to the café right now."

And she would too. "All right, all right. I wrote, 'Best friends are forever.'"

Her sister-in-law put her palm over her heart and smiled widely. "How *sweet!*" Then she declared, "I *knew* there were sparks when you guys met."

There *had* been sparks, but Kenzie had doused them with cold water.

"So what did Jared say?"

"Haven't you been listening to anything I said?" Kenzie complained. "He thinks I'm the worst! There's no use. Not after this."

"That doesn't sound like you. Your motto is 'never say die.'"

"Jared thinks I'm an underhanded, conniving, evil witch."

"Talk to him. Tell him what you told me—that you were just talking with Tracy—that you didn't mean this to happen."

"I tried, but he won't listen. Tom won't listen to me either."

Mandy's face fell. "So much for boy meets girl and falls in love and they grow up and fall in love all over again."

Sad but true. As an adult, Kenzie had hoped many times to run into Tyrone and discover they still cared about each other. But it was time to face reality and admit defeat.

"Try talking to him again," Mandy advised.

"I did—just now, and you should have seen the look on his face. Besides, even if I could get him to listen, I don't think it would change a thing."

"That's a good defeatist attitude. Where's that feisty Kenzie we all know and love? *You've got to try!* Jared was interested in you, and I know you like him. And the night Sara sprained her ankle . . . well, I noticed the way you two looked at each other. The romance vibes were simply *gushing* from you guys. Now there's no guarantee that if you talk to him things will work out. But if you don't try, I guarantee nothing is going to happen. Oh, come on, you've got to try! Do something! Take some steps!"

A gleam appeared in Kenzie's eye. She sat up straight. Stiffened her backbone.

Frightened, Mandy clapped a hand to her mouth. "I didn't mean to say that. I did not say that."

"You're absolutely right. I can take steps." Newly energized by her sister-in-law's speech, Kenzie felt a determination in her bones.

"Oh no," Mandy moaned. "I've created a monster."

"Don't worry—this isn't going to be like last time," Kenzie assured her. "This time I'm going to think before I act. All I have to do is plan out exactly what steps I'm going to take."

CHAPTER THIRTY-ONE

JARED SLAMMED THE DOOR AS he came into the house, making Corey jump. When his son glanced up in alarm from the kitchen table, Jared asked, "Done with your homework?"

"Almost. I only have to finish my math. Zach helped me with the first ones, and I only have six more to do."

"Where is Zach?"

"In the front room."

Zach was hunched over a book, long hair dangling in his eyes. He glanced up, dog-eared his page, and stood, wiping the hair out of his eyes. Jared paid Zach well for babysitting since the high-school junior had a knack for getting Corey to do his chores *and* his homework.

After Zach left, Jared returned to the kitchen and put some hamburger on to fry. As it began to sizzle, he pulled an onion and two potatoes from a bin in the pantry.

Jared took out a knife and slammed the drawer shut with a bang. He peeled the onion under cold water—the way his wife had taught him—then fished out a cutting board and began chopping. He scraped the bits of onion into the pan with the hamburger and started on the potatoes. The loud *thwack*, *thwack* of the knife on the wooden cutting board was satisfying. When a piece of potato fell to the floor, Jared grabbed it and threw it forcefully in the garbage.

"What's the matter?" Corey asked.

"Nothing's the matter. Why?"

"You look mad. And you keep banging things."

Jared caught himself. He had to stop this—he was alarming his son. He got angry so seldom he hardly knew how to deal with these volcanic emotions bubbling inside him. Jared put the potatoes on to cook, then sat beside his son. "I'm sorry. You're right. I am upset."

"Why?"

Jared hated to cast a shadow on his son's dreams, but it was probably better for him to hear it now rather than later. "There's been something I've been meaning to tell you. I haven't because I kept hoping things would work out, but now it doesn't seem like they will. We're probably not going to sell our home in time to buy the house we wanted."

It took a minute for Corey to digest this. "We're not going to move to that house?"

"Right." His muscles quivered; anger thrummed behind his temples.

"Is Sara's mom going to buy it?"

"Yes. Some people were interested in our house, but Kenzie talked them out of it." As soon as the words were out of his mouth, he wanted to take them back. He was being unfair. Carlos and Tracy were only one couple out of many who had seen the house over the past months. But still—

Part of his anger was because he'd been so attracted to Kenzie. There had been something in her voice and in those eyes that he'd gotten caught up in. Then she'd played her dirty trick, and now because of her, he wasn't going to get the house he'd counted on buying.

Corey looked stricken. "I thought you bought the house."

"I put an offer on it, but we had to sell this house by December 24 in order to have enough money to buy it. There's a couple who are coming to see it tomorrow, but that's our last chance because our time is almost up." Jared could almost see the wheels going round in his son's brain. He got up to stir the hamburger before it burned to a crisp. The can opener whirred as he opened a can of cream of mushroom soup.

"Why don't we pray about it?" Corey asked.

Turning, Jared was about to say it was too late, then caught the trusting expression on his son's face. "Sure. Just give me a minute." He stirred the soup into the hamburger, turned the burners on low, and sat across from Corey. "Do you want to say it? And remember to thank Heavenly Father for our blessings, and ask that if we can't have that house to help us find one that will be good for us."

Pushing his math book aside, Corey planted his elbows on the table and clasped his hands together tightly. "Dear Heavenly Father, we're grateful for our blessings. Will Thou bless us to sell this house so we can buy the one we want? Before the deadline is up? We really like that house. And will You—uh, Thou—bless Sara and her mom to find a house? In the name of Jesus Christ, amen."

When his son glanced up, Jared almost needed sunglasses to protect his eyes from Corey's radiant expression. "You forgot to ask God to help us find another house."

"I don't want another house."

His feelings exactly. Still, he wanted to protect his son from disappointment. "Remember, sometimes God tells us no."

"You have to believe, Dad."

Getting up, Jared went to drain the potatoes. "Like in the magic book?"

"Yeah. Sara's grandma believes in magic."

She probably believed in fairies too. "Say, if your math is done, why don't you clear the table and set it while I finish up."

While stirring the potatoes into the hamburger mixture, Jared had an idea. "You know what we need?"

Corey perked up. "A dog!"

Jared hid his grin. "No, we need a distraction—something to take our minds off the house. What if I invite Pam and her daughter over to watch a movie?"

"What movie?"

"I don't know. We'll find something at Redbox." He called Pam as Corey set out plates and utensils. She answered on the second ring.

"Jared!" Pam's voice was full of pleasure.

"I know it's kind of late notice, but, well, do you want to come over and watch a movie?"

"Tonight?"

"Yeah. I know it's kind of last minute."

"I'd love to!"

"Great. I'll pick out a movie that the kids will like. What kind of movies does Kaity like?"

"Oh, well. Just about anything." The tiniest bit of enthusiasm disappeared from her voice. But it didn't take long for her to rally. "We'll stop and get some ice cream."

"That'd be great!" But as soon as Jared hung up, he began having second thoughts. The tiny bit of a letdown in Pam's voice when she realized they weren't going to be alone finally penetrated. He'd been content to let things drift even though Pam seemed to expect something more. She sought out chances to talk with him, and her eyes sparkled each time he asked her out. He shouldn't have called—it wasn't right to string her along. Jared hadn't wanted anything more than a friend to spend the evening with, but the deed was done.

When Pam and Kaity arrived, Jared had made popcorn, and later they dished up bowls of ice cream. The evening was enjoyable enough, but guilt made his stomach jump whenever Pam's hand sought and held his. Jared enjoyed the movie, and when it was over, he and Pam carried the bowls into the kitchen while Corey and Kaity talked in the front room.

"Thanks for coming over," Jared said as he rinsed the bowls. "Corey and I needed something to take our minds off the house." He'd told her at work that it didn't appear like he was going to be able to sell his house.

She smiled warmly. "Glad I could help."

Lest she make more of the evening than he intended, Jared added, "Thanks for being a friend."

Pam leaned against the counter. "A friend? I thought we were a little more than that."

Oh, great. Now he'd opened up a can of worms. During the past year, Pam had made it plain that she liked him. The only trouble was that the feelings weren't there for him. Oh, he liked her well enough, but his feelings didn't come close to those he'd had for Robin. And they didn't compare to how he'd begun feeling toward Kenzie. He stopped himself right there. No, he had *not* fallen for Kenzie, not when she'd acted so low-down—

"Hello! Earth to Jared!" Pam said lightly.

"Sorry, Pam. Guess I've got a lot of things on my mind." Jared looked at her. Maybe he should try a little harder to make a go of it with her. He really did enjoy being with her. She was fun and good company. Then he sighed inwardly. If he had to talk himself into a relationship, something was wrong.

"I know you're upset about the house. It must be very disappointing."

It was. "I guess I'll have to start looking again. I should have asked for more time to sell my house, but I didn't think there would be any problem." Then a big one had come up—Kenzie. Jared looked at Pam. The time had come to be straight. He reached out and took her hand, making Pam smile. But as Jared searched for words, her smile faded until there was nothing left of it. Her eyes became guarded, and she seemed to brace herself. "It was really nice of you to come over—as a friend."

For long moments they gazed into each other's eyes. Then Pam bit her lip. "Is it Kenzie Forsberg?"

"What? No!" Jared's voice was loud and emphatic. "Absolutely not."

One of Pam's eyebrows raised. "Methinks thou dost protest too much." She gave a little shrug. "It's okay. I think I realized a long time ago we weren't going anywhere—though I still hoped."

"You've got to have a lot of men interested in you."

"A few," Pam admitted without conceit. "I've turned a lot of them down, but now I think I'll start saying yes."

Squeezing her hand, Jared said sincerely, "You're going to make them very happy."

CHAPTER THIRTY-TWO

KEEPING SARA ENTERTAINED WHILE HER leg remained elevated was proving tricky. It was impossible to play board games, and Sara soon tired of reading. Watching movies helped pass the time, and since it meant her daughter watched more than usual, Kenzie consoled herself that today was the last day she had to have her ankle above her head.

After breakfast, Kenzie helped Sara with some homework then handed her Poppy the Penguin and put in a movie—*The Muppet Christmas Carol*. As the opening credits rolled, Kenzie went to sit in a chair by her mother, who was crocheting.

Holding her crochet hook with one hand, Elaine used the other to spread the nearly finished afghan over her lap. "What do you think?"

"It's lovely," Kenzie said admiringly. Her mother had used a ripple pattern, choosing soft-blue and steel-blue yarn with white in between. "Mandy's going to love it."

"It always takes me longer to make an afghan than I think. For a while, I was beginning to worry if I could have it done by Christmas, but I'm nearly there." With an air of contentment, Elaine set to work again, her crochet hook darting in and out. Without raising her head, she said, "We haven't had much time to talk—seems like you're always gone."

A small stab of guilt hit Kenzie. It was true—she *had* been gone a lot. "Things have been so hectic—sorry."

"No need to be sorry," Elaine said mildly. "I know you've been worried about getting Tom's house. It was nice of him to say he'd sell it to you if the sale to Jared fell through." She glanced up. "Jared hasn't sold his house, has he?"

"Not yet." Kenzie's voice was low.

"So you'll get the house then—just like you wanted."

Her mother's words echoed and clanged in Kenzie's mind. *Just like she wanted.* Buying Tom's house *had* been what she'd wanted—and yet now that she was so close, sadness washed over her like a long, slow wave of ebb tide.

"You're not exactly turning cartwheels," her mother remarked.

"I feel sorry for Jared. He wanted Tom's house too."

"I know. He mentioned it a few days before you came." Elaine glanced up. "Your father and I stopped by his café and had a sandwich one day. Jared came over and talked with us about the house. He was so excited and full of plans. He said it's always been a dream of his to live in Lake Forest." Elaine bent to concentrate on a cluster stitch and missed seeing Kenzie's stricken face. The hook flashed in and out as she went on, "Jared's pretty taken with you. I noticed how he looked at you when we went to the school play. Goodness! I've never seen him talk so much. Jared's always been a touch shy, you see. When we had lunch at the café, he couldn't take his eyes off you."

She glanced up momentarily. "And wasn't he thoughtful when Sara got hurt? You'd have thought she was his own daughter the way he took such good care of her. Jared likes you—that's for sure. And I can tell you feel the same way—you always look so happy when he's around!" Her mother wore a serene expression as if there was nothing peculiar about two people being at odds yet still liking each other. Still, Kenzie had no idea she'd been so transparent.

"A mother can always tell when her daughter is in love," Elaine said complacently.

There was no sense denying it. "But now Jared thinks I'm awful."

Elaine's hook stopped. "Why? What happened?"

Glancing over to be sure Sara was totally engrossed watching Scrooge visit his childhood school as Rizzo the Rat and Gonzo the Great looked on, Kenzie told her mother about her visit with Tracy Perez.

"I said a lot more than I should have," Kenzie admitted. "Tracy was so friendly, and we just clicked. I kept rambling on and on—telling her things that could influence her not to buy Jared's house. Somehow, I couldn't seem to stop myself. I kept thinking about my friend's terrible experience and told her all about it. So it's my fault that she and her husband decided not to see Jared's house a second time."

"Well, you didn't go there to talk her out of seeing Jared's house, and you never mentioned it specifically."

"No, but I did talk up the other houses and tell her she ought to get three bedrooms. But I didn't know at the time that Jared's only had two. I also told her to get a house with a garage."

"Did you know Jared's house didn't have one?"

"No. I only saw his house on Tom's computer for a few seconds. But still—why did I talk so much about the problems of restoring an older home when I *knew* Jared's home was old?" Grimacing, Kenzie moaned, "I'm a *terrible* person."

"Stop it. You didn't set out to stop the Perezes from buying Jared's house."

"But I feel so guilty." The disappointment in Jared's face haunted her still. Kenzie bit her lip, knowing she had hurt him deeply.

"That's because you've got a good heart. You may have gone overboard, and as much as I hate to admit it, it does sounds like you took advantage of the situation—but not to the degree that you ought to be tarred and feathered." Elaine reached the end of the row, snipped the light-blue yarn, then tied it off. "So now that you realize you could have done things better, I'm sure you will next time. You simply got carried away. You have a tendency to act first, think second. You're a lot like your father in a way—only he tends to talk first, engage brain second."

The comparison rankled. Kenzie didn't like being compared to her father.

Elaine began a new row with the steel-blue yarn. "Did you apologize to Jared?"

"Yeah, but I think I'd have to be sentenced to the guillotine before he'd forgive me."

"Give him time. He really does like you."

They sat in silence for a time. Then Kenzie said quietly, "I found out something the other day. Remember that boy I used to play with when I was a kid—Tyrone?"

Her mother looked up with interest. "Of course. He was such a sweet boy. I thought of him when you set out your reindeer. You two could hardly bear to be separated. I hardly saw you those two summers."

"He's moved to Lake Forest."

"Really? Good heavens!" Her mother blinked. "Have you talked with him?"

Kenzie nodded. "He doesn't remember me though."

"Oh, that's impossible! You two were the best of friends." Elaine's blue eyes were astonished.

"I didn't tell him who I was. He only knew me as Izzy, but I stopped going by that nickname in high school. I found out who he was a couple of days ago. He changed his name too. Now he goes by Jared Rawlins."

The afghan fell to Elaine's lap, and her eyes were astonished. "Jared? Our Jared? But how?"

"I don't know, but when we were little, he said he hated his name and wanted to change it when he grew up. I guess he did."

"Are you *sure* it's him?"

Kenzie explained about the skates in the window, the inscription, and Jared telling Scott that the skates were his.

"Oh my." Elaine relapsed into silence for a minute. "It's hard to take in. Jared is Tyrone. You know, I always did like Tyrone. He was such a nice boy, and now he's grown into a nice man."

"But you hardly ever saw him. How do you know he was a nice boy?"

"I got to know him a little when we had that picnic. And again when we all went to the carnival. And I saw him a few other times." Elaine smiled impishly. "I didn't tell you at the time, but when you started going every day to meet this boy, I got a little worried. You two were always so busy playing that he never came to the house, and well, I wanted to make sure everything was all right. That's why I suggested we have a picnic, so I could spend some time with him."

"Is that why you invited his mother?"

"Yes, I wanted to meet her too." Elaine paused to reminisce. "As I recall, we had a very good time. And after we ate and you two went off to play, his mother and I had a nice, long talk. Turns out she wanted to meet me as much as I wanted to meet her. It was a comfort to both of us."

"Is that why you and Dad took us to the carnival—to keep an eye on us?" Kenzie sounded peeved.

"We thought it would be fun for all of us to go together," Elaine replied blandly. "We had a good time, didn't we? Watching the sea lion show, eating Navajo tacos, and going on rides. And as I recall, a few weeks later we took you two for hamburgers—in fact, we did that a couple times."

Tyrone's mother had also invited them on outings, Kenzie remembered, treating them to tacos or ice cream and taking them to the movies a couple of times on Saturday afternoons.

"A nice boy," her mother repeated, chaining four and flipping the afghan over. "Imagine. Tyrone is Jared. I wish I'd recognized him, but after twenty-six years or so, what's to recognize? All I remember is a little boy with long hair. And he wouldn't recognize me either. My hair's gray now and short. And I've put on a few pounds. I hardly recognize myself! Besides, I only saw him a handful of times each summer. Still, I'm surprised Jared didn't remember our last name and put two and two together."

"He was ten years old, Mom. I probably told him my last name once, but we didn't get into last names. He called me Izzy, and I called him Tyrone."

Elaine looked at her intently. "When are you going to tell him you're Izzy?"

"I'm not sure I will. Besides, what would be the point—with him being so upset at me?"

"I suppose, but he might like to know." Elaine peeked over at Sara, who was giggling at something in the movie. "I know you said Jared wouldn't listen to you about the Perezes, but you ought to try again. Surely he wouldn't stay angry if you could explain it to him."

"I've *tried*, and he's not interested. I don't know what else I can do." Still, Kenzie had never been one to sit back. And ever since she'd talked with Mandy, she'd been trying to come up with a plan of action. Her first idea, trying to talk Tracy into seeing Jared's house again, certainly hadn't worked out.

"I'm sure you'll do what's best," Elaine said, going back to her crocheting. "Just make sure you think things through first."

CHAPTER THIRTY-THREE

ALLEN HAD BEEN SHOPPING ALL morning, and so far the aversion he felt toward walking around stores had only increased. Elaine had told him a hundred times not to try to do all his shopping in one outing, but spreading it out was the equivalent of slowly peeling off a Band-Aid. Far better to rip it off with one swift yank. The pain might be momentarily greater, but at least it didn't last as long.

Besides, he usually had very little shopping to do—Elaine did most of it. Unfortunately, today she'd given him a list—a long one. Good thing she knew him well enough to write down what stores would be most likely to carry the things she wanted.

Whenever Allen got bogged down with purchases, he headed to the car and threw them in the trunk before starting off again—feet dragging. To passersby, Allen probably looked like a man heading for the gallows.

After a wearisome morning, he was back at the car with more sacks. Once he stowed them away, Allen checked his list. Only a few things left. The most important one was a thing called a natural light lamp. Elaine had once mentioned wanting one when she was having a hard time seeing when crocheting at night. Allen wrote that tidbit down on a little piece of paper he kept in his wallet—a record he kept whenever Elaine happened to mention something she liked or wanted. Elaine was amazed on birthdays, anniversaries, and at Christmas. She always complimented him on his phenomenal memory but wondered why he could never remember where he'd left his glasses. Allen never felt the need to explain that his memory was as long as the paper it was written on.

He looked up and down the sidewalk. What store would be likely to have such a lamp? What he needed was a phone book—a good, old-fashioned phone book. Tom had shown him how to look things up on his cell phone, but he preferred the real deal of a phone book he could heft in his hand. He could stop by Tom's office—his son could look it up on that fancy phone of his. However, his stomach had been rumbling for some time. He'd best get some lunch before his stomach decided his throat had been slit.

Heading down the sidewalk, Allen thought he saw a familiar figure cross the street. He made it to the intersection just as the pedestrian light began to blink a stop, but he hurried on even though it made his hip hurt.

The woman sure looked like Kenzie. Man, she was some fast walker—even with her head down. What was she thinking? It was lucky she hadn't plowed into somebody and knocked them flat.

When Allen judged he was close enough for her to hear, he bellowed, "Kenzie!"

The woman turned, and Allen was awfully glad it *was* Kenzie. He'd look like a proper fool if it had turned out to be some other slim, tall woman with honey-blonde hair.

When he caught up, Kenzie asked, "What are you doing here?"

"Christmas shopping."

"But it's not Christmas Eve."

"Close enough." Maybe Kenzie could tell him where to find one of those strange lights, but first he asked, "Where's Sara?"

"Home with Mom. She promised to let Sara help her make Thumbprint Cookies.[5]"

"How's she going to do that lying down?"

"Mom's going to mix the dough and take it over to Sara so she can roll it into balls and put her thumbprint in them."

"Ah." Allen watched her. "I was going to get something to eat. Want to come?"

She hesitated, and for a moment Allen thought she might politely decline. It wouldn't surprise him. Ever since she'd arrived, Kenzie had avoided being alone with him.

---

5 The recipe for Thumbprint Cookies can be found at the end of the book.

"Sure. Where do you want to go?"

"I wanted a hamburger. How about The Grille?"

She agreed. When they arrived, the hostess walked them through the rustic restaurant with its exposed beams and sports paraphernalia plastered on the walls. After seating them at a booth, she handed them laminated menus. Allen folded his coat and laid it on the bench beside him. When she came back with glasses of water, he was ready to order. He wanted one of those quarter-pound burgers with bacon—the kind his wife never let him order when they were together. Kenzie ordered a grilled chicken salad.

After the waitress took their orders and bustled off, an uneasy silence fell. Allen searched for something to say that would get past the prickles he felt bristling from his daughter. But how did one talk to a porcupine? Wait, her work. Kenzie loved to talk about her job. He opened his mouth to ask her a question but remembered just in time that she wasn't at Midwest anymore and she hadn't started her new job. Great. Allen drank almost a full glass of water before he came up with something really brilliant. "How about the weather? Pretty cold, huh?"

"Yes. It's been real—cold."

Maybe he could talk about shopping. Women liked that. "I've been shopping all morning."

Kenzie blinked. "You don't have any sacks."

"I took them back to the car. Didn't want to carry them around and bump into people."

"The stores wouldn't be so crowded if you shopped earlier."

"And deprive your mother of the pleasure she gets from telling everyone that I wait till the last minute? Never."

More sips of water. He was water logged. Would the waitress never come? He started to drum his fingers on the table then remembered how it annoyed Elaine. Presumably, it would also irritate his daughter. He snatched his hand away.

Kenzie made a few comments about Tom and the upcoming party at the house on Saturday. He added what he could, and in between they darted looks at each other and watched passing waitresses and customers as if they were the most fascinating people in the world.

Finally the waitress brought their food. Allen squirted a mound of ketchup on his plate and dipped in some fries. He tried another line of conversation. "Your mother tells me you're going to get Tom's house after all."

"I guess. Jared still has two days though." Kenzie's voice had been lackluster but suddenly took on a little fire. "You look like you disapprove."

He did but was surprised it showed on his face. "Doesn't matter what I think. You wanted the house. Your mom said it had a lot of sentimental value to you, but I imagine it meant a lot to Jared too." He dipped a trio of fries in ketchup. "You could have bought any home you wanted. You didn't need to run down Jared's house to those people."

When Kenzie set her fork down very deliberately, Allen knew he'd said the wrong thing. "I'm sorry, Kenzie. I didn't mean it like that. Your mother told me all about your talk yesterday, and it sounded like you hadn't discussed his house as much as you talked about how much trouble older homes were to remodel. And you've got a point there. It can be a pain in the, uh, wallet. It's up to people to decide for themselves what they want to do." Then, in case he hadn't made things perfectly clear, he added, "Besides it's not your fault his house hasn't sold."

Kenzie opened her mouth, then closed it, dropping her gaze to her plate. He plowed on. "Look, Kenzie, I've wanted to talk with you for a long time, but each time you shy away. I say this with all the love in the world, but sometimes talking with you is like trying to talk to a clam."

Another mistake. His daughter stared at him with an icy expression and pursed lips. Not good.

Allen tried again. "I know you've been angry with me."

"Oh, do you?" Kenzie shot out. "I don't remember you ever mentioning it before."

"No need. Your actions showed it plain enough." Allen stared at her steadfastly. "You said the other day that I'd made some horrible accusations. That was back about the time when you had decided to get a divorce. Can you tell me what I said that hurt you so much?"

Kenzie's eyes about goggled out of their sockets. For a moment he wondered if she might get up and stalk off. But no, she finally squared her shoulders as if determined to forge ahead. He struggled to figure out that expression on her face. It looked like a cross between pain and shock, but then what did he know?

"You can't be serious," Kenzie said in apparent disbelief. When he didn't reply, she pressed, "You *honestly* don't know? You said *horrible* things—things that tore me apart—you can't possibly not remember! How can saying such terrible things not even register with you?"

The force of her word pushed him back in his seat. Allen tried to stir his dim memory, but there was nothing. He must have said something monstrous—but what?

His daughter shook her head as if to clear it. Then she mumbled as if speaking to herself. "I've been so angry and upset for two years, and you don't even remember what you said? Unbelievable."

He was about to point out that Kenzie being angry and upset was her own doing, but he stopped, warned by Kenzie's slitted eyes and the uplifted line of her chin. Allen clamped his mouth shut. He had to tread lightly. One more wrong word, and Kenzie would go flying off. Obviously, she'd built whatever he'd said into the mother of all insults. "I'm a great one for putting my foot in my mouth. Your mother has told me more than once that I ought to have my tongue cut out."

His jest was not well received. In fact, Allen was glad Kenzie hadn't ordered a steak, or else she might have used her steak knife to carry out her mother's wishes.

Kenzie glared stonily at him. "You really don't remember what you said? We talked the day after I told you I was getting a divorce, the morning Mom went to the grocery store."

Allen knew she was waiting for an explanation that would make sense of it all, but he had to be careful. If he answered no, Kenzie could unburden herself—get it out of her system. But he mustn't be too vigorous in saying he didn't remember because clearly his lack of recall cut her to the core.

"I said a lot of things," he admitted. "As to which hurt you the most, I can't say." Which was true. Even though he couldn't even remember what he'd said, he did recall telling Elaine about it after she'd come home. His wife had hurled abuse at him for days.

What a mess he'd made. It all started when Kenzie and Sara had arrived for an unexpected and unannounced visit. Something was up— he could tell from Kenzie's red eyes and how she deflected questions about Larry. But it wasn't until Sara went to bed that Kenzie had revealed what was going on.

The three of them sat in the family room. Allen recalled how Elaine's hands tied themselves into a knot when Kenzie told them she and Larry were getting a divorce. As for himself, he'd gone numb with shock. He'd liked Larry from the first time Kenzie had brought him home. Easy to get along with, always up to going fishing, and didn't have to fill every moment with conversation. Larry had been the ideal son-in-law—friendly, willing to help clean out the gutters, and knowledgeable about the Chicago Bears. He and Kenzie always seemed happy. The reasons Kenzie gave for their divorce were vague at best, and Allen spent hours that night staring at the ceiling, trying to figure out what could have gone wrong as Elaine sniffled beside him.

The next morning, he'd played croquet with Sara. Later, when she went to play with friends, the only way Allen could hold anxiety at bay was to keep busy, so he started pruning the forsythia. He was half done when Kenzie came outside. For some reason, he could still see her as she'd been that day, a bright harbinger of spring in her bright yellow blouse, dangling white earrings, and long hair blowing about in the breeze.

Setting his pruners aside, he went with her and sat in the lawn swing. Shaded by a beech tree, they talked, although now Allen couldn't remember now exactly what had been said except for the part about Larry refusing to see a marriage counselor. What Allen did recall was how badly he'd wanted to fix things for his daughter. He was used to taking care of and mending whatever was broken—it was part of his job description as a father. He'd repaired the rim on Kenzie's bicycle when it got bent, the swing set when the chain broke, and the wheel when it came off her scooter.

But this. This was far beyond his capabilities and doubly out of his area of expertise. Give him a wrench, saw, and screwdriver, and he could work miracles. But relationships? He was either putting his foot in his mouth or trying to pull it out. No, Allen couldn't repair his daughter's broken marriage—no matter how much he wanted to.

Coming back to the present, Allen's eyes were troubled as he peered at Kenzie. It was probably best to let her tell him which of his unfortunate statements she'd glommed on to this time. Oh, things were bound to have become twisted over the years. They usually did. But really, did that matter? Not as long as Kenzie got out what had been bothering her for so long.

Allen kept his voice soft and low. "Why don't you tell me what you remember?"

Taking a very deep breath, Kenzie began. Her voice was shaking a little, like her words had been boiling inside for a long time—which they had. There was also a mechanical note there as if she were repeating a speech she'd memorized long ago. At times, she spoke in little gasps as if she were having trouble getting enough air. He listened carefully, letting her talk without comment, and finally she got down to the core of it.

"When I told you Larry and I were getting a divorce, you blamed me for the divorce. One hundred percent."

With a jerk, Allen sat up straight. He'd thought himself prepared, but this took him off guard. He couldn't let this out-and-out fabrication pass. "I never blamed you!" Allen declared with some heat. "Where did you get that fool idea?"

"From *you*!" The anger and bitterness in her voice startled him as well as a passing waitress who glanced at them in alarm. "When I told you we were getting a divorce, you asked if I was working too many hours and said I must not have been giving Larry the attention he needed."

"I said *that*?" Allen was reeling.

"Your implication was clear. You thought I'd neglected him and that if I'd been a better wife, Larry wouldn't have left me. You felt the divorce was all my fault." Kenzie spoke in a very precise voice. Her eyes were like ice chips, and her lips trembled. She wasn't done, and Allen's stomach twisted, wondering what she had left unsaid. Kenzie paused, caught in the grips of some strong emotion. Then she whispered, "You told me I could have something done to keep him and that a man doesn't leave unless there's a reason."

The pain in his daughter's eyes was like a shot to his chest. Kenzie's face was white, and she fell silent. Allen looked down at the burger nestled alongside golden fries and swept the plate aside, putting his elbows on the table and his face in his hands.

No wonder Kenzie hadn't come back for visits. No wonder she could barely stand to talk to him these past years. Had he really said such things? Ah, if only the tongue had an eraser on the end of it like a pencil.

In light of what he'd figured out later about Larry, it was easy to comprehend why Kenzie had been so outraged. The only trouble was—Allen couldn't remember saying those words. But he must have. Her memory seemed crystal clear. Allen lowered his hands. Cleared his throat. "I don't remember saying or even *thinking* that it was your fault. I wish I could say you misunderstood, but since it's so clear in your mind, all I can say is I'm sorry. Divorce is never just one person's fault unless—" He stopped in the nick of time. He'd almost said, "Unless one of them is having an affair." But he couldn't say that because Kenzie hadn't wanted him to know. He had to keep up the pretense that he was still clueless, although he'd eventually figured it out even though Elaine hadn't told him.

Their waitress approached but must have seen the tension on their faces, for she turned and scurried off.

Then, miraculously, a piece of the conversation came back to him. "I remember saying that you two needed to work to make your relationship better and that it might help if you were more patient and understanding. I didn't mean to *blame* you—I was only trying to come up with something that might help."

"You were trying to *help* by focusing on what you thought *I'd* done wrong." Kenzie spoke with tight-lipped disdain.

"That's because *you* were the only one there. I was trying to figure out what you could do to make things better. If Larry had been there, I would have done the same thing—try to figure out what he could do to make things right!"

"Nothing I did or didn't do would have made any difference. Larry had already decided to leave."

In the ensuing weeks, months, and years after Kenzie had hightailed it back home, Allen began to suspect that Mandy, Tom, and Elaine were hiding something from him. Allen wasn't an intuitive man. In fact, he was abysmally slow at picking up on things, but gradually he began piecing together bits of conversation until his suspicions crystallized and he realized that Larry had had an affair. But Allen continued to feign ignorance since it was clear Kenzie wanted him left in ignorance. But at times, it was hard knowing his own family left him out of the loop. Still, Allen accepted it and said nothing because in some cosmic way, it seemed no less than he deserved for hurting his daughter that day. But it was time for the truth to come out.

Clenching his jaw, Allen stared into his daughter's eyes and ground out, "I know."

His daughter caught her breath. She swallowed deeply. Obviously, it was difficult for her to process that he knew the full story. "But how?" she whispered. "Who told you?"

"Nobody told me. I heard a word here, a comment there. Sometimes it wasn't as much what was said as what *wasn't* and *how* it was said. I finally put two and two together."

"I made Mom promise not to tell you."

Ah yes. That promise had been a real sticking point in his craw—one that had angered him for a long time. It wasn't right for her to ask Elaine to keep a secret like that from him. Still, Allen admired Kenzie for not shirking from telling him the truth. Nearly a year ago, when Allen finally confessed to his wife that he knew about Larry's infidelity, Elaine had wept in his arms. It had been hard on her to keep silent. Never before had there been any secrets between them. Elaine explained why she had agreed to it—tearfully saying Kenzie needed someone to talk to but that she wouldn't, not unless her mother promised to keep it a secret. And so Elaine had promised—so she could comfort her child. And now, Allen had lived with it long enough to flush the anger out of his system.

Kenzie spoke softly, "You never said anything."

"I figured I'd already said enough to last a lifetime." Allen rubbed the back of his neck. "I'm sorry I made it sound like the divorce was your fault. I was only trying to fix things—to think of some way you could save your marriage. I didn't know back then that Larry was with someone else. You said you still loved him, and if you wanted him back, then that's what I wanted. So I tried to think of things you could do to make your marriage work. But, as usual, I worded things poorly."

"It hurt to think you blamed me for the divorce."

"I'm sorry. I must have been exceptionally thickheaded that day. I didn't mean to say it was all your fault."

"So many times the things you say come out badly—and I say that with all the love in the world."

A corner of his mouth twitched upward. Ah, Kenzie was sharp all right—she could always get the best of him. "I liked Larry, sure, but I *knew* you. There was no way it could have been all your fault." Allen paused. "I must have been thinking out loud—always a mistake. You'd told me what long hours you were working, and the thought crossed my mind that you might have grown apart because you were gone so much. If Larry had been here instead of you, I would have said the same thing to him. I was trying to think of how you could salvage your marriage."

"It wasn't possible to salvage it." Kenzie's voice was low. "Not when he'd left me for another woman."

Although Kenzie sounded reconciled, Allen was still furious at Larry. "I'll never be able to understand it. Larry had the most beautiful, loving wife in the world, and it wasn't good enough for him? He had to go find another woman? He was a blinking idiot." One who had caused his daughter endless pain.

Although Elaine had tried to shield him, Allen knew about the midnight phone calls and Mandy's hurried trips to Chicago. He knew about the therapists and the antidepressants. He'd also seen—albeit from a distance—how Kenzie had thrown herself into her work and knew it came from an attempt to dull the pain. Allen had sorrowed over their estrangement yet was hamstrung when Kenzie rebuffed his clumsy attempts to make things right. Whenever Elaine wanted to drive up to see Kenzie, he'd gone, but there had been times Elaine had gently told him she would make this or that trip by herself. It pained him to be left behind—to know that was what Kenzie wanted—and he tried not to get angry over it. But he'd never been able to control his anger at his former son-in-law.

Allen wagged a finger at Kenzie. "Larry was crazy as a loon. I can't think why he didn't know or appreciate what he had at home. One day, he's going to look back and kick himself. He'll wake up and regret it— you mark my words." Allen's words skidded to a stop. "I'm probably saying the wrong thing again."

"Actually, you're saying all the right things," Kenzie said softly.

When he looked at her, Allen saw that his daughter's face had changed, softened. Her shoulders had relaxed. And when she spoke, it was as if some of the ice around her heart had melted.

"I'll tell you something I haven't even told Mom yet. Larry called me about four months ago. He said he was sorry and wanted to know if we could start over, try again."

"So his lady love left him, huh?" When Kenzie nodded, he said, "I hope you told him where to go and how fast he could get there."

A small smile hovered around Kenzie's lips. "Something like that."

"Good for you!" Allen stood and went around the table. He was pleasantly surprised when Kenzie rose so he could give her a big hug. He held on, ignoring stares from nearby customers. "I'm so sorry, Kenzie," he whispered into her hair, feeling her tears soaking into his shirt. "I was a fool for saying those things and a triple fool for letting this go on so long."

"I'm sorry too. I had such a hard time after Larry told me he wanted a divorce. And then, when I thought you were blaming me for everything, I had a little bit of a nervous breakdown."

He pulled back to look into her face. "I didn't know they came in sizes."

Kenzie smiled then—a real smile. They sat, and Allen called the waitress over to warm up his lunch. As they continued to talk, and without either of them fully realizing it, the long road between them shifted and rearranged itself until there wasn't any distance at all.

CHAPTER THIRTY-FOUR

PEEVED, JARED FROWNED AT THE KitchenAid mixer as if it were a wayward child. Taking off the cover, he peered into the bowl, debating his next course of action. His first impulse was to toss it in the garbage can. But surely the cookie dough could be salvaged. Right now, the Sugar Cookie[6] dough was too crumbly, which meant he needed to add liquid. But milk or water? And how much? Corey stood on a stool beside him, anxious to spring into action with his pile of cookie cutters. He appeared hypnotized as the metal spokes sliced their way through the dough.

Without stopping the machine, Jared splashed a bit of milk in. Suddenly bits of watery dough started flying through the air. Corey shouted with laughter as his father turned the machine off.

Jared groaned. Why hadn't he put the cover on? He began picking blobs of cookie dough off the counter and throwing them in the bowl. Then he fit the cover on tightly and let the machine grind away for a minute or two. He didn't like making sugar cookies. The only reason he did was because his wife had made it a Christmas tradition and he didn't want to disappoint Corey. But he was frustrated today and had been ever since Tom had told him that his last hope, the couple who saw the house yesterday, wasn't interested in it.

He stopped the machine then yanked off some paper towels and cleaned the bits of dough off the floor. When he checked the dough, it seemed too sticky. He tossed in more flour, then put the cover on and pushed the button. When the doorbell rang, Corey was off like a greyhound.

---

6 The recipe for Sour Cream Sugar Cookies, which is different than the one Jared has trouble with, is found at the end of the book.

A woman's voice said, "Hi, Corey. Is your dad home?" It couldn't be, but it sounded like Kenzie Forsberg. What could she be doing here?

"Yeah, he's in the kitchen. I'll get him."

Running in and doing a hockey stop without skates, Corey slid on some spilled flour and would have fallen if Jared hadn't grabbed him. "Sara's mom is here," he announced.

Jared scowled. Great. The cherry on top of a perfectly rotten day. And he hated cherries. Jared had no interest right now in talking with anyone, least of all McKenzie Forsberg. Reluctantly, Jared walked into the front room, wiping his hands on a towel tucked into his waistband. Corey followed like a little shadow.

Huddled in her black coat, Kenzie stood by the door, hands deep in her pockets. Her hair fluffed out from under a black cap. The cold made her cheeks charmingly pink.

"Hello," Jared said politely.

"Looks like you're doing a little baking."

He was surprised. "How'd you know?"

"Um, you've got a little bit of flour there." Kenzie brushed her jawline to indicate the spot.

Jared rubbed at his face furiously. Must she *always* put him at a disadvantage?

"You got it," Kenzie assured him. "Any harder and you'll hit bone. I, uh, was passing by and wondered if you were going caroling tomorrow afternoon." When Jared hesitated, Kenzie added, "Sara and I are going with my parents to Heritage House—our group is the Candy Canes. I don't know what group you were assigned, but really, you can go with any of them." Kenzie was forced to take a breath; then she went on. "I also wondered if you'd like to come over to my parents' home afterwards. Mom and Dad always have a little get-together—but then you knew that, didn't you?" Her cheeks turned pinker. "Anyway, so I stopped by because, uh, Mom wanted to get an idea of how many people were coming so she could have enough, you know, cookies and hot chocolate."

Why was Kenzie rambling on and on? It wasn't like her. There had to be something behind it. He'd gone to the Dahlquists the past couple of years and was already on their list of invitees, so her pretext of stopping by to invite him was pretty thin. She had stopped by for a reason—but what? She must feel pretty secure to step into the lair of the enemy, the person who was trying to buy the house she wanted.

"We're going, aren't we, Dad?" Corey piped up.

Turning so Kenzie couldn't see his face, Jared directed a frigid glare at his son. Then, in a firm voice that brooked no dissent, he said, "I haven't decided yet."

"But we went last year!" Corey whined.

"I *said* we'd see." Jared spoke in a stern parental voice.

This seemed to fluster Kenzie. "Oh, well, of course. It's a busy time of year, isn't it? So much to do—but we'd love to have you come if you can."

Why would she love him to come? So she could gloat over getting Tom's house? No, even though Jared was upset, he couldn't quite imagine Kenzie as the kind of a person who would gloat.

When Kenzie glanced at the book, *Christmas Magic*, which was on the end table, Corey noticed and went over and picked it up. "Sara lent me this book. Have you read it?"

"Oh, yes, about a hundred times to Sara. I love it."

Opening the book, Corey pointed out a group of singing animals. "I like that picture."

Jared took a step closer to see, but his thoughts were not on the book. He was irritated by his inability to figure out why Kenzie had come by and invited him to the party. Then again, perhaps he was making too much of it. Perhaps Elaine *had* asked her to stop by.

As Kenzie listened to Corey go over his favorite parts, Jared remembered how he and Kenzie had talked at his café and the night they'd spent together when Sara sprained her ankle. He'd enjoyed her company immensely. And how pretty she looked, bent over the book with Corey.

Then Jared shook himself mentally. He would *not* get sucked in by her again. He had to remember Kenzie was responsible for him losing the chance to buy the house he and Corey had set their hearts on. A little voice crept in, telling him the Perezes might not have bought his house even if they had seen it again, but he pushed it away. As he eyed Kenzie, it occurred to him that it was possible Kenzie didn't think she'd done anything wrong. That riled him. Boy, she had a lot of nerve coming here.

Closing the book, Corey handed it to Kenzie. Clasping it to her chest, Kenzie asked Jared, "How did it go yesterday?" He was puzzled until she added, "Tom was going to show your home."

"Not good. Tom said they weren't interested."

Kenzie frowned, looking regretful, but surely he was misreading her expression.

"I, uh, was wondering if we could talk." Kenzie glanced at Corey, who stood watching them. "About your house and what happened with Tracy Perez."

Oh boy, he didn't need this. Jared had heard all he wanted. "I'm kind of busy right now. Corey and I are making sugar cookies."

She smiled, and Jared steeled himself against the unexpected warmth that came from her bright, interested expression. "That sounds like fun! And it explains the—" She made a swishing motion by her jaw.

Self-consciously, Jared rubbed his jaw again. "Yeah, I'm good at making messes."

"Need any help?"

What was this? Kenzie had managed to steal the home he'd made an offer on, and now she wanted to be friends? Didn't she understand how low-down and underhanded she'd been? And now she was acting as if she'd done nothing wrong!

"No, thanks." His voice was chilly. "We got it."

Her face flushed, and she shifted weight from one foot to the other. "Oh, okay. Well, I better get going then. Hope to see you at the caroling and then at my folks' afterwards." She turned to Corey. "Now don't eat all the cookie dough, okay?"

After the door closed, Jared squared his shoulders and stalked into the kitchen. His insides were roiling. He didn't bother to check the dough again but dumped it onto the counter. The dough had had its chance. He wasn't going to fuss over it anymore. Corey climbed on the stool.

The dough was still a bit sticky, and Jared threw flour on and attacked the dough with the rolling pin, rolling in short, angry bursts.

"What's the matter, Dad?"

"Nothing." A piece of dough rolled itself around the rolling pin, and Jared peeled it off and threw it on the counter.

Corey looked at him doubtfully. "Why can't we go caroling and over to Sara's house for hot chocolate and cookies? We did last year."

There was an accusing tone in his son's voice that Jared didn't like. "I'm not sure I feel like going."

"Because you're mad at Kenzie?"

Taking a deep breath, Jared stared at the dough, which was thin in some places and thicker in others. It took all his willpower not to gather it up, mash it into a ball, and throw it across the kitchen. "Yeah."

Corey eyed his father stoically. "Because she's going to buy our house?"

Jared cut his eyes toward his son. "That's it."

"We can find another house, can't we?"

If Corey wasn't going to start cutting out cookies, then he would. Jared grabbed a star and pushed it into the dough. "I don't want another house. I wanted Tom's house."

CHAPTER THIRTY-FIVE

THE PUNGENT SMELL OF LEMON ammonia filled the air as Kenzie scrubbed the tile floor in the kitchen. She worked fast, knowing her mother might wake from her nap at any time and protest that Kenzie was working too hard. Yesterday, Kenzie had dusted all the blinds, and earlier this morning she'd vacuumed, knowing her mother would appreciate a sparkling-clean house for the party. Kenzie had also found time to play Monopoly with Sara, who was ecstatic at finally being able to sit up. Two of her friends, Kaylee and Ali, had come over to play games with her.

Done.

Kenzie poured the bucket of rinse water down the sink drain and put the mop in the utility room. Checking on the giggling girls, she reminded Sara to prop her leg up on the ottoman. "I'm going for a walk in the woods and then into town. Grandma will be up soon, and Grandpa's in the office if you need anything."

She kissed Sara, told her father good-bye, then grabbed her coat off a hook in the utility room. After putting her purse in the car, she went around the side of the house and through the backyard gate. It would be good to have a few quiet moments to think things through one last time. Kenzie hated people telling her she acted impulsively. She determined that this was *not* going to be one of those times.

Walking through the oak, maple, hickory, and pine trees was like being cocooned in an oasis of solitude. The air was so still and wind-less that the whirring of a magpie's wings overhead was audible. She rounded the bend and neared the pond, which was surrounded by a light coating of shimmering snow. How often she and Tyrone had come here and spent delightful hours skating. How utterly remarkable that he had come back to Lake Forest. But then, maybe not so amazing. Tyrone had told her a number of times that he wanted to live here forever. A number of crows flew over, their raucous cries loud in the air. A few lit in a gnarled oak tree and tilted their heads at Kenzie as if curious to know why she was ambling around the pond.

She thought back to the unexpected lunch with her father and how they had opened up to each other. It was still hard, in a way, to realize that her father had only been trying to fix things, that he hadn't meant to blame her. Her breath fogged the air as she considered. She certainly hadn't taken his words that way at the time. And yet Kenzie couldn't doubt his sincerity yesterday. She didn't like to think that she'd exaggerated the incident, but in her emotional frame of mind it was possible. Had she built it up—going over and over it—until reality had become twisted and distorted?

The past two years had been such a struggle to simply hold on. It had been so easy to focus her pain and anger on her father. Someone who couldn't talk back because she wouldn't allow him to be part of her life. Perhaps she had used him as a scapegoat, someone she could direct her grief and anguish toward. And now, after talking with him, Kenzie believed him when he said he'd only been searching for solutions. That was her father—Mr. Fix-It. While growing up, Kenzie had learned not to go to her father if she wanted to talk something out because he was always set on finding a solution rather than listening to how she felt. For answers, she might turn to her father, but for heartfelt discussions she had gone to her mother.

The tranquility of her surroundings was balm to Kenzie's mind. On her second trip around the pond, her thoughts turned to Jared. From the very first, when she'd met Jared at the school play, she had felt a strong attraction which had grown slowly but steadily—even after the fiasco with Tracy Perez. Kenzie shook her head, still embarrassed at how she'd rambled on and on at Jared's house. It had been hard to dredge up the courage to offer an olive branch and invite him personally to her parents' party. Jared's cool treatment hadn't been easy to take—even if she did deserve part of it. Kenzie had hoped that by reaching out through small acts of friendship, she might eventually break through the barriers Jared had put up. But perhaps she was fooling herself. It was quite possible Jared would never forgive her.

A small cloud of discouragement hovered over Kenzie as she left the pond and headed home. The chill of the day entered her heart, and she shivered. Would all of her overtures be met with coldness? If only they could get back to the friendship of their youth—or even to before that wretched day when she had spoken with Tracy. Before then, she and Jared had been able to talk effortlessly with each other. She'd felt so free, so easy and comfortable with him. Had he felt the same way? Kenzie yearned to get those feelings back, but how many times could she reach out before giving up?

Suddenly, she stopped on the snowy trail as an epiphany hit her. Could her father have possibly felt the same way? During the past few years, he had reached out to her but only to give her advice on rotating her tires, putting in a toggle bolt to hold the towel bar, or hanging a new set of blinds. Enveloped in her own pain, she hadn't appreciated that her father's efforts were his way of reaching out to her and had kept him at arm's length. Thinking about it from a new perspective, Kenzie doubted she herself would have had the stamina to keep trying as long as he had.

Kenzie pulled her scarf a little tighter against the icy breeze. Since telling Mandy she was going to take steps, Kenzie had spent a lot of time thinking, but it hadn't been until recently that she'd come up with a plan—and this one was a doozy. Kenzie had thought about it long and hard, then prayed and received a confirmation that she was doing the right thing. Although her family might not understand, at least no one could accuse her of acting rashly. Well, actually they probably still would, but that was all right. She was a big girl and could stand by the decisions she made.

Her walk through the woods had crystallized Kenzie's resolve. Doubt had fled. She pulled out her phone and, using her teeth to pull off a glove, texted Tom. Kenzie told him she was on her way and wanted to talk to him. She'd tried to talk with her brother before, and he'd pushed her away.

But not today.

She wasn't going to take no for an answer today. If Kenzie had to strap him down and gag him, Tom was going to listen. In fact, he was going to get an earful. He didn't understand, and why? Because he'd never given her a chance to explain. He and Jared were too busy being angry to listen to her side of the story.

Kenzie chuckled to herself wryly as the similarities of this situation and the cold war with her father struck her. She hadn't been willing to listen to her father the past two years, and now Tom wouldn't listen to her, but he was going to today. Yes, she'd done a lot of things wrong but not as many as Tom thought. She wasn't as black as he and Jared had painted her. If only Tom and Jared had let her tell her side of the story.

She went up the driveway with purposeful steps—adrenaline surging. Kenzie could have jumped into a boxing ring with Muhammed Ali in his prime and knocked him for a loop. She was going to float like a butterfly and sting like a bee.

In Lake Forest, she strode down the sidewalk toward Tom's office, pausing at an intersection. A young couple, their faces bright and happy, hugged each other as they waited for the light to change. On the street, other couples walked hand in hand, chatting comfortably. She crossed the road and, walking past a restaurant, glanced though the window to see a middle-aged couple sitting close, talking as they ate. Kenzie sighed wistfully.

Jared was the first man since her divorce that Kenzie had felt a special connection to. She had fallen for him and felt interest on his side as well. There had been sparks, lots of them, but unfortunately, at least on Jared's side, they seemed to have burned out. And now, it might be too late to repair the damage, especially since Jared still believed she had deliberately torpedoed his chance to sell his house. If only Jared had listened to her. If only their chance at a relationship hadn't slipped away. But she was prepared to accept reality—once she'd put her plan into motion.

As she threw open the door to the realty office, the chimes crazily bumped each other, making a cacophony of noise. She glowered at them. One of these days, she was going to yank them down and use a hammer on them.

Kenzie marched into Tom's office, glad he was alone. "I want to talk to you," she announced, giving him a clear, unflinching look and planting herself into a chair.

"What have you done now?"

Her lips compressed. "Nice to see you've got such a high opinion of me."

"Well, based on your past record . . ."

"You don't even know *what* my past record is because you've never listened to me. You've been too busy being my judge, jury, and executioner. You keep putting me off, but you're going to listen today."

Tom put his hands out in a conciliatory gesture. "Look, it's over and done with. Let's just forget it."

"I don't want to forget it—I want you to hear me out. Do you realize that you've never allowed me to explain the whole thing?"

There was a pause before Tom admitted, "I suppose I haven't." He made himself comfortable and crossed his arms against his wide chest. "All right, sis. Go ahead."

"Before I start, I need you to put a crowbar in that closed mind of yours and pry it open."

Tom's mouth twitched, and she could tell he was trying not to smile. Starting at the beginning, from when she'd stopped on the sidewalk—beguiled by posters of exotic locations— Kenzie explained the dropped package, helping Tracy inside, and the instant camaraderie which had sprung from their common grounds of searching for a house. Kenzie made it plain she hadn't gone to the travel agency to stop the Perezes from seeing Jared's house. Yes, she'd gotten caught up, and, yes, she'd gone on too much about her friend's terrible experience with remodeling. And although she had advised Tracy to get a three-bedroom home, she hadn't known Jared's only had two. And, yes, she knew she was planting doubts in Tracy's mind. It was wrong to do that. She was sorry.

Kenzie paused in her recital, glad that Tom appeared to be listening. She went on further, explaining that when Tracy asked about homes, she'd pulled out the papers she'd been carrying around in her purse. She'd been wrong to talk up those houses, knowing they were a far cry from Jared's, and to speak in favor of a garage when she didn't think Jared's home had one. Kenzie didn't minimize her self-interest but laid out her visit objectively.

"I know I was wrong in many ways," Kenzie said a bit defiantly. "So give me ten lashes, but I'm not quite the hard-bitten scoundrel you seem to think I am. I felt terrible about what I did, and I have apologized."

Tom had laced his fingers together and took a few moments, absorbing the information. "Yes, you have apologized. And I see that I assumed a few things. When I was showing you houses and Jared's came up on the screen, I thought you'd seen the specs and knew it only had two bedrooms and no garage. And when Tracy called to cancel our appointment, I was sure you'd gone there to talk her out of seeing Jared's house and stop the sale. So now I have to apologize. I'm sorry, Kenzie, I should have listened to you."

"Thank you. Now I need your help."

A realtor gleam came in his eye, and Tom sat up straighter. "You've been looking at the list I gave you and found a home you want to see?"

"Close. Let me explain—"

CHAPTER THIRTY-SIX

STANDING IN FRONT OF THE mirror in her bedroom, Kenzie plumped her hair with her fingers, then smoothed it. She turned sidewise and sucked in her breath to flatten her stomach. Too bad she couldn't hold it all evening. Although Kenzie wasn't the slim reed she used to be, her figure was still good. The rust turtleneck with glittery threads running through it did something nice to her complexion, and she wore her best-fitting pants and gold heels. Kenzie leaned forward to apply her lipstick. All set. For the hundredth time, she wondered if Jared would come. And hoped with all her heart that he would.

She went to the kitchen, where her mother was arranging cookies on a glass platter. Elaine glanced up, and her eyes widened. "My goodness, Kenzie. Don't you look pretty!" As she opened another container, Elaine asked, "Would you put the rest of these cookies on plates and put plastic wrap over them? Your father is going to have a heart attack if I don't finish getting ready. You know how he hates to be late."

"Sure, Mom."

Elaine scurried off as Sara wandered in, a bit awkward in her walking boot. "Can I take this off tonight?"

"Absolutely not. The doctor said it was important to keep the boot on all the time."

Picking up a cookie, Sara bit into it. "Can I help?"

"That would be great." She showed Sara what to do, then checked the oven to make sure her mother had put the ham in and set it to timed bake. She had. The ham would be ready to take to Tom and Mandy's house, where they would have Christmas Eve dinner after the party.

Her father came out wearing a shirt and a tie with a Christmas-green sweater. He looked at the clock with narrow eyes. "Your mother is always the last one ready," he groused.

"Because she was getting the cookies ready, Dad," Kenzie replied. "Would you put these plates on the table?"

She and Sara got their coats, and Allen bellowed, "Elaine, we're going to be late!"

As if on cue, Elaine appeared, pulling down the sleeves of her gold jacket. "Don't fuss. It's only quarter to six, and it only takes five minutes to get there."

"By the time we park and walk in, we're going to be late," Allen grumbled. Elaine rolled her eyes, and they all bustled outside.

It was a long-standing tradition in Lake Forest to go caroling at assisted living centers on Christmas Eve. The number of volunteers had grown so much over the years that a committee had been formed to divide the carolers into groups—with each one given a holiday name such as the Candy Canes, the Saint Nicks, or the Holly Berries. At first the volunteers had simply sung Christmas carols, but now each group elected a chair and planned a program that included readings or musical instruments.

The first time Elaine and Allen had participated, they'd invited a few couples to come to their house afterward. The gathering became an annual event, and although the number of invited guests had grown, it remained an informal affair. Even though many of them were in different groups, they still went to the Dahlquist home afterward to socialize.

This year, Kenzie and her family had been assigned to the Heritage House. Their group, the Candy Canes, had prepared a wonderful program. A number of songs included musical instruments such as violins, guitars, and flutes. The residents, seated comfortably on couches, chairs, and wheelchairs, listened, enthralled. Claire Garacochea, who was well-known for her angelic voice, sang a solo, "O Holy Night," which was so soaring it took Kenzie's breath away. Most of the songs, though, were a group effort, and the residents were encouraged to sing along.

Afterward, the group served refreshments and chatted with the residents. Mandy caught up with Kenzie at the refreshment table, where she'd gone to fetch more cookies for a white-haired gentleman who fancied the coconut macaroons.

"You look fabulous! Love your curly hair."

"And you look—pregnant!" They laughed, then Kenzie said, "Jared didn't come."

"He could have gone with another group."

"I told him we were coming here."

Mandy remained optimistic. "Maybe he had a special part with his group. And he still might come to the house."

Their group continued to mingle and visit with the residents. After a while, Kenzie's parents left to get things ready for their guests, and a little bit later Tom drove his family and Kenzie and Sara back to the house. Shrugging off her coat, Kenzie scurried to unwrap platters of cookies while her father saw to the hot chocolate machine.

As guests arrived, Tom and Kenzie took their coats and laid them across the bed in their parents' bedroom. The house was filled with lively chatter, and Mandy turned on some Christmas music. Heavenly scents rose from the hot chocolate, evergreen garland, and cinnamon candles that were scattered throughout the room. Multicolored lights blazed from the tree, and the room was alive with friendly faces. The house was full, and the ringing of the doorbell slowed then stopped.

At one point, Kenzie caught Mandy's eye and shrugged slightly while looking toward the door. A lot of people had come, but not the two she'd hoped to see. Then, as she went to the kitchen to get more napkins, the doorbell rang out. Kenzie stopped and strained to see through the crowd as her father opened the door.

CHAPTER THIRTY-SEVEN

ALTHOUGH JARED HAD SOME SERIOUS debates with himself, he finally stayed with the caroling group he'd been assigned instead of going with the Candy Canes to Heritage House. When he and Corey arrived at the Golden Living Center, they went to where the volunteers were already arranging themselves in rows against the west wall of the large common area. He waved at Pam in the soprano section, and she smiled back. Their audience was ready. Couches and chairs were packed, and quite a number of seniors were in wheelchairs. Others sat on short rows of folding chairs facing the carolers.

The chair had organized the program well. They sang "We Wish You a Merry Christmas" as a group, then scattered around the room to sing other songs directly to the elderly. Many times, they were able to coax the residents to sing along. The volunteers gathered back in place and sang more carols in between readings. The biggest hit was a local radio announcer who recited "'Twas the Night Before Christmas" with a deep, booming voice.

After the program, the volunteers mingled with the residents. As he walked around, chatting here and there, Jared noticed a tall man by Pam. Later, as he and Corey pushed a jovial fellow in a wheelchair over to the refreshment table, they passed Pam and her friend, who were talking to a pair of plump, white-haired women sitting side by side on a couch. After the man in the wheelchair picked out his treats, he asked to be wheeled over to talk to a friend. As Jared maneuvered the wheelchair past Pam, her friend put a proprietary arm around her waist and pulled her aside to make sure she didn't get clipped.

When the man was settled, Jared and Corey went back to get a plate of cookies to take around to residents who hadn't made their way to the table, either because of unsteadiness or because they were having such a good time chatting. A tap on his shoulder caused Jared to turn and see Pam.

"Hi, Jared. How are you doing, Corey?" Pam smiled at them. "Are you having a good time?"

"We are," he replied as Corey nodded. Handing the now-empty plate to his son, Jared said, "Corey, why don't you fill this up and take it around again."

After Corey darted through the crowd, Jared said, "It was a great program, wasn't it?"

"It sure was." Pam peered around as if searching for someone. "Well, I need to go, but I wanted to say hi."

"Got plans for tonight?"

"I've been invited to a family dinner."

"By that guy I saw you with earlier?"

"Yes. Nate Kristofferson. When Nate found out I don't have any family in Lake Forest, he asked me to his parents' house for Christmas Eve dinner. It's kind of intense for a first date, so I'm a little nervous."

"No need to be. Just be yourself, and it'll be fine."

"That's sweet of you to say."

Jared followed her eye to where Nate sat on the arm of the couch, talking easily to a lady with thinning silver hair. "You know, he looks familiar. Have you known him long?"

"He comes into the café a lot."

"To see you, I bet."

Pam's cheeks pinked up. "I think it's the food."

"I doubt that. I hope he's good enough for you."

She put a hand lightly on his arm. "Thanks, Jared. You have a merry Christmas." Then she left to join Nate.

Jared found Corey with a group of boys by the punch. "Ready to go?"

"I guess. Can I have another cookie first?"

"No more. The Dahlquists will have plenty at their house."

There were a number of cars lining the street by the Dahlquist home, but Jared managed to find an open spot. When they rang the bell, Allen opened the door and shook Jared's hand heartily.

"Glad you could come." He bent to search out and shake Corey's hand. "Nice to see you."

"Thank you." Corey left his coat with his father then dashed through the crowd until he found Sara, who was with her cousins by—what else?—the cookies. They palmed a few then disappeared down the hallway—probably to play video games in the office.

Allen took the coats from Jared. "Tom's boys were supposed to collect coats tonight but forgot two seconds after getting here."

"Hard to keep your mind on the job when cookies are calling."

"Exactly."

Allen Dahlquist was a genial host and lingered to ask about Jared's café and how business had been. When the older man left with the coats, Jared stood to the side and searched the family room with his eyes. Then, as if by magic, the crowd parted, and there she was, standing by the fireplace and chatting with not one but two men. One of them was an earnest-faced young man and the other slightly older—a prosperous-looking man in a neat blazer standing far too close to her.

Of course, it was only natural that a woman as pretty as Kenzie Forsberg would have men flocking around her. And she did look beautiful tonight, with a great figure and that long, gorgeous hair. She was nearly angelic—all she needed was a halo. Then Jared caught himself. Only angels had halos, and Kenzie did not qualify.

When someone moved, blocking his view, Jared moved sideways a few steps so he could watch her.

Tom came over, munching on a cookie. He nodded toward a table set up near the kitchen. "There's plenty of cookies over there. Mom put name tags on the trays, and I recommend this one. It's called the Ultimate Chocolate Chip Cookie.[7] I ask you, who in their right mind could refuse a cookie with a name like that?"

"Not me. I'll have to try one. Haven't had time to sample any yet."

"I saw you come in—and noticed where your eyes have been since then." Tom glanced toward Kenzie. "I'm going to have to ask you to

---

7 The recipe for Dawnelle's Ultimate Chocolate Chip Cookies is found at the end of the book.

put your eyeballs back in your head—that's my sister you're gawping at." Jared jerked his eyes away, but Tom grinned. "I was joking," Tom said with a wry smile, "but from your reaction, apparently I wasn't too far off." He bit at his chocolate chip cookie. "Why don't you go talk with her?"

"I don't think so." Jared crawled into his shell.

"She likes you."

Jared bristled inside. "Yeah, that's why she made sure I couldn't buy your house."

"I have a little news flash for you. Actually, both of us kind of jumped the gun on that." When Jared eyed him curiously, he went on. "I talked to Kenzie, and she explained all of it. I misjudged her motives. Her visit with Tracy wasn't planned and was a lot more innocent than I thought."

"Wait a minute, you were practically yelling at Kenzie for talking the Perezes out of seeing my house."

"Turns out I misjudged her. And, yes, I apologized for being a hothead."

Anger and confusion mixed together, nearly choking him. "Why should *you* apologize? Kenzie was the one who tried to tank the sale of my house."

"That's what I thought, but it turns out I didn't have the full story. Kenzie came to my office yesterday, and we had a good talk. Let me explain—"

Jared listened carefully, his mouth hanging open slightly as he took it in. It took Tom a few minutes. When he was done, Tom said, "So you see, Kenzie's actions weren't nearly as reprehensible as I thought. Sure, Kenzie could have handled things better, but she's felt really bad about the whole thing. And she did apologize."

Jared didn't know what to say. It took a bit of doing to readjust his mind-set and realize he'd misjudged her. Kenzie hadn't sought out Tracy and persuaded her not to buy his home. She *had* played up newer homes, but who could blame her when her friend had had such a bad experience and when she wanted so desperately to buy her childhood home? He would probably have done the same thing. But the part that bothered him the most was that Kenzie had tried, more than once, to explain, and he'd brushed her off.

Jared was so lost in thought that he was barely aware that Tom had gone on to talk about something else. He only caught the last part of Tom's sentence.

". . . so you've got it."

"Got what?"

"My house. Someone made an offer on your house yesterday afternoon."

The announcement rocked Jared back on his heels. *"Are you kidding?"* His face lit up at the unbelievable news. "So that last couple who saw it decided they wanted it after all?"

"It was somebody else—someone who had seen it before."

"Who?"

"Some single lady—I forget her last name right now, but her first name is Izabelle. She spelled it kind of strange—with a *z* instead of an *s*—but all the paperwork's been taken care of, so it's a bona fide offer." Tom held out his hand. "Congratulations."

Grabbing Tom's big hand, Jared shook it firmly. "That's great news!" It was a bona fide miracle is what it was. Then Jared threw an uneasy glance toward Kenzie. "Your sister's not going to be too happy."

"Well, Kenzie knew I was working overtime trying to sell your house."

"I guess—" Jared looked at Kenzie, and just then she looked in his direction. Catching his eye, she gave him a radiant smile. Was he dreaming? Why would Kenzie be smiling at him so big and friendly-like? Jared glanced over his shoulder to see if she was smiling at someone else.

No one there. His gaze went back to Kenzie, but she was talking to someone. How pretty she was. It had taken a lot of courage for her to come to his house and invite him to the party. And he hadn't been very nice in return.

"Kenzie's going to take this hard," he muttered to Tom. "She told me how badly she wanted your house. It means a lot to her. Maybe I could find another one."

"You'd walk away from my house for Kenzie?" Tom's eyebrows quirked upward. "You must like her more than I thought."

Jared looked at the Christmas tree, the front door, then his shoes.

"Well, well. What do you know?" Tom's deep voice was filled with awe. "I know I'm repeating myself, but you really ought to go over and talk with Kenzie." He leaned closer and in a conspiratorial whisper, said, "I saw her smiling at you."

"Maybe later." Jared shuffled his feet.

"Go on over. Ask her out, even. I bet she'd say yes."

Hope rose as Jared looked at Tom. "Do you think so?"

"Of course. What is it with you? You're not Quasimodo, and you're semiliterate. Besides, it's only a date."

"There's no such thing as 'just' a date."

"Come on, you've dated before. There's nothing to it."

"Yes, well . . . the thing is . . . ," Jared glanced around to make sure no one was in listening distance. "I've always been a little shy around women—even girls when I was little. There was only one girl I could talk to—the rest made me nervous."

"All boys are scared of girls. You're supposed to cover it up and do things to make them notice you. Didn't you ever pull a girl's hair?"

Jared shook his head.

"How about tripping someone you liked? Swiping a girl's notebook? Gluing a valentine to her porch?"

More negative shakes.

Mystified, Tom stared at Jared. "Geez, how'd you wind up with anyone?"

CHAPTER THIRTY-EIGHT

TRYING NOT TO BE OBVIOUS, Kenzie kept darting looks at the two men. Her brother had been talking to Jared for what seemed an exceptionally long time. Jared had a very readable face, and it was interesting to see the play of emotions that crossed it: first irritation then embarrassment. As Tom talked on, there was shock, followed closely by joy, then another emotion that was more difficult to read. At the end, Jared was practically scuffing his toes in the carpet.

Kenzie would have loved to sidle closer and hear what was being said, but she didn't dare. One time, Jared glanced in her direction at the exact moment she looked his way. A fizzy feeling like ginger ale bubbled up into a huge smile, and she'd almost giggled when he turned to see if she was smiling at someone behind him. And the friendly, slightly-in-awe smile Jared gave her in return was so cute. What was it about Jared that had struck her fancy all over again? Well, other than he was friendly and kind. And by what a wonderful father he was. Perhaps it was his innate goodness that ran deep and showed itself in so many ways.

When Tom finally walked away, Kenzie got two mugs of hot chocolate and carried them over. "You haven't made it to the refreshment table, so I thought I'd bring this over."

As Jared took one of the red mugs, his fingers brushed hers. "Thanks."

"Tom was over here quite a while. What were you two talking about?"

"I'm not sure," Jared mumbled, looking bemused. "Something about tripping girls." He took a sip. "Tom also gave me some big news. Someone made an offer on my house."

Earlier—standing in front of the mirror—Kenzie had practiced looking surprised. She displayed the final version—big eyes, round mouth, and raised eyebrows. "Really? I didn't know anyone was serious about it. Well, that's bad news for me, but you must be very happy."

She was glad Jared had the grace to appear divided. "Well, uh, yes," he said. "I'd reduced the price, so I'm sure that helped." He took a drink then said kindly, "I'm sorry. I know you really wanted Tom's house."

Kenzie arranged her features to look sorrowful. "I did, but there isn't much I can do about it. After all, you did put an offer on it before I did. Did Tom say who bought it?"

"Someone named Izabelle—spells her name with a *z*."

"That *is* an unusual spelling." A flicker crossed Jared's face, and Kenzie asked, "What?"

"It just hit me—Izabelle. I used to know someone called Izzy. She lived here in Lake Forest."

"Do you think it could be the same person?"

Jared considered. "I doubt it. That was a long time ago. But still— Izabelle and Izzy?"

"That's pretty close," Kenzie admitted. "So you knew a girl named Izzy. That's a different name."

"Yeah. She was a lot of fun. I've always been shy with girls, but I could talk to Izzy for hours. We were best friends."

The corners of Kenzie's mouth turned up. "So you liked her."

"I did. But you know how things are when you're a kid—it didn't really mean anything."

Kenzie's smile faded ever so slightly. "But you said you were best friends. You *had* to have liked her—"

"Well, sure. Izzy and I liked doing the same things. We spent a couple of summers together in the woods. She was the first girl I could really talk to." Jared appeared to grow uneasy under Kenzie's intense scrutiny, and his face reddened. "But we were just kids, it was nothing."

"Nothing?" Kenzie's fingers tightened around her mug until her knuckles went white. She fought to keep her voice calm. "You *must* have been best friends if you spent two summers together." Her voice caught as she added, "It *had* to have been something special if she gave you ice skates."

Jared blinked. "How did you know about that?"

Oops. "I, uh, saw some skates in your display window. And—and they looked old, so I asked Corey about them."

Jared accepted the explanation with a nod and took a drink.

A stinging sprang up behind her eyes even as Kenzie studied his face. She was pushing it, but she had to know. "So it wasn't important, then, your friendship with Izzy?"

The shrug Jared gave made Kenzie feel hot and then cold. Her mouth had gone dry, and he added, "We were kids. Kids make friends with everyone."

It was as if the world had exploded in her face and the pieces were still falling to earth. Feeling off-kilter, Kenzie fought to keep a neutral expression on her face. "I guess that means you weren't best friends after all." Before he could reply, she raised her mug. "I think I'll take this to the kitchen." She had to get out of there—fast.

In the kitchen, Kenzie set her mug down hard, then put her hands on the counter and leaned forward, fighting the pain by taking deep breaths.

Mandy came into the kitchen and said brightly, "I saw you talking with Jared—" When Kenzie didn't turn around, Mandy came closer, and her brows drew together in puzzlement. "It looked like things were going good. What happened?"

"Jared told me about Izzy and—and said they were best friends."

"But that's good. Isn't it?"

"No, it is *not* good." Kenzie's throat ached. "When I asked him if his friendship with Izzy was important, Jared sounded as if he couldn't care less. He—he said they were only kids. He made our friendship sound so trivial!"

"Oh, Kenzie." Mandy's voice was compassionate.

"I pressed him and said if they were best friends, it *had* to be something, but he made it sound as if it was nothing." Kenzie gulped. "Apparently, Jared and I remember things very differently. Sort of like me and Dad," she said, making a weak joke. She'd told Mandy about the talk with her father.

When Kenzie went on, there was real anguish in her voice. "All these years, I really, truly believed Tyrone and I had been best friends. I thought our friendship meant as much to him as it did to me." She shook her head as if to clear it. "So much for thinking Jared and I might have something special." Kenzie plowed on. "And the worst was when Jared said our friendship didn't really mean anything. He—he said it was *nothing!*" Kenzie's voice broke.

"Oh, Kenzie, I'm so sorry." Mandy gave her a hug. "But you have to remember that Jared doesn't know who you are. You've got to tell him."

"Why?" Kenzie said furiously. "Tell me why I should tell him— when he just said our friendship was nothing." Repeating his words made her stomach hurt.

"Maybe he's being macho." Mandy put a hand on her arm. "Why don't you tell him. See what he says."

Kenzie's lips began trembling. She didn't dare speak, so she simply shook her head and slipped away.

CHAPTER THIRTY-NINE

PUZZLED, JARED WATCHED KENZIE WALK away, her back very straight. What had just happened? Somehow, he'd blown it but didn't have a clue as to how or why. Kenzie had seemed so warm and happy when she came over, but at the end, hurt had been stamped all over her face. Jared went over the conversation, trying to figure out what could have upset her, but he couldn't come up with a single thing.

Maybe he should have tripped her.

Jared looked toward the kitchen, but Kenzie had gone around the corner. He couldn't let it end like this. He had to talk to her—find out what had gone wrong. More than anything, he wanted to bring back that bright, joyful expression she'd had when she had brought over the mug. Something was obviously bothering her; perhaps he ought to give her a couple of minutes.

A weird, uneasy feeling had taken up residence in his gut, and he moved slightly—just to keep an eye on her. He could see her now, although her back was to him. Mandy was there, talking to her. Then Mandy gave her a hug. Whoa, what was that about? Their faces were still turned away. Mindlessly he grabbed a cookie, watching Kenzie's every move. After eating, Jared couldn't even think what kind it was— it could have been made of sawdust for all the attention he'd paid.

Elaine came over, forcing Jared to turn and face her. They talked for a few minutes—painfully long minutes since he couldn't keep his eye on Kenzie. When Elaine left, he turned back, but the kitchen was empty.

Kenzie was gone. Mandy too.

Hurrying through the family room, Jared searched for Kenzie. Nothing. He peeked into the small front room, but she wasn't there either. Once or twice, people stopped him to chat, but he made some excuse and moved on. His eyes never stopped hunting for Kenzie as he made his way through the guests. He went back to the kitchen, which was still empty. Disconsolate, he turned away, and his eyes lit on the narrow table that stood against the wall. Jared didn't remember moving his feet, but suddenly he was standing in front of it.

It couldn't be.

The table was strewn with greenery, and amidst three glittery candles stood a small wooden reindeer. There was no way it could be the same one. He picked it up, a jolt running through him as he gazed at the blue eyes and the spots that he had painted so painstakingly. He ran a thumb over the wood. It was smooth and cool to his touch, and for a moment he was transported back in time, watching Tony Manzano cut out the reindeer and show Jared how to use different grits of sandpaper. When Jared had glued the reindeer to its oval base, he'd used too much, and the glue had oozed out, all thick and yellow. Tony had handed him a rag, telling him to wet it and wipe away every trace because stain wouldn't adhere to glue. Jared still remembered the thrill of satisfaction when he finished. He'd taken the reindeer home and, sitting on the floor of his bedroom, used a black pen to write on the bottom, "Best friends are forever." It was the same thing Izzy had etched into one of his ice skates.

Slowly Jared turned the reindeer over. The words were there. A little faded—but still there. *Best friends are forever.*

Realization scorched his mind like heat lightning. Turning with a jerk, Jared combed the room again. Kenzie was nowhere in sight. When he saw Elaine, he practically ran to her. After apologizing for interrupting her conversation, he held up the reindeer.

"Where did you get this?"

"Oh that's Kenzie's," Elaine said. "It's always been special to her. Why, she even brought it with her from Chicago—couldn't stand to be parted from it."

It was too much to take in. Jared had a thousand questions but couldn't voice a single one. He forced himself to marshal his thoughts. "Where did she get it?"

"A boy gave it to her. They were special friends. Very special." Elaine seemed to be watching him carefully, but he didn't know what to make of that.

"Do you know where Kenzie is?"

Looking around, Elaine said, "Last time I saw her, she was talking to Mandy."

With quick strides, Jared crossed the room to Tom's wife. "Have you seen Kenzie?"

Mandy's eyes locked onto his. Again, there were undercurrents he didn't understand but had no time for. "I talked to her a little while ago in the kitchen. She seemed upset."

Agitated, Jared ran a hand through his hair. Of course she was upset. Hadn't he been the greatest fool in the world? All those stupid comments. Saying they'd just been kids, that being best friends didn't mean anything—and worse—that their friendship was nothing. No wonder the light in her eyes had vanished.

When Allen walked by, Jared caught his arm. "Do you know where Kenzie went?"

"I think she went down the hall toward the utility room."

Jared hurried off, but Kenzie wasn't there. On the wall across from the washer and dryer was a bench with boots underneath. Above the bench, coats, scarves, and hats dangled from a long row of hooks. One hook was empty, and under the bench lay a pair of gold high heels.

Grabbing a coat, Jared headed out the back door. Kenzie was nowhere in sight. Maybe she'd gone to the woods. Izzy had told him she often went to the woods if she was upset. Maybe she still did.

As he hurried down the trail, his shoes slipped a little on the frozen surface. There hadn't been any recent snow, and he couldn't make out any recent boot marks. Maybe he was mistaken. And why would Kenzie come out here anyway?

Because he'd opened his big fat mouth—that's why. How many times had he walked these woods with Izzy? His childhood had been an unsettled one, and his friendship with Izzy had been one of the few bright spots. Jared had always treasured their friendship. How could he have spoken of it so disparagingly? The only thing he could come up with was temporary insanity—brought about by the presence of a beautiful, vibrant woman. He hadn't wanted a memory of a childhood relationship to detract from what had been happening right then—the miracle of a new relationship.

He went round a bend and, turning off the main path, headed for the pond. A few minutes later, Jared caught his breath. A still figure stood there, staring out over the frozen pond. As he came closer, his shoes made a crunching sound, and Kenzie whipped around.

"What are you doing out here?" she asked, her eyes widening in surprise.

"Looking for you."

Her eyes were bright, and Jared could see tracks of tears on her cheeks. Kenzie turned back to face the pond. Her stillness made him a little uneasy. In a small voice, Kenzie said, "I needed some time alone."

Reaching into his pocket, Jared pulled out the reindeer.

Kenzie's lips parted in a faint gasp.

"You kept it all these years," he said softly.

"You know how kids are—they keep things that don't mean anything."

Jared's gaze was long and searching. "You were Izzy."

She nodded.

"And you're also Izabelle."

"It's my middle name. Mom liked the different spelling."

"Why did you buy my house?"

"Oh, you know how impulsive I am." As Kenzie gazed at him, her tone became serious. "Telling you I was sorry wasn't enough. I had to show you."

"But you wanted Tom's house—badly."

"You did too." Her chin lifted. "And I can make a home anywhere." Kenzie peered at him. "How did you go from Tyrone to Jared?"

"Jared's my middle name."

"Ah." Her eyes crinkled, and the corners of her mouth curved up. "What about your last name?"

"My mother remarried after we left Lake Forest. My stepfather adopted me and wanted me to take his name. He was the only father I'd ever had, so I was fine with it." Jared looked over the frozen pond. Frosty crystals coated the branches of nearby skeletal trees, and the current of night air iced his face. "Remember how we used to go skating in the winter?"

Kenzie's face softened. "It was magical."

Reaching out, Jared clasped her hands in his. He counted it a victory that she didn't pull away. "Your hands are cold."

"Are they?" She sounded flustered, but her eyes were shining, and this time not from tears.

He drew closer until their foggy breath mingled in the chill air. "Tonight is magical too."

Kenzie's eyes flashed. "I thought our friendship was magical, but you said it was nothing."

Moving even closer, Jared murmured just before their lips met, "I lied."

CHAPTER FORTY

THE FOLLOWING WEEKS AFTER CHRISTMAS and New Year's Day were busy ones. Kenzie moved to Lake Forest and started her new job, while Tom, Mandy, and Jared moved into their new homes. Kenzie considered moving into Jared's old home but decided to rent it out. Her mother was delirious with joy when Kenzie accepted her parents' offer to live with them temporarily. Sara adored her grandparents and adjusted easily to a new school. Although Kenzie found her new position at Reliance Software stimulating, it was also demanding and kept her busy.

Scheduling playtime was difficult, but Kenzie and Jared made plans for a big family ice skating party on the last Saturday in January. The kids excitedly counted down the days, and they all met in the wintry woods on a frosty Saturday afternoon.

After skating madly around the pond during a game of tag with Tom's children, Kenzie stopped to catch her breath. There was a light, misty fog, and the bare oak branches shimmered with crystal-like frost as she went to sit in a vacant chair next to Mandy, who had a thick red-and-black blanket over her bulging stomach. Allen had brought a portable fire pit, and Kenzie took off her gloves, stretching out her hands to the dancing flames. She smiled as her parents skated past, looking like twins in their matching parkas and knit caps. Tom, wearing outlandish striped earmuffs, skated alongside them.

She told Mandy, "When I told Sara she couldn't skate today, she said I was the meanest mother in the world."

"Sorry, that title is taken," her sister-in-law told her. "My kids tell me *I'm* the meanest mother in the world."

"Sara's reminded me a hundred times that it's been five weeks since she sprained her ankle, and the doctor said it would take four to six to heal. But still—ice skating? On a recently sprained ankle? I called the doctor to see if I was being overprotective, and he voted against it too."

"My doctor did too," Mandy said, patting her stomach. "Besides, I didn't want to take any chances with this little guy."

Kenzie chuckled as she nodded toward the pond. "Sara was sure the doctor and I were plotting against her, but look at her now. She's the belle of the ball."

Jared had drilled two holes in the upturned edge of a snow saucer and attached a rope. Sara sat on the saucer cross-legged, skimming over the ice as Brian pulled her, skating for all he was worth.

"Look at that smile—she's having the time of her life," Mandy said. "Corey and my kids keep fighting about whose turn it is to pull her. Say, that was a cute idea you had to put green laces in Jared's ice skates."

"Who said I did that?" Kenzie asked innocently.

"The chances of Jared doing it are about a billion to one."

Just then, Jared skated to the edge of the pond, swishing to a stop in front of them. "Come on Kenzie!"

How could she resist such a handsome man? Kenzie pulled on her gloves and stepped to the ice. With swift, sure strokes, they glided along, passing her parents, who skated along more decorously. Then, still holding hands, Kenzie turned and skated backward—both of them in perfect rhythm. Their eyes rarely left each other's as they moved gracefully around the pond. They went around twice, then Kenzie let go of Jared's left hand, turning smoothly until she was side by side with him.

Corey took a turn pulling Sara while Tom played tag, skating madly as he tried to catch Brian, Adam, or Hillary. As Brian struggled to get away, he spun around and fell. One of the rules was no tagging downed skaters, so Tom went after the other two. When Corey wanted to join in, Sara went to sit with Mandy. Then, breathless, Tom asked Jared to take his spot so he could take a break.

He came to skate alongside Kenzie. "So have you made up your mind on any of the houses I've showed you?"

"Tom Dahlquist, you know there's only one house I've ever been interested in."

"I could talk to the current owner, but I don't think he's interested in selling."

When Tom grinned at her, Kenzie smiled back. He knew very well why she was holding back on buying a home. In fact, everyone knew. But Kenzie was content to take things slow, although neither she nor Jared doubted what the future held for them.

When Tom skated over to Mandy, Kenzie went with him. "How are you doing?" he asked. "Are you cold?"

"I'm fine. But I think Sara's ready for some action."

Tom eyed Sara, whose eyes lit up. "Well, why didn't you say so? Hop on." He grabbed the rope as Sara scrambled onto the saucer. Off they went.

Kenzie poured some hot chocolate and asked Mandy if she wanted some.

"If I drink any more, I'm going to have to go find a bush." As Kenzie settled into a chair, Mandy asked, "So how is Jared doing on the remodeling? It's sure nice of him to ask your opinion on *his* house." She winked. "I've been dying to ask if you're going to let him build a workshop in the basement."

"After extended negotiations, we finally decided Jared can do whatever he wants with the basement, and I can do whatever I want on the main level."

"Still think it's a dumb idea to have a workshop in the basement?"

"Not as much as I did, but it helped when Jared explained he has a dust collection system so there will be very little sawdust flying around." Kenzie sipped her drink contentedly, enjoying the crackling fire. "But I did tell him that if he gets a workshop, I get a new kitchen."

"Ah, blackmail."

"Blackmail is *such* an ugly word. I prefer 'extortion.'"

Mandy laughed. "So have you set the date?"

"Slow down! Jared hasn't even popped the question yet. We want to take our time. Besides, you're always telling me not to act impulsively." And truly, there was no need to act quickly. She and Jared shared a deep, always-and-forever kind of love that had its roots in those magical, childhood summers.

"I still can't believe you two got together when you always seemed to be at each other's throats over the house. It's a miracle."

"True, but 'love looks not with the eyes, but with the mind.' *A Midsummer Night's Dream*." Kenzie waved at her parents as they skated by. "Ah, isn't that sweet? Still holding hands after all these years."

"Because they're afraid of falling." Mandy giggled.

"So are you loving your new home?"

"It's heaven! Bedrooms for everyone, including this little bambino when he makes his arrival." Mandy patted her stomach contentedly.

Just then, Jared zoomed over and did a hockey stop, spraying them lightly. Kenzie and Mandy squealed and brushed off ice shavings. Kenzie took her cup over to Jared.

"Want some? It's nice and cold now that someone sprayed ice in it."

He drank what was left, then took her hand. They swung onto the ice, and once they'd reached the far side, Kenzie said, "Watch this!" She carved a figure eight into the ice.

"Wow, that's cool." Jared studied the design with interest. "What is it?"

"Whaddaya mean, what is it? It's a perfect figure eight!"

"It may be a figure eight, but I'm not sure how perfect it is. Let me try." He moved a few feet away and began. As he bowed his legs, he hit an uneven spot in the ice and slipped.

Laughing, Kenzie watched as Jared lay on his back with his legs spread apart, then raised his arms and spread them apart as if doing the *Y* in *YMCA*.

"That looks interesting," she said. "What are you doing?"

"Visualize, Kenzie, visualize. You did an eight; I'm doing a ten."

"Sorry. I can't see it."

He wiggled his arms and legs. "Hey, I'm making a perfect *X*!"

"I thought we were doing numbers."

"I am."

When he grinned up at her, Kenzie finally got it. "Roman numerals don't count."

She reached down to help him up, but Jared yanked her down. Laughing, they tickled each other and rolled over the ice. Finally they sat up.

"What are you thinking?" Jared asked. "Your eyes are twinkling."

"I was thinking about what I wrote on your skate. It's true—best friends *are* forever."

"I totally agree." Jared leaned over and kissed her.

Brian zoomed past, pulling Sara, who squealed with delight. Kenzie snuggled closer to Jared. "Can I ask you something?"

"Anything."

"Mandy told me that you and your wife were converts. What made you decide to get baptized? As I recall, when we were kids, you and your mom were Protestants."

"Remember those Primary activities you invited me to? I had a lot of fun. And whenever you told me something about the Church, I'd go home and talk with my mom about it." Jared smiled. "I never said anything, but you and your church made a big impression on me. So when some missionaries knocked on my door one day, I invited them in. The rest is history."

A snowflake lazily drifted through the air and was soon joined by more spindrift flakes. Holding hands, Kenzie and Jared gazed over the fairytale scene. Mandy sat by the glowing fire with Adam, both of them sipping hot chocolate. Corey, Elaine, and Allen glided along in a trio while Tom held hands with Hillary, teaching her how to skate backward. The sky overhead was sharkskin gray, and the misty fog softened the outlines of the pines and oaks that surrounded the pond.

"It's like a winter wonderland," Kenzie said, watching the skaters go round in the lazily drifting snow.

A snowflake lit on her cheek, and Jared kissed it away. "Now you need one on your lips," he told her.

"It might take a little magic for that to happen, and Christmas is over."

"If you believe, there can be magic all year long."

Kenzie tilted her head back and waited. It only took a few moments before a snowflake settled on her lips.

"Now *this* is magic," Jared whispered. Then he leaned close for a long, lingering kiss.

APPENDIX: COOKIE RECIPES

PEANUT BUTTER BLOSSOM COOKIES

1¼ cups brown sugar

½ cup butter or butter-flavored shortening

¾ cup peanut butter (creamy or chunky)

1 egg

3 Tbsp. milk

1 Tbsp. vanilla

¾ tsp. salt

½ tsp. baking soda

1 ¾ cups flour

½ cup white sugar for decoration

Bag of chocolate candy Kisses, unwrapped

Directions

1. Cream sugar, shortening, and peanut butter.
2. Mix in egg, milk, and vanilla.
3. Add salt, soda, and flour.
4. Form dough into balls, roll into white sugar, and flatten slightly with fork.
5. Place on greased cookie sheet and bake at 350 degrees for 10–12 minutes.
6. Remove from oven and immediately press chocolate Kiss into the middle.

MEXICAN WEDDING COOKIES

1 cup (two sticks) butter, softened
2½ cups flour, sifted
1 cup powdered sugar
½ tsp. salt

2 tsps. vanilla extract
1 tsp. almond extract
1 cup chopped walnuts
Milk as needed

Directions

1. Beat butter, flour, sugar, salt, extracts, and nuts.
2. Add slight amount of milk if needed, just enough so the dough sticks together.
3. Form dough into 1" balls, and place on ungreased cookie sheets.
4. Bake at 350 degrees for 15 minutes or until top is pale gold.
5. Cool for four minutes, then roll each cookie in powdered sugar. Store in airtight containers, sifting powdered sugar on bottom, in between layers of cookies, and on top.

GINGERSNAP COOKIES

¾ cup butter or butter-flavored shortening
1 cup brown sugar
2 eggs
¼ cup molasses
2¼ cups flour

¼ tsp. salt
1 tsp. baking soda
½ tsp. cloves
1 tsp. ginger
1 tsp. cinnamon
White sugar for dipping

Directions

1. Cream shortening and sugar, then add eggs and molasses, and mix well.
2. Add flour, salt, soda, and spices, and mix well.
3. Shape into small balls, dip the tops in white sugar, and place on ungreased cookie sheet.
4. Bake at 350 degrees for ten minutes. Do not overbake.

APPLE CIDER COOKIES

1¼ cups apple cider
1½ cups all-purpose flour
1 tsp. cream of tartar
½ tsp. baking soda
½ tsp. cinnamon
½ tsp. salt
½ cup butter, softened
½ cup white sugar

¼ cup packed light brown sugar
1 large egg
Optional: ⅓ cup grated apple

Dipping Mixture:
3 Tbsp. white sugar
2 tsp. pumpkin pie spice

Directions

1. Heat the cider in a pan until it comes to a boil. Reduce heat, and cook until syrupy and reduced to about 2 tablespoons, about 10–15 minutes. Set aside to cool.
2. Beat together flour, cream of tartar, baking soda, cinnamon, and salt.
3. Beat the butter with white and brown sugar in a separate bowl for 2–3 minutes or until fluffy.
4. Beat in the reduced cider, egg, and grated apple if desired. (The mixture may look slightly curdled.)
5. Stir in the flour mixture.
6. To make the dipping mixture, stir together sugar and pumpkin pie spice in a small bowl.
7. Roll heaping tablespoons of dough into balls (flour hands lightly if dough is too sticky), and coat in the dipping mixture.
8. Place balls on ungreased baking sheets. Bake at 375 degrees for 10–12 minutes or until the edges are set but centers are still soft.

THUMBPRINT COOKIES

½ cup brown sugar
1 cup shortening, butter flavor
3 eggs, separated
¼ cup water
1½ tsps. vanilla

¼ tsp. salt
2 cups flour
2 cups chopped pecans
1 cup jam

Directions

1. Beat sugar and shortening.
2. Add egg yolks, water, vanilla, and salt. Then add flour.
3. Beat egg whites until foamy.
4. Divide dough into 48 pieces, dip each in egg white, then roll in pecans.
5. Place on greased cookie sheet, and make a deep indentation with your thumb.
6. Bake at 350 degrees for 10 minutes.
7. Remove from oven, put small amount of jam in indentation, then bake 5–7 minutes longer.

SOUR CREAM SUGAR COOKIES

½ cup butter, softened
1½ cups sugar
2 eggs
1 cup sour cream
½ tsp. salt

2 tsps. baking powder
1 tsp. vanilla
½ tsp. soda
4½ cups flour

Directions

1. Cream butter and sugar, then add eggs, and mix well.
2. Add sour cream, salt, baking powder, vanilla, soda, and flour, and mix well.
3. Chill one hour.
4. Roll out dough ⅜" thick (approximately the thickness of a wooden spoon handle), and use cookie cutters to cut into shapes.
5. Put on ungreased cookie sheet, and bake at 375 degrees for 10 minutes or until edges are lightly browned.

DAWNELLE'S ULTIMATE CHOCOLATE CHIP COOKIE

½ cup shortening
½ cup brown sugar
½ cup white sugar
1 egg
1½ Tbsps. vanilla
½ tsp. salt

1 tsp. baking soda
¾ cup flour
1½ cups quick oatmeal
Chocolate chips
Vanilla or peanut butter chips
Coconut and/or chopped nuts

Directions

1. Cream shortening and sugars until smooth.
2. Add eggs and stir; then mix in vanilla, salt, and soda.
3. Add sifted flour, then mix in oatmeal.
4. Stir in chips, coconut, and nuts until fully coated.
5. Drop by tablespoons onto ungreased cookie sheet. Bake at 350 degrees for 12–15 minutes.

Note: These cookies are fabulous as is, but if you'd like a healthier version, cut back slightly on shortening, using only ¼ to ⅓ cup, and decrease baking time by 1–2 minutes. You can also substitute whole-wheat flour for up to half of the white flour without much change in the final product.

ABOUT THE AUTHOR

MARLENE BATEMAN WAS BORN IN Salt Lake City, Utah. She graduated from the University of Utah with a bachelor's degree in English. She is married to Kelly R. Sullivan, and they live on half an acre filled with flowers, quail, and fruit trees in North Salt Lake, Utah, in the foothills of the lovely Wasatch Mountains.

Marlene loves reading, camping, and flowers, and has a super-sized iris garden with more than 80 different varieties. Also an animal lover, Marlene has a pudgy Westie and an energetic Welsh Corgi, both of whom manage to coexist with her four cats.

Marlene has written a number of nonfiction books, including *Latter-day Saint Heroes and Heroines, And There Were Angels among Them, Visits from Beyond the Veil, By the Ministering of Angels, Brigham's Boys, Heroes of Faith, Gaze into Heaven: Near-Death Experiences in Early Church History,* and *The Magnificent World of Spirits.* Marlene also wrote the best-selling novel *Light on Fire Island* as well as three other mysteries, *Motive for Murder, A Death in the Family,* and *Crooked House.* You can learn more about Marlene and her books at www.marlenebateman.info